MW00745465

GINA FRENCH IS NOT A WASTE OF ROOFIES

2014

C. J. ANDERSON

www.krakenpress.com

FOR KAZIA

"You do not have to give people reasons to be violent, because they already have plenty of reasons. All you have to do is take away their reasons to restrain themselves."

—Roy F. Baumeister, P.H.D.
EVIL: Inside Human Violence and Cruelty

WHEN I WAS a little girl, I was an insomniac.

I'd lay awake at night staring at the ceiling trying my hardest to fall asleep. It sounds stupid to those who have never fought for sleep, but trust me, it's perpetual hell.

Time itself becomes your enemy.

On an average summer night the air conditioner roaring to life signaled the passing of another twenty minutes. Every third time meant another sleepless hour had gone by.

Ticking clocks were forbidden.

I would lay awake all night, estimating the current time and subtracting the remaining hours until I had to get up and start all over again.

I'd stare at objects around my room.

My dolls and posters of dolls would grimace back at me.

The harder I tried to sleep, the wider awake I became.

Around 6 A.M., I would suffer whatever a third grader's version of a mental breakdown would be.

I would kind of "zone out," like I was stoned, or a vegetable or something, and I'd sob uncontrollably as my mind went black and the morning sun burned white.

It was around this time that sleep would finally take pity on my shaking body, but it was truly a hollow victory as the alarm would chime me back awake in less than two hours and I'd be forced to zombie my way through another day at school. Another day spent nervously counting down the hours until I had to return to the sheets for a repeat performance.

Some nights my dad would sit at the foot of the bed, tell

me endless stories, hold my hand, pray for me, whatever he could. My mom talked to doctors and read books on childhood sleep disorders. I know they tried to help, they really did, but it didn't matter, nothing helped.

I was so fucking beyond help.

GINA

CHAPTER I

" AND THEN I pissed myself."

It was an honest answer, and although the delivery was intentionally "to the point" the psychiatrist didn't even flinch. He merely curled the corners of his mouth ever so slightly towards the humming florescent lights with what can best be described as a "pity smile." It was his way of gently letting her know that she had failed, and better have tried.

Gina sat.

Her knees locked together, both feet on the floor, arms crossed, eyes glued to her shoes. Everything about her body language reinforced her original opinion—this "mandatory visit" was as much a waste of the doctor's time as it was hers.

Still, they both went through the motions, both playing their parts to perfection. Each said what the other expected to hear and this brought closure on the official forms if nowhere else.

What did they want from her? When an average day at the job you've already come to despise suddenly becomes nine horny pent-up prisoners kicking you upside down and tearing at your clothes, it's not something you're going to— going to—

Christ, thought Gina, her trademark sarcasm was usually droll and lightning quick.

The doctor continued to secretly scribble in the folder marked "G. French" as she sat motionless on the couch. The baggy prison clothes she was given to wear after her "physical" rubbed against her already raw skin.

She sighed. Maybe it was the shoddy prison fashion that caused the riot.

The room was uncomfortably quiet and every second that passed reminded her how quickly the day was draining and how she just wanted to go home. Yes, today classified as a bad day, but she was lucky—she would survive; one of her co-workers wouldn't. She glanced up at the doctor as he continued to document his observations.

She thought about just asking him.

Despite the chaos and its aftermath, one question remained unanswered.

Graveyard Travis.

What happened to Graveyard Travis?

What happened to the lucky correctional officer who somehow landed the overpaid prison in constant lock-down 9 P.M. to 6 A.M. shift? Rumor had Travis as one of the C.O.s that took the worst of the riot and had been transferred off the grounds to a better quipped medical facility, which was far from what she wanted to hear. Even with Gina working evenings and Graveyard Travis's working nights, they still had their mornings together and over the last seven weeks had managed to hook up no less than three times a week with the record being six.

He was alive, she knew that much, and it was enough to make her smile.

The shrink finally tapped the tip of his pen in victory, shook the papers into formation and placed them on the table in front of Gina.

Signature time.

Five.

Six.

Seven.

Eight.

Christ.

He took the papers back and tackily handed her a business card with another time and date etched on the back.

Next week already. Fantastic.

She thanklessly exited the room and began back down the hall. Each step sent a slight pain shooting from mid spine, down her back, through her left thigh, and grinding to a fiery halt just behind her kneecap. It was annoying, but manageable and served as a reminder of what almost was. She caught a glimpse of her reflection in the glass door, she looked like complete hell but this was not the time to get all girly about her appearance. As she left the prison's East Wing and began south down the dreary corridor Gina relived the days events:

She punched her timecard.

She got some coffee.

She completed forty minutes of neglected paperwork.

She started her evening rounds.

She took a break.

She had to use artificial sweetener in her coffee as no one replaced the sugar in the staff room.

She went back to work and the sky came crashing down.

She awoke in the prison hospital.

She was escorted to the in-house shrink.

She headed back to the prison hospital.

Joy.

Gina continued to limp down the gloomy hall.

One more round of nods and signatures would push me that much closer to just going home.

She rounded a corner.

Once again she thought about Travis.

Gina burned for contact with someone who had an update on her . . . what? Boyfriend?

This overbearing urge for a man who reciprocally signed on for nothing deeper than a physical relationship slowly picked at her.

Back to the hospital.

As unpleasant as her post-riot physical had been, the hospital had been a useful buzz of between-doctor chatter. It was actually while she was on her back with her feet in the examination table's stirrups that she overheard someone on the other side of the curtain shout that Travis had been rushed to Sisters of Hope Hospital. Apparently his wounds were too severe to be treated in-house.

For whatever reason, the idea of grilling the doctors about Travis's condition beyond the casual limits of a concerned co-worker, at the time, seemed like a bad one. It's not like she was fooling anyone, the entire staff knew she was getting it on with one of the graveyard guys although everyone pretended they didn't, so Travis and Gina pretended they weren't, and work continued as normal with a giant invisible elephant held captive within the walls of the staff room.

As Gina's throbbing knee carried her around the last corner and the prison hospital doors came into sight, her breathing shortened and without thinking, she placed one hand against the wall for support. Her palm barely made contact before she snapped it away like the faded yellow paint burned hot. Regaining her balance on her wounded limb, she quickly looked around to see if anyone witnessed her moment of weakness.

Luckily, the hallways were empty.

Her secret was safe.

She contemplated a much needed cigarette.

A single smoke meant three flights of stairs and another six hallways, just to puff illegally behind the massive facility, under a massive loading dock, under a massive "No Smoking" sign. She rubbed her thigh. After walking incorrectly to keep pressure off the knee, the pain had now found a new home in her lower back which made her extremely uncomfortable, but in no way was it going to deprive her of her nicotine.

Ten minutes later she had shuffled through the halls and was happily huddled under the dock, clumsily lighting a cigarette and filling the tiny crevice with a beautiful mix of secondhand smoke and oxygen as she inhaled something beyond heavenly and exhaled it into the crisp November air.

The beauty of the season quickly turned on her.

While she tried to move around in an attempt to warm herself, the prison uniform once again became an unbearable antagonist and rubbed her cold, irritated skin to levels unimaginable. Her awkward "Warmth Dance" sent her lower back into spasms and caused her to abandon her cigarette in exchange for the warmth of the prison after less than a dozen miserable, choppy mini-drags.

Gone was her only reliable source of stability and reassurance.

She now focused on the final two stops before she could crawl into her own bed and sleep this goddamn day away.

***

Gina never understood why the rest of the prison staff called the in-house hospital "Crook U," but she laughed along like she was in on the joke.

The doctor asked her to sit, but she declined and opted instead to remain nonchalantly leaning against the examination table; the very examination table she was helped upon earlier that evening while the rape kit was administered. She did her best to act like today's events were no biggie; like her back wasn't an upsetting mess of pins and needles. One of the stirrups floated inches beside her shoulder. There was only one reason a medium security, all-male prison hospital would house such a female-specific examination table and that dark revelation suddenly and horribly washed over her. How many former employees did she share this humiliating experience with?

It made her dizzy.

The doctor flipped some pages and nodded over the clipboard's secrets.

"Well, Miss French," he started with a warm smile which disappeared a little too quickly for Gina's liking, "all tests came back negative and there was no signs of trauma inside or outside the vaginal or anal areas."

The doctor paused for Gina's reaction, but she gave none. While she understood the necessity of the procedure for safety and—more importantly—legal reason, she was pretty sure she could tell she wasn't violated after she lost consciousness. While she thankfully had no prior experience with the degrading act, she was pretty confident there would be some obvious telltale physical signs if somewhere between one and nine men forced themselves inside her.

Still, the SORT Team found her unconscious and in "a state of partial undress," thus rewriting her next few month's agenda into a series of exhausting medical and mental evaluations.

But, like those millions of times she had to answer friends of friends' questions about the safety of being a female prison guard at an all-male prison, her reply was prepackaged and bubbled over with a spooky confidence:

"I know the risks."

And Gina did know the risks, and although she never allowed herself to dwell on what could happen, she now had factual events suddenly replacing repressed fantasy situations, complete with an official paper trail. Now everything seemed reversed, like the visions were real and she was fictitious.

The doctor rose, placed his hand on her shoulder, offered a slight squeeze, and while avoiding eye contact he told her that she had done the right thing by urinating. The jarring reminder upset Gina and her mood continued to plummet. On top of the unnecessary internal swabs and samples, the realization that a condescending co-worker in an enamel trench coat—a disenfranchised young man who acted like he was doing the prison some giant favor by lowering his standards enough to practice inside this second rate prison facility—someone Gina dreaded sharing her evening coffee breaks with—had now spent a fraction of his life sponging her own urine off her own legs, was something more haunting. Something more than her mind could properly digest.

Her angry silence sent the message that his complement was not well received.

"I didn't piss my pants because I mentally revisited the *Defense Mechanism Handbook*, you stupid, stupid man! It wasn't a calm, calculated maneuver thanks to this facility's five-star training process. I pissed myself because I knew I was about to be raped. Repeatedly raped, and depending on a million split-second-under-pressure decisions made by my incompetent coworkers, I could have become an amalgamation of hostage and plaything for hours—passed around like currency, until they finally grew tired of me. And then, depending on the decisions made by the people in charge, the people sitting safely in their offices, my captors would realize how bleak the situation truly was, and while already serving life sentences, they would probably kill me to send a message if negotiations turned ugly like they usually did."

This was the statement she so desperately longed to carve into the doc's skull with that slim, pointy, pen-light thing he decided, after-the-fact, to quickly shine in each of her eyes in a sad attempt to look professional.

"They didn't rape my eyes either, asshole, but thanks."

And as the light momentarily blinded her she thought about cracking the code for him, denouncing the wisdom bestowed upon the staff from the almighty *Defense Mechanism Handbook* as, from what she could remember, urination didn't send waves of disgust coursing through the sea of obvious hate-filled lust. It didn't even slow them down. At best, the urine mildly amused them as the choking continued, as one particularly charming, saggy-tattooed-middle-aged man lifted the back of her head and smashed it back down against floor—repeatedly, as the other gentlemen tore at her clothes. Screw the *Defense Mechanism Handbook*, retaliation didn't even cross Gina's mind—despite all her training and her time passing Bruce Lee retaliation situational daydreams, when the events finally unfolded in real time, the fear left no room for a reaction of any kind. The fear was instant and overwhelming.

The fear paralyzed.

All training vanished and selfishly taking its place was the all-consuming embrace of said fear, fueled only by self-preservation—forced down with an impressive side helping of cranial damage.

Suddenly, as if remembering a birthday or anniversary two days too late, Gina's hand nervously ran up the back of her skull searching for that inexplicably forgotten wound. She cringed as her fingers unearthed the sensitive spot where her head had become one with the cement.

The combination of pain, anger and raw humiliation put the inquisition into Travis's health on hold. She needed to get out of there—now.

Winning the battle but losing the war, she thanked him through clenched teeth while escaping the examination room, which seemed to go from zero-to-claustrophobic in a matter of seconds, but the hallway brought no relief. She was too far into the flashback to turn it off. Her head throbbed as she relived her last seconds of consciousness before losing approximately six minutes and waking up on a cot in the prison hospital too scared to take physical inventory.

Her skull bounced off the floor again and again and again and again. Each moment of impact sent her mind skipping like a CD followed by a moment of nothing as it fought to catch back up and updated her brain of the progressing horrors.

"Come on, come on."

"Hold her down."

"Fuck the shoes."

"Wonder if the whore's clean?"

"Hurry up."

Gina shakily ducked into the little girl's room, locked herself in a stall, and with all the desperation of a seasoned addict, lit up another cigarette. She enjoyed long drag after long drag as she slowly slid down the smooth metal wall until she sat on the floor resting her head against the toilet tank.

She closed her eyes and carelessly ashed on the floor. Once she tasted filter, she opened her eyes just long enough to spark another.

Paying for the sins of others, the cigarettes fell one by one. Two, three, four, all reasonable limits were gone.

She inhaled until her veteran lungs screamed for release, which came with an intense coughing fit and eventually threatened vomit.

As her breathing regulated she somehow felt genuinely centered for the first time since some bitter headcase from Cell Block B knocked her to the floor as her co-workers were being swarmed three corridors over.

Was it planned? Calculated? Spontaneous? All she knew is that she wanted a cup of coffee to pass the remaining twenty minutes of her shift when she heard screaming. She began to move—then something hit her.

At the time, all she had wanted was another coffee to help run out the clock when the sudden screams pushed her forward. She remembered her head swimming with adrenaline and fear when she was knocked to the ground.

Then the fun began, and here we were.

Whenever a decent sized riot breaks out, months are wasted with in-depth interviews and conspiracy theories and the final verdict is always the same: nothing more than impulsive acts from impulsive criminals with no motives deeper than breaking the pulsing monotony. Besides, Gina gave up trying to find meaning in any of their actions almost one year ago to the date, when a new inmate she had never met before small-talked her close enough to the bars to drench her with a mug of bloody diarrhea. For him, it was some sort of gang initiation; for Gina, it began an embarrassing medical cycle with a month of anti-viral medication, followed with a six week, a three month, a six month and a one year blood test. Knowing an impressive twenty-to-forty percent of the inmates rock Hepatitis C make for some long sleepless nights as you await the results.

The conclusion? Serving life sentences provide zero incentives to behave.

Feeling almost human again and furiously indifferent about her chosen profession, Gina French collected herself off the bathroom floor and headed to the final necessary stop before she could free herself of this day.

***

In the small meeting quarters she was surrounded by police, her superiors, a SORT Team representative, lawyers and a government official. All madly digging their way through paperwork hell.

Her immediate supervisor stood up as she entered and offered her his chair. She declined and stood shamelessly in front of the group.

How many people in this room saw me covered in my own urine? she wondered, as her sudden bravado drained.

They led her into a side room, closed the door, and presented her with another stack of paperwork to be meticulously reviewed, approved and signed. She tugged at her sweatshirt which continued to scratch her skin as she nodded her way through the seemingly endless buzz of information as they verbally tripped over each other.

"The standard procedures were exercised as stated in the Riot Comprehensive Guide. The SORT Team responded with immediate force and the disturbance was contained and dissolved before the instigators had the opportunity to organize and section off territories, fortify their positions or recruit additional participants. The disturbance consisted of a total of seventeen prisoners, six of which have been moved to secure units and are currently being interrogated but initial information indicates the riot was a sudden unplanned reaction of a verbal altercation between Officer Claire—"

Gina's attention came and went until an overly dramatic pause demanded it back.

"Officer French? Gina? Officer James Claire suffered extensive internal damages and passed away in the ambulance during transportation to Sisters of Hope."

The statement caught Gina in mid-swallow. Although she was immediately told of a staff fatality when she awoke in the Prison ICU she had somehow been misinformed—she was under the impression the deceased was a faceless janitor and not a fellow correctional officer. Not Officer Claire. Not the fatherly old man with the gentle features and the infectious chuckle. Suddenly questioning every other fragment of information she had been fed, Gina managed to stop choking on her own spit long enough to finally force out her million dollar question:

"What about . . . Graveyard Travis?"

Christ, she totally blanked on his last name.

The sudden topic transition caused an uncomfortable silence while the Bad News Crew exchanged glances.

One man she had never seen before took a step forward while opening a manila file and locking eyes with Gina's immediate superior. "Officer?" He waited for someone to jump in. "Green. Officer Green?" someone offered, filling in the blanks.

"Green? Green, right?" Gina mentally filed the color/name.

"Yes, Officer Green," she loudly corrected herself. "What's the current condition of Officer Green?" she coughed out, trying not to sound like some lovesick little girl, terrified the opportunity to rhythmically pant his name will never present itself again.

The pages scurried through the manila folder guy's fingers at an impressive pace, followed by a less impressive monotone delivery.

The list of injuries read like a sociopath's grocery list:

"Minor trauma to the skull . . . cracked collar bone . . . two damaged ribs . . . three broken toes . . . "

Pause.

The first four wounds showed negative signs of long-term damage, however a severe puncture wound below the kneecap with a yet-to-be-determined object. Most likely a pen or pencil, would require rehabilitation with the possibility of permanent damage.

Confirmation that Officer Green—Graveyard Travis—was indeed okay seemed to relieve a substantial amount of pressure between Gina's ears, but it was quickly replaced by the lawyer's babble and paper-pointing fingers as she rapidly signed form after form as her superiors explained their courses of action and reaction to locate and protect one of their current four female employees.

After everyone witnessed her last signature, the pen was snatched from her hand and the papers were whisked away; gone forever from her sight, leaving another unusual silence with the promise of dismissal. The room was saturated with relief. As the door slammed, her immediate supervisor placed his hand on Gina's shoulder, the same shoulder that the doctor touched when he faked compassion—it was clearly that particular shoulder's lucky day.

"As you know, Officer French," he began in a tone that mirrored the one her dad used when he gave her *The Talk*, "employees taken hostage are allotted substantial time off for mental and physical recovery. However, in this case, this incident did not evolve into the state's definition of a riot. There were—from a technical standpoint, no hostages taken, as the response was immediate and the situation did not progress to the next level—waiting and negotiating were elements which did not come into play. We used force as soon as we could and from the reports filed by the SORT Team, it was the correct decision because they located you, the lone female officer just before—well, you were lucky they found you when they did. Anyway, in this situation we have extended your official leave of absence from two weeks to two months at one hundred percent of your wage for the first two weeks then fifty-five percent of your regular wage for the following six weeks as long as you continue your weekly psychological evaluations during this time. You are free to return at any time during the six week stretch and, um, thank you Officer French—you are free to go."

Gina nodded them away as she rose from the chair. The

shitty deal didn't surprise her in the least, but this financial grave they had just dug and tossed her into, forced another emotional 180. Surviving six weeks at fifty-five percent of an already depressingly low wage was going to cause forty-six days of fresh new financial problems. Or she could suck it up and come back in fourteen days.

"One more second please."

Completely defeated, Gina slumped back into her chair. Her head hung down but her eyes looked up and met her superior's nervous glance.

"Gina, expect a visit sometime in the next forty eight hours. Um, one prisoner is still unaccounted for."

Gina looked for traces of sarcasm and waited for the punchline.

It was her turn to break the silence as she shook her head, but he cut her off before she could even begin to formulate words: "We know, it seems logically impossible, but—"

From the "not officially a riot's" central location to the concertina wire surrounding the facility, Gina began to point out the obvious and was again cut off as her superior began listing the already long list compiled of theories, the most popular one being that he was still hidden inside the compound and it would only be a matter of time before the dogs flushed him out.

Gina had nothing to add. Her head continued to shake from side to side, but no longer out of confusion. Her face was visibly painted with comical bewilderment. Was it a riot or was it not a riot? Can you have a mini riot? A riot-lite? How bush-league was this place? Can someone walk across an entire prison and just leave while a riot may or may not be going on? For the second time today she scolded herself for beginning to care and decided to cease and desist. This couldn't be less of her problem.

Forgetting to protect her knee, she raised herself from the chair, and a sharp spasm shot through her leg, causing her to stumble forward and grab the desk for support. Manila

Folder guy helped her regain her balance and as she breathed down the pain and pulled away from his touch someone else explained that the facility would provide her an escorted ride home and would arrange to have her vehicle delivered tomorrow morning.

"Oh, and Officer French? One more thing: until we gather more information on the, uh, unaccounted for prisoner, we expect you will exercise strict professional confidentiality? We don't want to risk the media shedding unnecessary negative light on a very successful 'possible worst case scenario' operation. Let the reporters focus on the unfortunate incident involving Officer Claire for the next few days."

"You mean the on-the-job murder of husband and father—Jim Claire?" Gina returned with the identical detached monotone delivery.

"Go home and spend time with your daughter, Officer French."

CHAPTER II

T HE KNOB WAS filthy.

There was some sort of greenish-brown tint covering the face of the cold tap. The hot tap, however, seemed immaculate. "Makes sense," Gina noted and once again twisted the hot tap with the ball of her foot, sending a fresh stream of scalding water into the bathtub. She traced the large red H with her big toe. The tap-fixation continued.

The cold tap was filthy, the hot tap was clean, and the spigot matched the latter- polished and shiny. If she squinted hard enough she could make out a somewhat distorted and inversed image of herself and all things considered, she didn't look half bad. The spigot was a mixture of cold steel and deception. Feeling like the centerfold for *Lazy Magazine*, her MP3 player's headphones remained deep in her ears although the battery level was so beyond low it never even powered through a single song before shutting itself off. At the time, music was a decent idea—a much needed distraction, but forty-five minutes later it made no difference. Gina just stared straight ahead at the twisted faucet reflection as the newly added water slowly warmed her from her feet up to her neck.

Her cigarette extinguished itself about two-thirds of the way down as the sweat from her hand soaked the lower portion beyond . . . burnability?

After a few failed puffs, she giggled and flicked the fraction forward, missing her reflection in the faucet but hitting the wall and dropping into the water. She watched as it momentarily spiraled and danced under the force of the running water before it went under and came shooting back to the surface by her thigh. She snickered again as she closed her eyes and counted the other filters bobbing up and down against her skin, hidden beneath the bubbles. One rested against her rib cage, two tickled her feet, and another two were just like that prisoner—unaccounted for.

As obviously shitty as the day was, she seemed to be sweating out the negative energy. All that remained was warmth, white and silence.

She wondered if this was what purity felt like—purity and/or death. Maybe the two were interchangeable.

Her daydreams of being warm, pure and deceased were finally interrupted by the sounds of fumbled keys outside the apartment door.

***

Sitting at the kitchen table Gina now found a new fascination with a similar distorted reflection—this time the aromatic liquid in her coffee cup failed to invert her image, but instead gave it a bluish tint. Somehow it was Smurf Gina who demanded all her attention, not the baby who restlessly slept, snuggled deep between the ridiculously large folds of her ridiculously large housecoat. Out of pure guilt, she looked down at the precious little package inhaling and exhaling on her lap before looking back to the Blue Man Group version of herself and slowly back to her roommate's dramatic glance.

Hannah was such a perfect friend and when the times called for it—a loyal sidekick, but above all else, she was comfortably predictable at all times. Hannah kept pressing for details but was getting the rehearsed, stripped down PG version of the evening's events, knowing full well that by the time Hannah returned to the diner she waitressed at, artistic privileges would be in full swing and a new 18A version of the evening-news-making-story would be presented for consumption.

"Really, that's it. I got jumped from behind, they wailed

on me a bit—and then it was broken up," she offered her skeptical roommate as she shifted the weight of her daughter to a single arm, freeing up the other for another sip of coffee. As Hannah pressed on, playing the "It feels better to talk about it" card in her grade school substitute teacher voice, Gina caught her reflection rippling in the dark liquid and winced as the flashback of the sudden kick that sent her crumpling to the floor rattled through her brain. The kick that stole the air from her lungs and left her ripe for the pickings.

Hannah silently sat and waited. Gina said nothing, knowing full well she was being unnecessarily distant to someone who genuinely wanted to help, and although Hannah was a complete social freak when it came to sensationalizing gossip, this dynamic was the glue of their friendship—Gina was the performer and Hannah the reporter. Gina entertained the idea of opening up, of detailing some of the evening's more horrific moments, but more out of exhaustion than malice, the thought was abandoned. The conversation needed to shift. The unforeseen financial spiral needed to be addressed.

Hannah brushed it off, the looming holiday season promised both extra shifts and generous tips, which would cover the missing income. To illustrate the point, Hannah brought her coffee cup down in the middle of the table on top of the unopened phone bill and gently slid it towards herself, letting it fall off the table and symbolically (in her mind anyway) plummet to the floor, out of her roommate's sight.

The visual aid reminded Gina of another time; another life, where Hannah happily worked double shifts during Gina's short maternity leave. Gina felt no guilt, this is who Hannah was—she was a fixer; enthusiastic and blissfully loyal.

"Plus," Hannah excitedly offered, "you still get your checks from Dan."

The sentence ran out of steam midway though and the concluding word "Dan" was barely audible.

Hannah primed herself for damage control but Gina needed none.

Hannah knew select Friday nights were unusually hard on Gina, as agreed during the bitter visitation negotiations, every other Saturday Dan took the baby—took their baby— for the weekend, but this time around Gina secretly felt relieved for the future daughterless forty-eight hours. For the first time in her life she allowed herself to agree to Dan's claims of superior parental abilities.

Despite Gina's lack of visual concern, Hannah felt compelled to fill the silence: "I can call Dan. I'm actually surprised he hasn't called yet, I'm sure if he hasn't heard about the riot by now he will completely understand if you want to switch weekends and spend time tomorrow and Sunday with your baby. Yes, that's right Ryen is totally your baby, not his. I don't care how hard he's scheming for custody. She will never be his baby—he gave that right up the first time he bailed on you, he can't just come and go as he pleases and expect to have a place in Ryen's." Gina held up her hand, cutting Hannah off mid-sentence.

The silence was broken by a slight chuckle which manifested itself into full blown laughter.

"Jesus, Hannah, come up for air." Gina smiled as she rubbed her temple to heighten the effect of her statement.

The noise caused baby Ryen to squirm awake and the women were instantly silent. They watched as the tiny six-month old yawned through fluttering eyes before sighing back to sleep nuzzled deep into her mother's housecoat's warm white sleeves.

The coffee suddenly cold.

***

The knocking at the door partially woke up Gina, but left her disoriented. Ryen suddenly appeared inches from her face and cooed "Bye-bye Mama," without moving her lips then disappeared from sight. Hannah sat on the edge of the bed and readjusted the infant's pink toque before resuming

Gina's sudden intimate ventriloquism production. This time the baby swung forward, returning inches from Gina's face as an adult hand shook Ryen's tiny hand at the tiny wrist— "Bye bye Mama, see you Monday morning," and then Ryen was whisked out of her sight.

Gina lay in bed listening to the brief, but civil, exchange between Dan and Hannah during what sounded like a business transaction. Hannah lied about Gina's whereabouts and agreed to pass on a message of concern and relief about Friday night's "incident."

Incident? That's what we're calling it now?

Gina wondered if Dan sounded this phony and shallow their entire relationship and she just didn't pick up on it, or she overlooked it somehow because she fooled herself into thinking he was in it for the long haul.

Despite the legal arguing, Gina's pivotal Dan memory remained the numerous times he'd sink the eight-ball and put Gina, arguably the world's worst pool player, out of her misery. His celebratory tradition involved raising the cue above his head and proclaiming "I'm Dan. The man." Funny how his humorous self-confidence used to be the biggest turn-on but somehow didn't hold up over time.

The click of the front door yanked her from the dingy beer-filled pool hall and back to the emptiness of her bedroom. Gina concentrated on the footsteps as they faded down the apartment building's echoey hallway. She imagined Ryen bundled up and snug in Dan's thick arms—a place Gina herself was very familiar with. Dan's body was epic—thick and muscular—and imagining her daughter currently cradled in his arms sent Gina a flash of something she refused to admit was jealousy.

She finally rolled her carcass out of bed and easily counted the hours of sleep on one hand.

Standing in front of her giant oval bedroom mirror Gina disrobed from what little she routinely wore to bed and surveyed the damage: bruises and scratches littered her body, most new, some old, but all in all, she didn't look half as bad as she expected.

She upgraded her status from "carcass" to "passable."

Her hands slid to her stomach—the stretch marks were almost gone. Gina was far from a large woman and an eight pound baby girl didn't do her treasured abs any favors. Turning sideways brought a smile to her face. Four months. Four deceitful and disciplined months of taking advantage of Hannah's Aunt Kat's generous and open ended babysitting offers whenever she was called in to work early (ie—hit the gym), were finally paying off. Only six months had passed, twenty four weeks, and her stomach was almost back to where it was, before cells divided and life erupted inside of her.

Small steps towards the walk-in closet revealed a pain in her knee far less intense than yesterday's, but still justified starting the day chasing two pain killers with a diet soda.

Life itself is a series of justifications.

**

The sound of the hairdryer picked at Gina's now-fading headache as she removed the coffee pot mid-brew and with an impressive amount of speed, grace and practice, she filled a large travel mug and returned the pot with a very small volume of coffee casualties. The drips that didn't make it sizzled and danced, sandwiched between the burner and the bottom of the pot. Gina snatched Hannah's MP3 player from the table, held it up and shrugged her shoulder's in her roommate's direction. Hannah replied with a smile and a nod from over top the waist high partition that separated the kitchen and living room. The hairdryer was a lovely excuse to avoid conversation.

As Gina floated down the front steps she cringed, expecting familiar pain, but her knee held the weight with very little hesitation. Feeling proud of her body's ability to mend itself, she swaggered across the lot until she came face to face with her empty parking spot.

"Right . . . "

She squinted up at the dark sky as her hands searched her jean pockets for change.

The November rain began about ten minutes into her bus ride but nothing was going to break her good mood. As the songs from Hannah's MP3 player randomly flowed into each other, Gina winced at her roommate's bizarre taste in music. She could never understand how someone who lived their life in an unbreakable bubble of positivity could satisfy their musical needs with an elite diet of Rage Against The Machine, Nine Inch Nails and Marilyn Manson. The first three songs alone contained over twenty words she felt would cause Hannah to blush if asked to use them in a sentence. Gina tried to shuffle past the angry rock to something better suiting her mood when she remembered another unusual quirk about her unusual roommate: Hannah changed music styles with the seasons; fall's angry rock would eventually fade into winter's hits of the 50s and 60s, before dissolving happily into 80's classics in the spring. In the hot summer months, the MP3 player went into storage and Hannah listened to the radio.

After hearing every song's intro a third time, Gina finally relaxed the NEXT button and admitted what she knew all along; this hyper-angry, sexually-driven music couldn't have been more suitable for the all the joys that come with public transportation.

Despite the downpour that quickly soaked the clothes to her body, Gina smiled as she sprinted up Travis's front steps. *That's right*, she thought, congratulating herself, *I'm frick'n jogging already.*

About an hour before The Dan came to pick up her daughter (and the only time something other than a bad dream or door knocking aborted her slumber), her cell phone beeped with a new text message: Travis was on his way home from Sisters of Hope. The wound in his knee was cleaned and bandaged and there was nothing else they could do for him, so the hospital sent him packing.

She rang the bell, but then cursed at her stupidity and used the key in her pocket to let herself in.

Travis was in mid-lift, struggling to use a crutch and an elbow to raise himself off the couch, but his leg was having none of it. The giant bandage kept it straight and useless. "Don't . . . " Gina ran to him and helped lower him back down. They abandoned any attempt at an embrace and eagerly kissed each other deeply and forcefully, sputtering one word sentences while coming up for air. From the second she awoke after "the incident," she craved this moment, the unknown reaction. Would Travis cry? Would she? Was Travis going to be emotionally splintered? Would it be awkward that after months of casual sex, life finally forced the two of them into an adult conversation? Would new ground finally be broken?

As if still shuffling through music on Hannah's MP3 player, Gina searched Travis's face for answers but found none.

He seemed the same.

Was it possible that someone else could be as strong as she was? The thought of an equal male counterpart humbled and excited her—was it possible he shared the same perfected detachment to events beyond his control?

She slid her hand down to his puffy bandage.

"Are you—?"

"I'm fine, those dicks tried—"

"But—"

Silence.

The DVD Travis had paused spun back to life after the five minute window expired, sending them both jumping as audio sidetracked the awkward exchange.

Travis searched the couch for the remote control but Gina hopped up and turned down the volume manually.

Silence.

Eventually Travis said, "God, Gina. I heard they got to you just in time—they—"

It was Gina's turn to murder the conversation:

"Trav, I'm okay, it was nothing. But Officer Cla—James—"
Silence crushed their eardrums.

Gina helped herself to his fridge, and walked two perfectly chilled beers back to the couch.

She handed one to Travis and held the other tightly between both hands, imagining the golden liquid filling her tummy full of pain killers. She imagined a similar scenario next to her.

After their horribly failed first real conversation it was clear that communication was not the fusion, and since Travis was in no shape for sex, it was time to bust out the only other common denominator.

She tucked her legs underneath herself, causing the couch to shake and Travis to cringe from the movement as she tried to pry the cap off. "Th—They're not twist-offs," Travis managed to deliver sweetly through clenched teeth, as he steadied himself with his free arm. Gina watched as he took two deep breaths and nodded approvingly.

"Nothing shook out of place?" Gina asked, dragging each word out. She followed her act by dramatically lifting herself from the couch as slowly as humanly possible.

Travis sucked up the pain and slapped the back pocket of her jeans. The sound of flesh hitting rain-damp denim made a loud pop.

Gina spun towards Travis wearing a playful look of shock as she sauntered backwards to the counter that divided the kitchen from the living room. Instead of taking the ten extra steps around the divider she bent over and stretched her upper torso through the two-foot opening between the tall counter top and the low hanging cupboards. Even after her calculated display of flexibility, her fingers hovered a good foot short from where the bottle opener lay by the sink. This caused more laughter.

Gina offered some over-the-top grunting as she raised herself to her tiptoes and closed the distance by an inch.

The show must have gone on longer than she thought

because suddenly she felt a hand gently slide down the back of her jeans.

Before she could say anything his fingers had reached their mark.

The timing was obviously flawed—she immediately wondered what kind of a sick human being would let herself get felt up less than twenty-four hours after nearly getting gang raped, but she also wondered what kind of a sick human being would feel someone up who was nearly gang raped less than twenty-four hours ago. It was a viscous cycle.

This is so wrong. Wrong, wrong, wrong, she thought over and over in her head, until a slight change in finger movement caused her body to tense. She hit the back of her head on the hanging cupboard, causing a millisecond flashback of her skull smashing into the prison floor. Thankfully it didn't last and the pleasant sensation kept her in the present and the past in the past.

Her mind continued in rhythm with his hand. Wrong, wrong, wrong. Damn.

Gina's body finally betrayed her guilt and she gave up, thawing against his inappropriate touch. She popped the button on her jeans and lowered the zipper, giving Travis more room to work as she lay the side of her face down against the cool counter top.

I am not going to feel guilty about this, she justified, I survived a traumatic experience. I need some safety, I need to feel wanted—to be held.

Gina turned off her inner monologue as she lifted her chest off the counter top, silently inviting his other hand up her shirt.

Closing her eyes, she decided the tiring charade of pretending she didn't take a rainy bus ride across the city just to fuck had officially expired.

In Travis's bed the well-oiled routine was constantly interrupted by the flares of tender bruises and still healing scars. Body parts didn't respond to touch like before, forcing them to reinvent the wheel. Travis had always been the aggressor, but now Gina found herself on top, careful not to lower her full weight on him. It was like their minds had been transplanted into foreign bodies, forcing them to find compatibility between the past and the present. Cringes and shudders were answered with breathless apologies. Movements were hesitant and unsure.

The room seemed to be one hundred ten degrees as sweat soaked through bandages and covers were kicked to the floor—exposing the sin as the mid-afternoon sunlight bled through the windows.

Gina opened her eyes long enough to catch a glimpse of the sad union in his wall mirror. Their weathered bodies lacked confidence and seemed completely out of place in Travis's unusually clean bedroom. The act looked like it should have been taking place in the twisted wreckage of a horrible multiple-car collision; the two sole survivors celebrating their second chances right then and there.

This is some serious circus porn.

Minutes later Travis went. Each shudder sent his hand flicking away tiny invisible objects from the side of his vision.

Gina bit her lip as she peeled a soggy and foreign Band-Aid from her stomach.

Circus porn.

***

Things were back to normal.

Even with war-ravaged bodies, the physical compatibility overshadowed any missing degrees of emotional or verbal connections.

It had been over two hours since they finished, but they remained on the mattress, wrapped in the bed sheets. Neither even attempted conversation. Scientists would argue that the post-sex silence was identical to the pre-sex silence; however, the silence they now shared had context. It didn't need validation, nor was it searching for something unobtainable to fill it. It was the tasty silence of aftermath.

They suffered, they survived, they moved on.

The next few hours blurred together until the sobering sunset crashed the party.

CHAPTER III

ALTHOUGH GINA HAD nowhere to go, she decided she had overstayed her welcome.

After helping Travis back into the reclining couch, she showered, using her finger to write "Thanks for the Emergency Room Sex" on the fogged mirror, and gathered her things.

As she emerged from the bathroom, Travis grinned out from behind the red light of a camcorder which could easily have been the most expensive model on the market back in 1989.

She remembered an impressive amount of small talk they had at work a few weeks ago. His family had been pressuring him to finally dub years of home movies from High 8 to VHS and the irony of converting one outdated format to another was noted.

She smiled back into the camera and blew it a kiss.

Once again moving past the possible violation of an almost-rape victim thing, she noticed how relaxed—how at ease she was when they were together. How unusually happy. She briefly allowed herself to revisit the hell that was yesterday: swimming up from unconsciousness, somehow concerned for his safety before her own and wondered if all the negatives of a purely physical relationship somehow became positives for someone as messed up as she was. Maybe this was her last chance to connect with someone who seemed unshaken by the whirlwind of drama that attacked her life with an alarming regularity.

Her eyes softy searched past the red light into Travis's

single, visible eye. The camera followed her as she dropped her bag and walked over to the stereo. Punching the little green arrow with her finger, she brought a song reserved for background noise up to a commanding, eardrum-damaging level.

She slowly turned to face him and slid both hands to her shirt's top button. The smiles slowly faded from both their faces as Travis recorded over his baby sister's high school graduation.

***

Quietly, Kevin Conner appeared on the Marshal Service's Top Fifteen Most Wanted. Debuting at a respectable Number Thirteen, it was his profile that sent the story of his baffling escape nationwide.

Thus began the panic.

Serving a life sentence for double murder, the outstanding young man apparently straight-up teleported out of the prison complex during Friday's momentary loss of control which also resulted in the fatality of one correctional officer.

No signs of escape; no leads.

The Fugitive Safe Surrender initiative was highlighted in a giant bold font and seemed more like a punch line than a viable option.

The media began to swirl.

Gina was questioned three times by three different sets of investigators, and each time they treaded less softly around the whole attempted rape thing and during their final visit they practically demanded she remember every insignificant detail she mentally logged while on her back, pinned to the floor.

As much fun as reliving those particular events on a detailed, daily basis was, the truth—her truth—never changed: Conner wasn't one of the guys that assaulted her. As far as it came to Kevin Conner, she saw nothing—she knew nothing.

In fact, she only knew Conner as a man who would

occasionally nod at her as she did her rounds. "Quiet and quite boring, actually," was her official signed statement regarding her routine interactions with the immediately famous escapee.

The interrogations turned to monotony, then monotony turned to frustration and on the fourth and final visit she stood in the doorway and coldly broke it down to them in jot form:

Kevin Conner:
-5'11"
-African American
-one gimped eye, which in all brutal honesty, she found a little repellent
-no history of violence inside the facility—a model prisoner
-did not see him during the "incident"
-thank you

SLAM
On the phone, Travis was his usual level of vague, but he too had his own issues to deal with. While "the incident" exploded around him and on top of him, he also was pressed for detailed clarity and came up short.

Then the clouds rolled in.

With all reasonable situations exhausted the only logical scenario remaining would be one or two correctional officers aiding Conner in his escape. Although no one interrogating Gina ever verbalized the idea, somewhere during their third Q&A session Gina felt the hair on her arms stand up, like suddenly the name Gina French had slipped across the line separating victims and suspects. Travis felt the same way.

A full week passed. Gina counted down the days until she would be forced to decide. She would either embrace poverty for a six week stretch or return to a place so vile it overflowed into her dreams. The hallway was unavoidable; twenty minutes after punching her timecard she would stand on the exact spot she was attacked and undressed while on the clock. The chance of a repeat performance or subjecting herself to even more abuse and ridicule seemed reasonable and probable. She couldn't calm her fears down; the threat of rape was now constant.

As the days counted down, she knew she couldn't do it. Not just yet.

***

She watched Ryen's brown eyes fade as she rocked the tiny creature to sleep in her lap. The second the child's body relaxed into a deep slumber, she texted Travis. It had been three days since Gina's last interrogation and she was pathetically feeling starved for attention. While they appeared to be done with her, they continued harassing Travis for information they knew he didn't have. Gina smiled to herself as Travis returned a lengthy text complaining about the day's events. She had found a loophole—in person Travis Green often came across as a borderline mute, but give him a cellular phone and the man would text for hours. The interrogators were unusually harsh on him that afternoon, actually asking about he and Gina's rumored relationship. Not sure what that had to do with Conner escaping from prison, Gina chose instead to hop aboard Travis's Anger Train and lash out at the detectives:

"screw them
if I new 4sure where Con was
I wouldnt tell them
I would cash in on the 25k"

Bing

Travis's response was immediate:

"what r u talkin about"

Gina rolled her eyes. A complete lack of attention to detail was one of Travis Green's more frustrating bad habits. They had looked at the Marshal Services' Top Fifteen Most Wanted webpage together—twice—and yet because she didn't point to the words and read them aloud, Travis somehow missed the fine print about the $25K offered for information directly leading to an arrest.

She shook her head and texted back:

"chek the wsite $bags"

Gina waited for the "bing" signaling his reply. When it didn't come she studied the phone itself, waiting for the mail icon which precedes the "bing" to float across her phone.

Suddenly her phone rang.

Travis Green was ready to talk face-to-face.

***

Rain hammered the coffee shop.

The drive to Hannah's aunt's place set her back twenty minutes, but it was worth it; conversation minus fussy baby equals no interruptions. The traffic lights streaked through her reflection in the driver's side window. Even with the smoke in her mouth, Gina couldn't focus. Poverty loomed and brought a deep sense of desperation, but something in Travis's voice unearthed a new measure of hope and it sped her tired body forward, through intersection after intersection.

Travis would have something to turn all this around.

An ace up his sleeve.

Travis would be her savior after all.

Travis looked like complete shit.

His minor wounds were hardly an issue anymore, but the pencil-sized hole under his kneecap had become horribly infected and the poison had spread to the joint. His skyrocketing temperature had landed him another night in the hospital, but this time his bed and breakfast was not financially covered by his employers.

Ignoring his yellow-like complexion, Gina dropped into the dark booth across the table from him and searched his vacant face.

"Spill."

Travis silently stirred his coffee without looking up. Gina eagerly slid off her damp jacket and quickly surveyed the surrounding booths for eavesdroppers.

"You fucking know something, don't you?"

The steam rising from his coffee fluttered with her breath. Travis poured another unhealthy heaping spoonful of sugar into the chipped cup and resumed stirring.

"You're holding out on me."

A small smile spread across his face.

"Spill it, prick," Gina commanded, hoping the delivery sounded more flirtatious than impatient. The truth dangled somewhere in the middle.

Travis began, "Sometimes during the graveyard shift, to break the boredom."

"Oh Travis," Gina's jaw dropped, "you slept with Kevin Conner?"

Travis finally met her gaze. "What? No. I . . . "

The waitress appeared.

"She's a rainy one out there, ain't she?" the perky lady began while removing a pen and notepad from her apron.

Travis broke his stare and dropped his eyes back into his coffee as Gina restlessly shifted and smiled angrily at the waitress and her terrible timing.

"I swear it's been raining off and on for—"

Gina's hand shot up, her open palm suddenly hovered half a foot in front of the waitress's face.

"coffeethankyou."

The smile drained from the waitress as she stared into Gina's hand. Shifting her weight from one foot to the other, she mustered a synthetic smile and continued to waste Gina's time—this time on purpose. "Let me tell you about today's special, hon. Okay, first we have our famous late-night pot roast, served with—"

Gina squirmed in her chair, anxiously wiping her hand over her mouth and tucking her hair behind her ears as the waitress continued, holding every vowel, stretching every syllable.

"No, no pot roast—thank you, no, just a coffee, please . . . Brenda?" The pitch of Gina's voice raised with the name delivery; as if it were a question. The waitress looked down at her once-gold name tag pinned just below the uniform's faded collar. Turning slightly towards Travis, Brenda subtly brushed her hand across her large breasts before straightening the engraved rectangle and picking a piece of crud out of the B's groove with a giant red fingernail.

The power play began.

Travis turned away, but not before Gina read his face: he was annoyed by another of her impromptu catfights—her bizarre ability to steer every conversation into the surreal. He started to say something but got cut off as the waitress bent across the table to collect an empty creamer. Gina scraped a fingernail over her tooth and she too looked away as the side of a red and black checkered breast eclipsed Travis's face from her sight.

Brenda finished her little show, straightened back up, and began smoothing her uniform with her hands; continuing to not-so-subtly run her hands over her chest and thighs in front of Travis while smiling coldly at Gina.

"So, that was just a coffee, honey?" were her words but her tone said something else; something more along the lines of, *You think you're better than me, you skinny little bitch?*

Gina reached down the table, slid an upside down coffee mug/saucer combo in front of Brenda, noisily flipped the mug right-side-up and pointed inside the empty mug implying that the waitress needed visual aid to pull off a task that was beyond her comprehension.

Brenda stuttered to retort but Gina's pointing became

43

more animated, climaxing with an over-the-top encouraging smile—as if the waitress was a puppy Gina was teaching to fetch.

The complete, unfiltered lack of respect caught Brenda off-guard and she stormed away—defeated.

Gina watched the waitress retreat back into the kitchen then quickly raised herself off the vinyl-covered bench, leaned across the table and stuck her own breasts in Travis's face, "Let me get those empty creamers, big boy," Gina delivered with an off-key imitation of the waitress's husky voice. She sank back into the booth and threw her arms open. "What the fuck? Seriously, what the fuck Who does this happen to?"

Travis brought his coffee to his lips, set it back down without taking a sip and raised his hands in exhausted agreement.

Gina continued to shake her outstretched arms then brought closure to the whole production with a final "fuck."

Travis checked for the waitress then snapped his game-face back on and whispered, "Gina, Conner—I . . . okay, okay, okay—about a year ago, maybe fourteen months, Conner, well, one night I was—"

Gina snapped her arms closed across her chest. Her irritation bled into Travis as she nodded him on. He continued to drop his words.

"Conner was—I mean he—"

"You know how he escaped?"

"No, I—"

"You helped him escape?

"What? No, no. I just—"

"Just?"

"I think, I mean, I have a pretty good—"

"Here you are, sweetheart!" loudly interrupted the exchanging whispers.

Brenda had returned.

Travis closed his eyes, leaned back and locked his fingers

behind his head. Gina, arms still crossed, slumped further into her seat and rolled her eyes up at Brenda, whose smile beamed from ear-to-ear. Brenda ignored the timeless waitress protocol and opted not to bring the actual pot of coffee to the table and fill the pre-placed mug Gina so loving prepared for her, nope, Brenda returned with an actual pre-poured cup of coffee. Pre-poured from someplace out of Gina's sight. Pre-poured from someplace probably evil. Gina's eyes rolled down and fixed on what appeared to be a normal cup of coffee as her mind spun a quick montage of Brenda parading her beverage through the kitchen while grubby cooks lined up and spit into the mug.

With a hand on her hip, Brenda raised a white bill above her head. "All right, two coffees? Will there be anything else?" Her confidence meant the game was officially over and Brenda was wearing the gold.

The horrible gurgling sounds of the tattooed cooking staff ungluing unspeakable horrors from the darkest folds of their black lungs slowly graduated into a smuttier version of the coffee's origin, one where the kitchen staff, now crowding around Brenda, cheer her on as she places the coffee mug on the dirty kitchen floor, hikes up her black and red checkered skirt, squats over it, and with pinpoint accuracy, urinates right into Gina's java, before she triumphantly picks up the cup and exits the kitchen.

Gina blinked away the coffee's questionable beginnings and with her back against the wall, she retaliated. With both hands firmly wrapped around the mug's warmth, Gina slowly raised it to her lips and loudly sipped at the liquid before she closed her eyes and swallowed with orgasmic glee. Gina's eyes slowly fluttered back to life as she dreamily rolled her pupils to Brenda and sighed, "Oh my God, Brenda, it's delicious."

Despite the crushing blow, Brenda continued as if Gina still feared the unknown and backed away smiling down at the cup of coffee nestled in the hands of her least favorite customer.

The second Brenda disappeared around the corner, Gina's bedroom eyes snapped back to rage, snapped back to Travis and then with the flick of her wrist, the presumed spit/urine/coffee cocktail soared into the planter separating their booth from the next.

Travis quietly sipped his pee-free coffee.

More silence.

Gina rubbed her head. Her patience dripped down the fake plants alongside her discarded coffee.

"Okay, okay," she began, while she carefully unfolded the fancy napkin wrapping just enough to allow her tongue to slide across the fork, knife and spoon before returning the cutlery to the unused placemat one booth over, "I lied and begged for a babysitter and drove here through the rain, I need caffeine and I'm ten seconds away from walking into the kitchen and breaking my foot off in Brenda's ass. If you wanted your way with me you would have invited me over to your place and not this shithole, so I'm guessing this is serious, I'm guessing this is either about our jobs, our pretend relationship or about Kevin Conner—so can you please, please just get to the goddamn point?"

Shocked by the demanded conclusion, Travis nervously stole another look around.

"Christ, Travis, no one can hear, no one is listening—do you know how Conner escaped or not?"

Stunned by her raised, condescending tone, Travis nodded.

His eyes turned as serious as his tone:

"Gina, I don't know how he got out, but I think—I think I know where he went." Travis held up a hand and repeatedly rubbed his thumb across his middle and index fingers. "I think I know where he is."

Rain hammered the coffee shop.

***

Gina tries to stand when someone shoves her back down from behind.

"You ain't going nowhere."

Her first thought is to protect her spine and she rolls over just in time to take the stomp in the stomach instead of the vertebrae, but the blow cheats the oxygen from her lungs.

A thousand hands grope.

Her soul screams but her mind translates her pleas to a garbled "Huhhhhhhhhhhttttthhhhhhhhh," as spittle runs down her cheek.

"Come on, come on."

The hands are so cold on her skin.

She defiantly tries to sit up but a giant hand catches her throat mid-lift and slams her head and shoulders back down.

WHAM

Her skull meets cement.

"Hold her down."

The vision is a blur of angry, unattached hands: most continue to invade, others, curled into fists, land blows.

Her shrinking lungs remind her of bigger problems.

"Fuck the shoes."

THUD

"Wonder if the whore's clean?"

Tears stream.

"Hurry Up"

THUD

Gina's eyes snapped open.

As the cobwebs in her vision faded she realized she actually woke up midway through the night terror, but subconsciously chose to remain in the dream, letting it play out.

This was scarier than the nightmare itself; she spent her days running from the experience, but now it had caught up to her. It found her at night when the race was over. Laying in the darkness, she relived it again. Every detail was forever burnt into her brain. She could effortlessly recreate it. Imagining the rest of her life coexisting with the memory usually overwhelmed her, so in select moments of bravery she tried to embrace it—hoping for closure through overkill. She inhaled the hoard of stank breath. She offered herself to every selfish hand. She watched as every hovering set of eyes reduced themselves to sadistic slits. Somehow nine individuals combined their horrible years of intense sexual inactivity into something tangible and cruelly offered it to her against her will.

"I know the risks."

Looking back through history it now seemed like her favorite "don't screw with me" catchphrase played out like a punchline to a joke everyone told behind her back.

"I know the risks."

THUD

"I know the risks."

THUD

***

The darkness seemed angry and ready to pounce. Gina rolled out of bed and shuffled towards her only point of reference—the crack of light under the door.

Spilling into the safety of the hallway's sixty watt bulb, her mind seemed relieved, yet suddenly deprived.

Coffee time.

She was exhausted but under three hours of sleep was nothing new for her; if anything, it was almost routine and, as always, curable with the right amount of caffeine. A slight chill turned her back towards the open door of her bedroom. The light from the hallway bled deep into her room and chased the demons to the far corners.

As Gina retrieved her housecoat, she caught her image in the giant mirror. She sucked in and turned sideways so the light from the hallway hit hard against her stomach, making its smooth definitions prominent. Prominent and inspiring. If she covered the fading stretch marks with her hands, all signs of carrying a baby past term were finally gone.

Losing herself in the warmth of her humorously large housecoat, she crept down the area which was a hallway by name only as three strides took you past the three bedrooms and one bathroom and put you in the kitchen. Gina's toes sunk into the worn gray carpet as she stopped and peeked in the second room: the baby's room. Curled into a ball in the middle of her crib, Ryen's tiny tummy rhythmically expanded and deflated. The word "Mother" still seemed more like a nickname than of an official title, but every so often the little pink reason for her body image insecurities stirred feelings of unrelenting pride. That flawless collection of flesh and blood came from inside her. How completely adult of her.

Sneaking into the kitchen revealed Hannah asleep on the couch. Still in her gaudy waitressing uniform she drooled onto the cushion as the blue light from a late night infomercial playfully bounced off her features. Gina got sucked in and spent the next five minutes watching the ULTIMO KNIFE 3000 cut through everything in its path. Except for another ULTIMO KNIFE 3000.

Gina balanced the pros of coffee production against the negatives of waking up her slumbering roomie.

It was a tough call indeed.

Gina's eyes landed on the bristle board hanging beside the fridge. "The Showcase", as they called it, displayed photo highlights of the friendship as it spread across two decades.

Picking a penny off the floor, she decided luck would choose her course of action.

Amused by the sudden game she created, she whispered to Hannah, "Heads I make coffee, tails I get my lazy ass dressed, hit a coffee shop and let you sleep. It's all up to the penny now, Hannah; don't hate the player—hate the game," and with that Gina flipped the coin into the air. In her mind it went straight up and down, landing back in her hand, head-side up, but in reality she fired it hard left, sending it noisily into the sink. Hannah's eyes shot open. Gina bit her lip and smiled as the sound of the penny spinning in the sink got slower and quieter until, after what seemed like a decade, it finally came to a complete stop. Hannah blinked a few times, turned to face the back of the couch, and fell back asleep.

The coffee percolated and bubbled, filling the tiny apartment with the Godlike aroma of Irish Cream flavored Java. To curb what little guilt she had, Gina pulled the plug mid-brew. The machine puffed and fizzled. With her free hand, she blindly grabbed a mug from the cupboard that, as of last month's count, housed forty-six handled masterpieces. 90% of the dishes in the apartment were either baby-related or coffee mugs. It was a sincere reflection on their lifestyle. She examined the mug she chose at random; the thick black words "Gina French Is NOT A Waste Of Roofies" jumped out from the shiny white finish. It took her back to an evening when foreign beer was cheap and this particular catchphrase owned the night as Gina and her girlfriends kept dancing long after the music had stopped and the ugly lights had been raised. The phrase had started as a playful dig, after a round of shots promising no men, no drama tonight, a stranger had asked Hannah about her friend, to which she replied, "Who her? Oh, Gina—ya, she's a waste of roofies."

The quote was relayed back to Gina who feigned offense and rebuttal: "Gina French is NOT a waste of roofies." The following afternoon Gina painfully awoke on the floor of the apartment, the inside of her mouth tasted like the back of a stamp, and Hannah presented her with the "one hour" custom made mug as they laughed and drained the digital camera's batteries, flipping through the pictures, hoping to remember the hours the alcohol had stolen.

Gina slid the balcony door open and entered the night.

Sitting on a rattly lawn chair she used her barefoot to slide the overflowing makeshift ashtray within reaching distance.

Traffic whizzed through the busy street below. Downtown was a blur of lights and smoke and she waited for the last set of taillights to disappear in the distance before overhanding the dented tin of cigarette butts into the darkness.

One.

Two.

Three.

She had reached seven before PING, RATTLE, RATTLE. A new record.

Lighting a cigarette and ashing into a virgin tin can, she followed the trail as she gloriously emptied her lungs into the night air.

Gina poured her first cup of coffee and swore for forgetting the sugar, but decided to suck it up and drink it hardcore black as she had already sank into the lawn chair's Gina-sized groove and sugar didn't seem to justify movement. Nor did a house fire, a sniper or the apocalypse.

Sitting in silence with her two favorite crutches, she was now complete and had no other morning routines or memories to distract her. It took a while, but the present had finally caught up with her.

Travis had become increasingly obsessed with the $25K reward and as a result, Travis's plan had become increasingly insane.

It was all based on a passing comment that was made over a year ago. More than twelve months ago! Casual conversation, small talk, filling time—nothing more. Boredom ate at the prisoners every second of every day, crafting them all into attention seeking liars. However, Travis had printed maps from the Internet and had actually managed to put together a compelling argument. They studied the region and the few spottings the media were reporting coincidentally supported Travis's theory—Conner was definitely heading north. There were millions of variables and the reliability of these sightings were questionable at best, but still, Gina could see in Travis's eyes that through betrayal, he felt he deserved to be right. Travis thought he had a certain rapport with the inmates; that he was less despised than the rest of the staff because he would wander the halls late at night and pass the time conversing with them. Travis was clueless enough to think that the criminals could see past his uniform and see that Travis was what? In his own way, "just as much a prisoner as they were?" Did he really think that? Was Travis that stupid? Gina didn't despise Travis's backwards strategy; in his shoes she probably would have done the same thing as cutbacks, the threat of privatization, and the false sense of security when the entire prison was locked-down for the night, left Travis pretty much lone wolf during the shift. If something ever went wrong, it would be him against them. Not good odds. Gina wondered if Travis actually believed that. If he truly thought in that situation these killers and rapists would just . . . what? High-five their favorite CO as the brutality burned safely around him?

Instead, years of fake friendships ended with a pencil of truth painfully protruding from his naive knee.

CHAPTER IV

THE PLAN.

Lake Timor.

A quick Internet search told stories of a small community which "once was". In the eighties, people predicted Lake Timor would be the next vacation destination. Rich families bought land and erected giant cabins. Actually, rich and stupid families bought land and erected giant cabins. Time revealed the land itself was bad, weak and unstable; unable to support the sudden billions of dollars of attention. Future retirement homes sank. Walls cracked. Foundations crumbled. The structures worth salvaging were physically moved west to stable ground, but most were left broken and abandoned. Lake Timor West is still kicking ass and taking names; growing and expanding every year, however, what ever became of the first draft? What happened to Lake Timor East? A question suddenly worth asking, indeed. When you're on the run, do you try to get lost in the shuffle of a large center or do you go into seclusion; avoiding all human interaction? Other than his crime and his disfigured eye, Conner was completely average in every way. Was it possible this was a perfected character trait? Was Conner's greatest ability to remain chameleon-like? To disappear in the crowd? To slide unnoticed through the background? Had he played them all?

Travis was convinced he was right. Gina was convinced Travis had lost his mind. Although his argument made more sense each time she went over the details, the mental picture of her and her crippled screw buddy going on a road trip to flush a murderer out of an abandoned lakefront community still seemed beyond comical. How very Hardy Boys. She imagined Travis yelling "Gina" as she snatches one of his crutches out of his mid-air toss and strikes Conner over the head with it. Comedy.

The best part was that Travis couldn't really remember much about the actual conversation surrounding the random name drop.

Gina felt a guilty smile creep through her lips—that had to be where Travis's "hey brother, let's rap, you can tell me anything" rapport he thought had with the inmates soured: he was a terrible listener.

Lake Timor.

The conversation apparently wasn't memorable in any way, it blended together with the billions of other stories he had heard from the sleepless inmates. Travis rarely saw any sort of action or negative energy from these men during the nights. This slowly caused Travis to side with the shrinks and authors who judged the penal system from a safe distance. Society's popular theory which started surfacing around the time Gina was hired was that the majority of the prisoners were, themselves, helpless victims. Victims of poverty, victims of a lack of education, victims of whatever. Victims living a double-life. During the day prison life was all about reputation and intimidation, but as Travis testified on a regular basis, during the darkest hours of the night, most of them were just depressed, bored young men who craved contact with their children, wives and girlfriends.

Gina covered the odd graveyard shift over the past few years and the difference in the men was indeed, night and day, however, she didn't believe the hype. A monster too tired to lash out is still a monster. Even evil needs downtime.

Gina was a walking reminder that she had been right all along; Travis was a limping one.

Gina carelessly burned her tongue as she took a giant sip of coffee. The sting derailed her train of thought and made her realize she was mentally procrastinating—she passed her criminology classes years ago. The back stories were no longer relevant; the current score read like this:

1. Kevin Conner escaped from prison.
2. Travis may have known where Conner was or where he was heading.
3. There was a $25K reward for information leading to his capture.
4. She was about to hit a gigantic financial recession.

This seemed like a no-brainer: hand over the info and wait by the mailbox for the check—however, with her wages cut and the creeping suspicion her name had indeed been added to the list of suspects, all that remained was anger. So much anger. So much complicated anger. Travis took his sweet-ass time coughing up the name of the lake and would his tardiness cement his guilt with the authorities? The unknown was just that.

So what was Travis's whispered proposal?

To wait until his body rejected the poison and he would be able to walk, then the two of them, clutching pitchforks and torches, would pay a visit to Lake Timor East to flush out Frankenstein's Monster. It seemed like she should be sewing them some matching, tight-fitting superhero uniforms. The idea flip-flopped between "ludicrous", "beyond ludicrous", and a "worthwhile longshot".

Gina playfully rolled the cigarette between her fingers and studied it.

Over her shoulder and through the sliding door the flickering TV grabbed her attention a second time and she envisioned advancing Kevin Conner on a rotting dock, armed with an ULTIMO KNIFE 3000, effortlessly slicing through anything Conner desperately tried to put in between himself and the unstoppable cutting utensil:

A tomato.

A smaller knife.
A hardcover book.
A tailpipe.
Slice
The showcase would continue until Conner produced an ULTIMO KNIFE 3000 of his own.
Then it would be on.
Her imaginary knife-fight faded into a daydream where the makers of ULTIMO KNIFE 3000 offered her a multi-million dollar endorsement deal after she used the revolutionary forged steel, smooth handled, all-in-one cutting instrument to apprehend the country's most notorious escaped killer. Her face would be plastered on the UK3 packaging; white teeth smiling out from behind the staggered serrations.

Lighting a second cigarette, Gina imagined the media coverage of the two scorned and jaded correctional facility staff members spit out by the system who pulled off justice's biggest coup by locating the missing—no, capturing—the missing convict. Sadly, but honestly, that was the newspaper headline that immediately popped into her brain as Travis finally revealed his Master Plan.

The Plan.

Although she asked to see the list of meds he had been prescribed, his idea had the possibility of an attractive outcome: the shock, the controversy. Handing Conner over to the police themselves would make True Crime footnotes; forever etching their names in news trivia.

Each time Travis repeated the $25K dollar amount, Gina's mind sank deeper into the incredible ripple effect.

It would be their legacy.

Gina and Travis.

Lake Timor.

Initially people would be relieved, then outraged. Coincidences would lead to speculation and theories of involvement, of guilt, but none would be legitimate; after all, they actually were innocent of Conner's escape. Eventually their incredible story would have to be taken as fact.

Then the negotiations would begin.

They would stand united, holding all the cards.

Talk shows.

Book tours.

Gina was practicing her dramatic huff she would reserve for those awkward moments when someone would beg her for an autograph, when a sudden too-late-to-be-night-but-too-early-to-be-morning cold wind blew up her housecoat.

She shivered back to the present.

She was getting ahead of herself.

Again.

The waiting was going to be excruciating. Travis was looking at another two to three weeks at least. That would mean another two to three weeks at fifty-five percent of her income and the guaranteed financial headaches it would cause.

She could not return to work.

As another barrage of headlights approached and transitioned into taillights, the possibility, no matter how unrealistic, to turn this all around goosebumped her skin.

This could be it.

This could be the one.

$25K.

Her only ticket out of this place.

Out of this life.

Over her shoulder some naive bitch was clapping along with the studio audience after doubting that the Ultimo Knife 3000 was capable of cutting through the yellow pages.

***

The following week brought another unconfirmed sighting (which pegged Conner still heading north) and another wave of speculations from Conner trying to return to the scene of the crime (geographically impossible), to Conner speeding to connect with a prison pen pal (just stupid).

The following seven days also brought another wave of pointless, time wasting interviews/interrogations where Gina would be, once again, forced to relive the past while regurgitating the same story. Over and over. Verbatim.

***

Gina hit the gym with a new passion.

Weights were added.

Reps increased.

She penciled her name under "Aqua Fitness Strength Training" and "Cardio Kick Boxing Fitness."

Each push-up bought an exciting new scenario of Conner's capture.

Each bench-press flashed a heroic moment.

Travis would hesitate but her reaction time would be lightning-quick.

Conner would be worried about Travis, he wouldn't even see her body shots coming hard and fast as she beat Conner upon the head and upper torso.

Conner would crumple.

Conner would beg.

Each dead-lift spawned a different version of Conner's pathetic soliloquy as they burst through the front doors of the cabin with the fresh footprints ending his high stakes game of hide and seek.

"He almost got away," she'd tell the news reporters as she scrunched up her face and showed them the inch between her thumb and index finger. "Almost!"

For the first time ever she tackled the chin-up bar. Her arms felt like they were going to explode out their sockets, but she pressed on. A couple of fitness club regulars passed by on the way to the stationary bikes and she caught the taller one checking her out; watching her body tense and relax as her head rhythmically dipped above and below the silver bar.

The final five reps came easily.

The cool water mixed with the thickness of her saliva. Satisfied with its density, Gina wiped her mouth with the back of her hand, and studied Hannah's MP3 player. The duo passed her a second time and once again tall guy turned his head to study her before brilliantly continuing the rotation, trying to create the illusion that his eyes initial destination was the giant wall clock. Trying and failing. The attention motivated Gina and all initial thoughts of calling it a day were discarded. With the push of a tiny button she resurrected the afternoon's soundtrack. Leaning against the wall she began stretching her legs as she primed herself for another spin on the treadmill when she noticed that the gym was suddenly empty. Looking around, she saw the familiar collection of regulars at the front of the club, all necks stretched upwards to the hanging flat screen televisions. Dread festered in her stomach as she turned to the set in front of the ellipticals.

The MP3 player's deeply jammed ear buds blocked the television's audio, but the caption's white letters burned through the blue background that framed the bottom of the child's picture.

"POSSIBLE ABDUCTION"

"Fuck," she mouthed, as Trent Reznor screamed hate into her skull.

***

Within twenty minutes she was back on Travis's couch talking a mile a minute as they watched the events unfold on live television. While the news anchors and reporters and police officials strongly reinforced that there was no evidence linking Baby Amber's disappearance to the prisoner on the run from the law. Their lies were exposed by simple geometry. The child was there one second, then gone the next. Gone from her own backyard less than a two days' drive from the last gas station Conner was presumably spotted—a mere three days ago.

News station after news station, story after story, they visually connected the dots while verbally stressing the lack of connecting evidence. Spreading panic while reminding the viewers to remain calm. The unrelated disappearance of the young child always followed a story about Kevin Conner.

Every time.

Every station.

No matter how unrelated.

Once the stations began to loop their initial abduction stories, Travis and Gina slid beside the computer and searched online for updates. The Marshal Services Top Fifteen Most Wanted had indeed been updated.

As well as jumping nine spots from thirteen to four, Kevin Conner's small print reward had nearly doubled.

$40K.

The number smiled back at them.

Travis squeezed Gina's tiny hand under the blanket.

CLICK

The images on the monitor hummed, clicked, then disappeared.

They sat in silence.

Gina's stomach gurgled. Sleep depravity and liters of dark caffeine had rotted her stomach, but she ignored the pain.

Travis's breathing had sped up.

They were both thinking it.

Gina turned to face Travis and studied his profile. There was a seriousness in his eyes that was foreign to Gina. Before this latest twist, The Plan was somewhat of a fantasy with a two week window for common sense to obliterate the notion; to split it at the seams of better judgment.

Travis remained staring forward at the dark computer monitor as he spoke.

"I can't ask you to go alone."

Gina remained silent.

"The kid, Gina, God—the child, should we just—call the police?"

Gina's sleep-deprived mind fragmented all the information in an attempt to somehow organize it all. The Plan, the reward money, Conner, the child, Lake Timor.

The risks.

"Are they closing in on him, Gina? Does he need a hostage, or—or does he—is he?"

Gina could no longer suppress the putrid thoughts of Conner touching the trembling child.

The images played out with disgusting familiarity.

The confusion.

The tears.

The fear.

The helplessness bonded them.

The helplessness motivated her.

Rage exploded within Gina and suddenly the daydream began. It was the same daydream she played out before every final exam, every job interview and every time she needed to do something unpleasant that she didn't particularly want to do, but had to do.

It begins in a boxing ring. She bounces up and down in the corner, tossing haymakers into the air and getting ready to drop her shiny red robe as the ring announcer calls her name. He nods at her and begins with her weight, hometown and win/loss record before thundering, "GINAAAAAAAAA," holding the hard A for a good three seconds before pounding, "FRENCH," into the rectangular Memphis microphone hanging magically in the center of the ring. The robe drops, her arms go above her head and the crowd reacts accordingly. The stadium lights and flash photography blind her. Suddenly the photo op is over. Gina explodes to the center of the ring where she spits out her mouth guard, slides off her protective headgear and kicks it into the audience. The response is deafening. She swaggers back to her corner, pounds the top rope with her glove and screams at the timekeeper to ring the bell. The officials try to replace the dripping mouth guard but she refuses to cooperate and screams to start the match. The crowd is on their feet. Replacement headgear is slid under the bottom rope, but Gina kicks it back out to the floor, and the response is deafening. She screams a second time for the timekeeper to ring the bell, to start the match, to let her go without protection. The officials tire of her verbal abuse, angrily point their fingers, shrug their shoulders and signal for the bell. The crowd's decibel level shatters her eardrums as she charges forward, open-eyed into the blinding lights, ready to kill anything that moves.

The sound of applause faded into the silence of the living room.

Adrenaline popped the veins in her arms.

Gina stared straight ahead.

"No. No police."

$40k.

"Trav, I'll need your backpack."

CHAPTER V

CRACK

Gina winced at the thunder.

The wipers cut back and forth across the windshield, obliterating the enormous drops as they rattled the tiny sedan.

To keep her thoughts from the possible horrors of the future, Gina immersed herself in the horrors of the past. Forty-eight hours had collapsed into themselves since the decision was made. Two days of frantic loose end-tying left her physically exhausted but mentally stuck in overdrive.

CRACK

Each time the thunder boomed or the lightning illuminated the road she was back in a different place, reliving a different event from the last two days of her life. Her memories were a massive jumble. The order was all wrong but each event raced through her brain with vivid clarity. Reminders of what she was risking.

CRACK

Back at the correctional facility. Accepting the pay cut and the paperwork involved.

Fifty-five fucking percent.

She could feel her innocence being silently debated by the masses. The law's lack of leads sent Gina's status tumbling from victim to possible conspirator, and now to what? Fugitive on the run? There was some irony worth noting. Gina morbidly smiled at the facial expressions her employers would make if something terrible happened to her during her secret trip. Would that upgrade her status back to victim? If

Travis was right, if everything fell into place she would take down her own personal Axis of Evil: her asshole employers who abandoned her, the no-talent police force that rejected her, and all her so-called friends and family members who took pride in pissing all over her when she failed out of cop school and settled on that job at the correctional institution in the first place. Even if the odds were a million to one, if Kevin Conner was indeed holed up somewhere at Lake Timor, the payoffs for this risky little recon adventure made rolling the dice absolutely mandatory. This could be her time—she was due. Time to prove everyone wrong.

Gina smiled as she slid the pages across the table and shot them an unenthusiastic "thank you," as she confidently never broke eye contact. Her complete lack of intimidation was a silent victory in itself. Gone was the disoriented little rape victim. Next time she saw these dicks it would be them unenthusiastically thanking her for doing the work they were unable to do as she returned infants and escaped convicts to their rightful owners.

Lighting a cigarette and puffing arrogantly as she displayed her name tags and bar codes for the officer working the gate, Gina looked back at the massive structure which jeopardized her wellbeing every time she punched her timecard, yet somehow, barely paid her bills. The red scanners beeped and popped as her info entered the system for what she knew would be the last time. Sizing up the rundown facility behind her the word "hate" didn't quite do it justice.

Reminders of what she was risking.

CRACK

***

Hannah held Ryen as Gina frantically stuffed clothes into Travis's large, multi-pocket backpack.

"I know the timing is terrible," Gina rambled, "but I gotta get out of here for a few days and clear my head, you know? I hope you understand." Of course she understood. Ryen cried as Hannah replaced the soother and coaxed the child's screams into coos. "Plus, I'm going to hit up my folks for some cash to help smooth over this rough patch, maybe you won't have to work as much if I can get a few months rent out of them." Gina's apologetic smile was met with a trusting nod from her roommate. Of course it was. Nothing further needed to be said; the sales pitch had been accepted without hesitation. However, Gina decided to take the pity game to the next level and rubbed her eyes, offering, "The nightmares, Hannah, the hands . . . " Hannah bit her lips shut and nodded along. They both swallowed hard.

Gina zipped up the backpack (brimming with an oddly exclusive black wardrobe) and they embraced. Hannah whispered, "You—we will get you through this. Take your time, kid, don't worry about Ryen. She's in good hands. Get better, she needs her mommy healthy."

Gina kissed her daughter on the forehead and silently cursed Hannah's final comment. Motherhood was the only chink in the armor of The Plan. It went without saying that juggling the complex duties of single parenthood with an impromptu road trip (with intentions of bringing down a convicted killer) would probably be questioned within the pages of some of the stuffier parental magazines, but Gina kept focused by consuming the searing heartache of the abducted child's parents. Those who missed the missing. She could imagine no greater hell than the helplessness of that situation—the not knowing, and the slightest possibility of being the one to end their suffering roared as loud as the adoring crowd in her boxing daydream.

Once again the tiny voice inside her head begged her to just call the police with the Lake Timor theory and speed up the process for the sake of the child, but with each passing day it was quieter and less frequent. This trip had an ugly selfish side which was easily buried underneath a heroic pile of self worth.

Gina took the stairs two at a time as she sprinted out the

complex and into the night. Tossing the backpack into the car she imagined Ryen delivering her first word while she was off playing detective. Would it be "Mama"? and if it was—where would it land? On Hannah, or Hannah's aunt? Ah, Aunt Katherine; Aunt Kat was a daily highlight of Ryen's young life. Be it an actual visit or just the chance to coo at the large, ugly blue-hatted picture of Aunt Kat on the bookshelf, Ryen's eyes lit up in the presence of the old lady. Good old Aunt Kat: the hyper-reliable retired nurse, (of all things) who eagerly jumps at any and every opportunity to babysit at the drop of a hat (ugly-blue or not) free of charge, in exchange for—in exchange for what? A tiny slice of infant companionship? Gina remembered hearing something about how faulty uterine walls or collapsed fallopian tubes paved a childless road for the gentle widow.

But Gina couldn't be sure—the story was too fucking depressing to sit through.

***

CRA-KOOOM

The car skidded slightly and Gina rode the brakes, centering it back between the lines as she noticed the breakneck speed the last flashback caused her to subconsciously excel to. Even with the brights locked on, the highway took a hard cut into complete darkness thirty feet from the front of the car. She leaned forward, pressing her face as close to the windshield as possible, as if that would magically push the blackness further back. No dice. She yawned. Her body was exhausted, but her mind remained razor sharp. The memories continued randomly and vividly as if a surgeon had peeled back her skull and was making a game of haphazardly pressing his finger into the tender pinky-red folds of her brain—popping images and conversations into the forefront of her mind with no segues or connections. Gina flicked the headlights back to normal then back to bright. Normal bright normal bright normal bright and suddenly she was at the kitchen table in the house she grew up in. Sitting like a lady of all things, back straight, legs crossed, hands in her lap while she smiles politely into the blackness of her mother's skeptical eyes.

CRACK

Her father didn't even need the elaborate story Gina concocted on the long drive over, he just handed her an envelope of money and a seven week old birthday card, which also contained a significant amount of cash. The first trip home after "the incident" didn't make things more awkward with her parents; though, in all fairness, it didn't actually make things any less awkward either. The tension was still there. It floated thick in the kitchen. It crept into the open cupboards and behind the oven and silently observed. When she was a teenager her older brothers both moved out, just got up and abandoned the family, leaving her alone with the misery of a stressed father juggling a career with a mentally degenerating soul mate. Why did her brothers inherit Dad's patience and luck while her own life seemed to mirror her mother's disturbing path: a life of escalating humiliations? She could remember the first time her mother forgot the car and walked home from work, and the time she almost choked to death at this very table after filling her mouth too full of scalloped potatoes. Nobody realized how completely fucked up it was struggling to become a woman while watching your own mother deteriorate into a child. The fact that her mother's vacant stare forever haunts both brother's wedding photos offers a small amount of comfort.

Dad returned to the table with a steaming pot of stew and three bowls. Gina ate quickly, silently giving thanks for her mother's condition as Mom's random outbursts provided the much needed distractions. Her father's probing was predictable and embarrassing; he used this scare, as an incentive to turn a new leaf. An excuse for career advancement.

It was all business with Dad.

They almost raped your little girl, Daddy, Gina thought,

stewing into her stew as her father helped guide her mother's spoon. *Some emotion would be nice.*

Although very much Daddy's Little Girl, her resentment reached the boiling point as she stirred her supper with her clenched spoon.

Did he just call it a "scare'?

As the word left his mouth the giant bulge on the back of Gina's head flared.

"Scare?" Attempted rape? That's what constitutes as a "scare" around the house these days? Who the hell was he to downplay what happened? "Scare?" A life spent earning his way up the ranks of the police force seemed to be the only thing in his life he was genuinely proud of. When push came to shove, it sure as hell wasn't his daughter. At one time his love flowed smoothly, although entwined with expectations, but everything hit the fan after bad grades and poor attendance removed her from the academy. It was then it became obvious how badly her back-up career veered off the family plan he had mapped out for his children. *Geenie, how could you disgrace the family?* she imagined him thinking. His perfect little family fantasy shattered—the mighty Senior Constable raised two strapping sons who followed his footsteps to a tee and took the oaths and served the force as Dad proudly looked on, then along came the daughter, the poor, dress wearing penisless girl. The failure. Poor, pathetic little Gina. So much wasted potential. An afterthought in the annual Christmas newsletter. Heaven forbid she had any sort of hand in her own future beyond the dictatorship of this Nazi-like family. Sure, she wanted to make drastic life changes, but she had to do so without the support of her parents, unlike her brothers. They have memories of a different mother, a normal, fully functional mother, who cooked and took them to the zoo and bought them ice cream.

Her brothers could bring their friends home after school without worrying that their father would call to them for help because Mom had had another "accident."

It was so unfair. Sometimes her mother wore a diaper and somehow she emerged as the family disgrace because she didn't follow the family protocol and exchange her individuality for a goddamn badge.

Because of her two DWIs.

Because she partied away her share of her grandmother's inheritance.

Because she had a baby out of wedlock.

She would never forget how her heart shattered when she finally worked up the courage and shakily admitted her lack of self-control to her dad. The shock momentarily tore down her father's clear and emotionless army-voice as he repeated her statement back in question form, replacing "pregnant" with "knocked up."

Anger dripping off every word.

Syllables pussed contempt.

Her life was officially split in two sections—everything before he said "knocked up" and everything after.

Suddenly, finishing the bowl of his stew seemed like admitting defeat. Like time was healing. But time was and always would be Enemy #1 in this house—looking at her mother's stew drenched chin cemented that. Gina cursed herself for agreeing to stay for lunch. This stop was a business transaction, nothing more. This house was like an ATM; she punched in her PIN, got her cash and past that, she had no reason to stay. Some part, buried deep in her brain, was silently hoping the "scare" would have somehow mended the ever-growing father-daughter rift but she realized that opportunity would never present itself. Now she was out a precious hour, an hour she could have used to get closer to Lake Timor; closer to restoring the peace of mind to people who deserved it—because no one in this house did.

***

CRACK

Sheet lightning bled out the memory.

Gina's eye's watered and her mind exploded with fury as

she realized the sting of her dad's rejection could still, after nearly two years, affect her this way. The way he judged her when she was at her absolute lowest. How could a father look at his daughter with repulsion? Like she was a dirty tissue? Gina's sleeve violently wiped the tears from her eyes before cranking the car stereo's dial. She sniffed and pounded her fist on the dash as Rage Against The Machine vibrated her teeth.

She lit a cigarette as she nodded her head in tune to Hanna's "borrowed" CD.

CRA-KOOM

"Wonder if the whore's clean?"

Gina slowly surfaced from the nightmare as the hundreds of violent and violating hands synthesized into a single gentle touch. Travis seemed lost and distant as he continued to run his index finger up and down her naked back.

Tracing her spine.

Circling every dark bruise.

Lightly dragging his nail across every scrape.

Every wound.

Still under the illusion of slumber, Gina silently watched as he struggled to pull himself forward and shakily kiss the lump on the back of her head.

The shitty thing about a reoccurring nightmare is how violently it can hijack any dream at any time. No matter how safe and warm her dreams started—the hands found her and dragged her back into the darkness. This time they came for her as her mind recreated an evening where binge drinking had led her and Travis to a lovemaking session in his shower. As if her subconscious had scolded her for having the audacity to attempt to recreate happy moments, this time the transition back into the nightmare was a sharp one. It started with Travis suddenly grabbing her by the throat and slamming her down on the shower floor before the smooth curtain and fog faded into prison walls and Travis propagated into the familiar mass of sneering convicts.

Shaking the debris of the horrible new twist that took place during her four hours of broken sleep, she studied her man as he slowly slid from the bed, hobbled around the room, scratched his belly button, lit a cigarette and rearranged the junk covering his dresser until removing a semi-clean mug, pointing it in her direction and whispering her name.

Gina nodded and closed her eyes, stretching out her limbs and sinking into the white sheets. The feeling of warmth brought a feeling of weightlessness. Yes, coffee. She was stalling and knew it. She had already overslept. The road beckoned and she refused to answer. Someone else could deal with Conner, the kidnapped child, the bills, and the responsibility of it all; she promised never to raise her head above the covers ever again. She would begin an exciting new life forever in Travis's bed where it was warm and safe. She could hear him remove and return the coffeepot.

"Don't make me do this," Gina silently begged.

She imagined him standing naked in the kitchen with a sleepy look on his face as he stirred in the artificial sweetener. Out of view, his practiced and permanent look of encouragement was probably wiped clean—replaced by a war bride's worried scowl. As Gina sank further into the sheets her mind flashed back to the exact second of her dream when Travis's touch cruelly snapped from passion to torment as he slammed her to the floor and began sadistically banging her skull into the ground. Trying to suffocate the negative she focused on the real Travis—imagining him sweetly balancing a cup of coffee in each hand as he limped his way out of the kitchen.

Suddenly, in her mind, Travis's face distorted.

The same angry smirk from the dream flashed across his face as she listened to his bare feet ineptly slap the hardwood as he got closer and closer. Gina didn't move or breathe as panic took over. She heard him enter the bedroom and somehow through clenched eyes and cotton sheets she could see him standing over her, that crazy look in his eyes, hovering, waiting for the exact second she peeked out from underneath the covers before pulling the fake mask of concern back over his horrible lying face.

How much did she really know about Travis? Would he have helped Conner escape? What's in it for him? How did she fit into whatever plan the two of them may have concocted? Were his injuries legitimate? Was he guilty? Was she going to take the fall? Was The Plan a set up?

She could hear him breathing right above her. She imagined him standing there with that angry and amused look in his eyes as he circled the dual cups of scalding hot coffee inches above her. The thin sheets offered no promise of protection against her bare skin should he decide to pull the trigger prematurely on whatever sick plan he had in store for her; deciding The Plan, the long road trip, and the promise of wealth was going to take too long to play out, he was suddenly bored and he wanted immediate results and he would speed the game up and seize the moment and pour the scalding hot liquid on her then yank back the covers and watch in amusement as she screamed and thrashed as her naked skin boiled and blistered as he breathed in her agony before Conner emerged from underneath the bed and crawled on top of her as Travis cheered and pumped his fists into the air while capturing the moment on his outdated high-eight video camera and the two of them would laugh at how easy it was to manipulate the trusting little whore while—

"Gina?"

She slowly lowered the covers and came face-to-face with a non-threatening mug of coffee. As the exchange took place she studied Travis's eyes. Doubt had planted its seeds. She bore into his soul and could only find the broken man whose recent emotional acceptance finally caught up to the physical freedom she gave up months ago.

She had no reason to distrust Travis, for no other reason

than the idea of including someone attempting to pry your kneecap clean from your leg as part of your master plan seemed an unnecessary ballsy detail.

But the seeds had been planted.

After placing his coffee on the dresser, a completely unarmed Travis limped his way over to the closet.

Watching him struggle to lower himself onto the floor, one hand firm on the bandaged knee, Gina imagined Travis and Conner finding an empty corner while the riot exploded around them, Travis quickly dropping to the floor, slapping himself in the face, clamping his teeth around the sleeve of his shirt and frantically nodding as Conner nodded back, wound up and drove the pencil straight under his kneecap. Forcefully, but carefully. Right on the practiced mark. Conner jumped back to avoid the initial spray of blood. She imagined Travis rolling in pain, pulling the pencil from his wound and waving Conner away, Conner nodding back and running down the corridor with Travis's key ring safely in his hand.

The theory now seemed more amusing than it did factual, but the image of Travis's evil grin, a look of pure malice that possibly crept across his face every time he turned his back to her—that image seemed to fit like a glove and refused to subside.

Before she could write the next chapter in her elaborate conspiracy theory, Travis sat on the edge of the bed, placed something between her hands then pressed her palms together. His large hands completely encompassed her tiny ones.

She felt the cold handle of a revolver.

KRAKOOOOOOOOOM

Gina began pulling out unorganized wads of bills from her jean pocket and smoothing them out in front of the cash register. The gas jockey with a "Robertson" name tag impatiently drummed his fingers on the glass-covered scratch and win tickets while alternating his focus between the flustered blond and the long line of cars forming at the pumps behind her. Gina struggled to count the cash, balance the overpriced necessities the sad little Gas Bar provided, and answer her cell all at once, but failed at all three. She continued stuffing bills onto the counter until he finally brought his grubby hand down and wiped the cash off the side and into his other equally grubby hand. Separating the unorganized clump of cash into the till, he huffed past her to serve the more organized customers.

"Miss French?" the official voice flatly inquired through the cell phone.

"Yeah, yeah, sorry—yes, you're speaking to her."

Gina clenched the phone between her shoulder and ear, grabbed the plastic bag of groceries and stacked her bottled water atop the Styrofoam cup of coffee while trying in vain to swing her hair out of her eyes. Her cell began to cut out.

"Miss French, I represent Mr. Daniel Rosser. We talked[. . .]the week?[. . .]arrange another[. . .]three of us can reopen the discussions[. . .]"

Gina leaned back against the door which offered less resistance than she anticipated and she stumbled outside, shrugged her entire body left; miraculously re-balanced the water/coffee totem pole, and braced herself as the door began to swing back towards her elbow.

"I'm sorry—what?"

An elderly gentleman holding a newspaper over his head suddenly appeared and caught the door pre-impact and held it as she continued to struggle with her purchases and the phone.

"Thank you," Gina whispered accidentally into the phone.

"Miss French?" the phone cracked.

The rain was finally starting to let up and was now nothing more than a light drizzle, but the aftermath of a two day downpour splashed up and soaked her pant legs wherever she stepped.

"Hello? Yes, it's me, sorry—"

As she readjusted the phone on her shoulder and pressed the water/coffee tower against the wall for stability she caught the gas jockey's glance before he snapped his eyes back to the rolling numbers on the pump. Robertson's satisfied smile indicated he was enjoying the show.

"Miss French?" the voice on the phone angrily crackled. "HELLO, MISS FRENCH?"

"Sorry, I'm just—just a second—" Gina lowered her body placing the grocery bag on the wet ground while still balancing her liquids against the wall. All she needed was one free hand to—

CLICK

Gina felt the smooth plastic bump compress against her chin.

Silence.

"Christ."

Gina snatched the phone with her free hand and frantically menued through the call log.

RECEIVED CALLS

DIAL

Beep beep beep beep

CLICK

REDIAL

Beep beep beep beep

CLICK

REDIAL

Ringggggg . . . ringgggggg . . . ringgggggggg . . . ri—CLICK

"You have reached the mailbox of—"

CLICK

REDIAL

Ringggggg . . . ringgggggg . . . .ringgggggggg . . . ri—CLICK

"You have reached the mailbox of—"

Gina brought her hands to her face, then turned and windmilled her arm, pretending to chuck the cell into the abyss behind the station, but instead she snapped the phone shut, clenched her eyes closed and lightly tapped its corner against her forehead as she regained composure.

"Breathe, just breathe."

CHAPTER VI

LIGHNING ILLUMINATED THE earth.

One
Two
Three
Four
Five
Si—
KRAKOOOOOM

Once again thunder tore the sky.

It was fantastic.

Both the thunder and the lightning managed to hit on perfect down beats as De La Rocha continued to stick it to the man.

Gina grabbed her phone and held it up into the light from the dash.

Searching for service . . .
Searching for service . . .
Searching for service . . .

Frustrated, she gave up again and tossed it onto the passenger's seat. Even if she got through, the lawyer would be long gone from the office by now.

Finishing the last sip of another surprisingly tasty gas-station-brewed coffee, she unrolled the window and chucked the Styrofoam cup from the car, watching it bounce and roll and disappear in the rearview mirror, then wiped her face with the pure rainwater.

With one hand on the wheel, her free hand rummaged through the all-black contents of the shotgun-riding backpack trying to find the emergency back-up cigarette pack. Her hand blindly dug for what seemed like hours and produced zero results. The itch slowly grew from a reminder to a full grown necessity as she began removing articles of clothing until her hand finally brushed the familiar cellophane smoothness. Using her nails, she tore open the packaging and had a cigarette jutting from her mouth in a matter of seconds, all while her eyes never left the road. As she jammed the built-in cigarette lighter and waited for it to pop back up with a red-hot click, she scanned the black mess now covering the passenger's seat.

Gina screamed Rage Against the Machine lyrics out the window, then popped her seatbelt, leaned back in her seat, slipped her hand under the bottom of her shirt and removed the .38 from the waist of her jeans.

She used the barrel to flip down the driver's side visor, then pointed the gun at the roof of the car and pressed the chamber against her cheek. She studied her reflection in the tiny mirror. She wondered if this is what the movie poster would look like after she sold the rights. Would Hollywood let her play herself?

"I'm gonna find you and take. You. Out. Motherfucka," she sneered at herself.

Her mind curved with the road and she fantasized about what kind of a media nightmare she would be.

"Miss French, Miss French can we get some quick thoughts? How did you not only find, capture, and return Conner back to the authorities, but rescue Baby Amber as well?"

"Sure, I'd love to comment, little Miss Reporter—the drive was fucking awesome, there's some surprisingly quality coffee available at those shitty little gas bars along the way. The baby is fucking lucky I got there when I did, and Conner is a baby-stealing bastard asshole, next question."

She decided she would take every opportunity possible to drop the F-Bomb in every interview. Make them edit and censor her remarks. No matter how crude she would be, every news station would still beg her for a sound bite.

She would be a conduit.

People that watch the six o'clock news are the same people who are too scared to leave their houses and create lives of their own, so they watch reporters exploit the actions of people who explore life's possibilities and force change—people like herself.

High school kids would turn her interviews into a drinking game, tipping glasses every time a word was beeped-out.

The C-word had remained dormant long enough.

CRACKKOOOOOOOM

One

Two

Three

Fo-whoooooooooooosh

The lightning was getting closer and the rain was coming down thicker. She was driving right into the worst of it. She jutted the revolver back into the waist of her jeans and rolled up the window as Evil Empire returned to track one. Ejecting the CD, she studied the still compressed cigarette lighter and concluded this storm was gearing up to be an absolute cunt.

CLICK

***

KRAKOOOOOOOOOOOOOOOOOOOM

The hotel sucked.

Her supper was from a vending machine.

The shower helped, but not as much as the mickey of Jack Daniels she purchased at the downstairs gift shop. Although no stranger to alcohol, it was her very first dance with Jack and he was a bitch of a partner.

Each swallow stung her throat and bulged her eyes.

Her proud plans of drinking it straight from the bottle were now watered down by a diet cola as she sat on the lumpy bed watching outdated porn. Outdated, yet, somehow free, porn.

Jack's method of transportation was far from the smoothest she ever experienced but she admired how quickly she had arrived at her destination.

The tiny room began spinning in no time at all.

She could no longer blink away the haze.

The situations on the television were no longer recognizable—she could no longer tell who was doing what to whom. Using the remote control nailed to the nightstand, she clicked off the TV and pulled the covers over her head.

She giggled herself into a deep, assisted slumber and tried not to dream about rape, her possessed boyfriend or another full day of driving.

KRACKKKK

The thunder continued.

***

The bells jingled as she entered the tiny all-night diner. She glanced up at the fitting wagging eyes and tail Kit Cat Clock which hung dusty on the wall.

1:15 A.M. Good God.

Minus the gas and bathroom stops, she had put in a full fourteen hour day of driving. Fourteen hours. With that realization, Gina felt like she was entitled to her first real meal of the day—or as close to a real meal as this place could muster.

Sliding into a booth, she felt all the sleepless locals and passing through truck drivers eye her with intrigue. She could not have looked more out of place. Although she tried to imagine how truly disgusting she really looked after the fourteen hour drive, she didn't hesitate to momentarily bask in the attention. She stretched her arms behind her back, jutting out her chest as she rolled her head and rubbered her shoulders. Although stretching for the yokels had started as a show, after she playfully massaged her neck she became aware of the legitimate strain the long hours of highway driving actually had on her spine. She rubbed deeper and just before she shut her eyes she spotted some gritty-looking bespectacled trucker blinking at her from across the room. She waited as his glance slowly returned to her face and when his eyes finally met hers, Gina's facial expression snapped from "complacent" to "you are so busted" and he embarrassingly looked away.

She continued to massage her neck and shoulders, wincing as she worked out some of the larger kinks. In the darkness she imagined the entire male population of the restaurant suddenly congregating in front of her table. Anticipating the reveal, she would open her eyes and be met by the group's desperate—familiar—expression of overpowering physical need.

This time she welcomed the flashback turned fantasy.

This time it brought a huge smile to her face.

Now she was the one with the secrets.

Tucked in her jeans, she had half a dozen ways to rewrite the ending.

One hand continued massaging her road-ravaged neck and shoulders, while the other slipped under the table and tapped on the bulge just above her waistline. Sliding her fingers past the handle, she traced her iliac muscles that made her oh, so proud. In her favorite pair of low cut jeans the definition was unbelievable. It was like someone took a T-Square and a jiffy marker and drew two diagonal lines from the top of her jeans to just above her hip bones.

The left one now served as a holster, running parallel with the revolver, forcing the barrel to point straight to the part of her body the inmates tried to take for themselves. Tried to make their own.

Her smirk came easy.

My, how the tables have turned.

Now, if anyone came looking to take, they would find a quick metallic and phallic punishment.

The dark, but rewarding, fantasy of how things would have been different if she had then what she had now was cut short as her fries arrived. Tipping the bottle of ketchup, Gina scanned the room again and realized she was already old news; the locals and truckers had returned to their newspapers and travel mugs and small town tales. Taking her first bite of deep-fried goodness she promised to return to that particular daydream later. It was going so well.

She was just about to rape a rapist with her gun.

In the restroom she washed her hands and face before she stepped back, lifted her shirt and studied the handle peeking out of the denim waist. For the first time in a long time she finally felt a slight connection to her family. She had no idea packing heat was so liberating.

Empowering.

Gina dropped her shirt bottom as the door swung open and an elderly lady with an obvious hip displacement faltered into the washroom. The old woman smiled politely as she passed and lumbered into a stall.

I could kill you, thought Gina, *and you would never see it coming.*

***

KRAKKKKKKKKKKOOOOOOOOOOOOOOOOOOMMM MMM

A road sign warned her of an upcoming exit and listed all its possible destinations.

Lake Timor was second from the top.

The car became claustrophobic and unusually bright.

Gina drove past the exit and pulled onto the shoulder.

She killed the engine, popped the seatbelt, turned 180 degrees around, knelt on her seat, and stared at the back of the large highway sign. The lightning momentarily shone a spotlight on the turnoff. The sign, the exit, the immediate future, and an estimated fifty-two and a half hours of arrogance and self-built bravado drained from her now shaking body.

Tears violently streamed down her face as she shook— from the cold?

From the fear.

She pulled the gun from her waist and held it with both

hands—waiting for another adrenaline boost which never came.

You're gonna die up there.

Gina began to sweat.

She closed her eyes and tried to breathe as she continued squeezing confidence from the revolver.

Nobody knows where you are.

Gina was sweating fear.

The crying started suddenly and violently.

Travis has set you up and you are all alone.

She reached for the glove box which harbored two-thirds of her alcoholic travel companion, but she was unable to wrap her fingers around the bottle as her nails scraped the rough plastic.

And you're going to die up there.

She gave up, rested her head against the steering wheel and let it all in.

I am so afraid.

Saliva dripped from her mouth as she heaved and moaned.

She let it all out.

The fear ate her as the darkness, rain and noise buried the tiny car parked in the middle of nowhere.

You.

Are.

Going.

To.

Die.

Die.

Die.

The snap of the thunder timed itself perfectly, drowning out the raw screams of a terrified little girl.

KRA-KOOOOOM

***

Gina leaned forward with both hands gripping the cracked sink in the truck stop restroom. Her face sneered at its own reflection inches from the mirror. The light flickered on and off in rapid succession four or five times before correcting itself. The bright-red veins in her eyes seemed to pulse along with the hum from the on-again-off-again faulty light fixture.

The floor was covered with discarded paper towels, the majority unused.

A plunger lay on its side in the corner.

Graffiti adorned every inch of the walls.

"it's not about the money but the music you see"

"tony waz here"

Despite the obvious bacteria she stuffed the crusty rubber stopper in the drain and sent the contents from her pockets spilling into the sink.

Loose change.

A lighter.

Cigarettes.

A black sharpie.

Jack Daniels.

A pair of cheap black binoculars.

A map.

A picture.

Gum.

The revolver rattled against the porcelain last, resting atop the pile.

She pulled her shirt over her head.

The light flickered again.

She continued to read the walls.

"we ain't new ta this we're true ta this"

Her friendly yellow T-shirt was replaced with a sour black version.

"sharon roe is easy."

"doug j is a homo."

"that, ladies and gentlemen, is a skank."

Her trendy jeans hit the floor.

The light flickered on and off for a third time casting an odd shadow on her bellybutton ring.

"jill sux cox"

"hate. hate. hate. hate. hate"

"you never know when you're gonna need a brick."

Weighing the pros and cons, she separated the silver loop protruding from her inny, slid it free from her skin and dropped it on the floor.

She buttoned up her black jeans but her belt caused debate. The bellybutton ring was a no-brainer, but If things got physical would a belt come in handy or would it work against her? If she needed to run, would it be something Conner could easily grab? She had no idea, trying not to over think things, she stuffed it into the backpack.

"it's not you it's gatorade i'm quenching"

"jesus saves"

"your mom"

The black hooded sweatshirt was last and as her head emerged she found herself face-to-face with the mirror once again.

Her eyes looked vacant.

Dead

Gina was officially out of prep.

"in my defense people were loving it."

"god i feel for you."

"you can't say that to a former fattie."

One by one the contents of the sink were repacked until only three things remained:

The Jack Daniels.

The .38 revolver.

The photograph.

"gravity is a lie, the earth just sucks."

"13/11/74"

"hide your brains."

Gina held the revolver up to the light.

It sent a hard shadow against her face.

She cocked it open, removed and held each bullet against the light.

The thunder barked just outside of the door.

"chris stetson, spring 97."

"no more dc."

"it's already gone."

Satisfied, she returned the gun to the waist of her jeans, guiding it down along her iliac. The familiarity of the sensation brought the first glimmer of feeling back into her numb body.

She wondered if it would ever be possible to go back to her old life without the safety of this new addition permanently hiding in her jeans.

Her perfect little secret.

"alice, chris, tina and trish."

"babies in the back seat cause accidents and accidents in the back seat cause babies."

Gina twisted off the cap and took a cautious swig of J.D.

Of all the questionable things she ever did with her body, this affair with Jack was the lowest and the worst timed. She craved the full blown effects of his sting but had to settle for just a tease. She swallowed hard and continued to observe the wisdom of the bathroom walls.

"don't believe the hype."

"watch out for father goose."

Still unsure of Jack's power, she brought the bottle to her lips twice more and each time pulled it away after long debate. She needed to lose the edge, but it was no time to get lost in his embrace. No matter how badly she craved it.

She capped it and shoved it into her backpack.

"i'm the original hot-male."

"chrissy hates life."

As she retrieved the picture from the sink, the light

flickered again, this time the performance seemed to last twice as long as before.

"buck authority."

She raised the Polaroid to her face.

"excuse me miss, you dropped something. my jaw."

She stared at her two dimensional daughter.

A mini version of herself.

"every song on the radio i try to listen to reminds me of you and i."

"put the kids to bed."

A combination of genetics and broken promises.

"payback is a bitch."

Everyone said she had her smile.

Her eyes.

"the fan just hit the shit."

Her fearless persistence.

"they say you suffer for your crimes. if i'm not suffering, maybe it wasn't a crime."

"everything i do is wrong."

Her.

"aloha loverboy!!!!!!!"

Fearless.

"i need you like heat."

Persistence.

"when the oil really runs out, or when the water supply is fatally contaminated, people will look back on our era as the culprits responsible for their suffering. the future will have its own version of satan, and it is likely to be you and me.

r. baumeister"

Gina retrieved the sharpie from her backpack, popped the cap, and in big block letters scrawled "gina french is **not** a waste of roofies" across the mirror itself. She took a step back and floated the sharpie sideways in front of her face. Closing one eye she used it as a ruler, studying the consistency of her penmanship with glowing approval before simply relaxing her fingers and letting the marker casually spiral to the floor.

All that remained on the gritty porcelain was the snapshot. Her final reason to go forward was carefully folded and slid into her back pocket.

CHAPTER VII

Kooooooom

The thunder pushed her forward.

Lake Timor West.

The community slept as her car glided through the streets, undetected and cloaked in the downpour. As she passed each cabin the realization of her lower class status simmered into self-pity before beginning to boil as motivation.

These were mostly summertime homes. Three-story castles adorned with giant verandas and balconies overlooking the lake. These enormous structures were bigger than the house she grew up in and that made it hard to ignore the rising bitterness.

The dark mansions taunted her as she continued the drive. Every so often she would see a car or two in a driveway—the giant mini vans were the current models, pimped out with Kleenex boxes and personalized license plates advertising grandfatherhood.

Luxury boats shared the driveways. Badges of the elderly.

I'm going to buy one of these, she silently promised to herself. She thought this comfy little community overrun by distilled geezers could use a sassy young woman parading around these parts.

Drunk off her ass twenty-four-seven.

The old men would be unable to peel their eyes off of her perfect, youthful appearance.

The elderly ladies would gossip about the famous bitch.

The mothers whose bodies sagged from age, multiple births and steak and lobster suppers would complain behind her back.

On those warm summer nights, she would lay on her back and learn the constellations as she drank herself to sleep on the beach. Lake Timor's residents would be forced to draw up a schedule—yes, an actual schedule, on paper. Everyone would take turns making sure Gina French's cigarette was extinguished before rolling her on her side, eliminating the possibility of choking on her own vomit and dying in her sleep.

Imagine what a death on the beach would do to their precious property value.

She loved the idea of forcing these wealthy wenches to babysit her.

The dark sedan loomed forward through the rain.

Gina approached the last cabin on the block. Compared to the rest, it was embarrassingly small but the thing seemed to be made entirely of glass. She had to squint through the rain to make out any sort of paneling in between the gigantic panes.

The predictable sign that hung from a post halfway up the cobblestone walkway leading to its drawbridge-like front doors read "Welcome To The Hapinners—This Is Where Things Hapinn."

She leaned over far enough to firmly press her fist against the passenger window and extended her middle finger.

Her mind spun but on the spot she couldn't think of something derogatory and clever she would write on her sign, but now she knew she had to have one. Hell, once the money came in, maybe she'd buy an adjoining property, knock down the neighboring cabin and just fill the lot with the world's longest walkway—that would allow her to hang one of those fucking signs every ten feet or so.

By the time she rescued Baby Amber, brought down Conner, sold the story to Hollywood and started her literary career, she'd be able to afford it and more.

Independent wealth—something these Lake Timor West money hungry prostitutes would hate her for more than anything else.

They had to marry into money, but not her. She'd be young and free and alone. Gina's only full time job would be flaunting her carefree life in their faces.

She would make history by jumping from blue collar, surpassing upper class, and creating an entirely different social category all together out here in Lake Timor.

Her happiness came with no strings attached.

"Elevated class," she mouthed to herself as she watched the glass house disappear in the rearview mirror.

Thick trunks and wet leaves blurred brown and orange as she sped down the winding road. The trees were enormous and demanded respect, preventing what little light the moon could offer after the clouds and rain had their way with the sky.

The trip to the lake's failed east side was less than a five minute drive, but you could get out and spray paint a line across the road exactly where the money stopped. Without warning the car bumped and jerked as the road became cracked and uneven—a never ending reminder of obvious neglect.

As she neared the forgotten side of the lake, her heart broke with abandonment.

She killed the headlights as she approached the spooky settlements.

Lake Timor East's design was pretty much identical to that of Lake Timor West—unnecessarily large cabins loomed side by side, most just as empty as the ones across the lake, however these produced a different type of empty. These were hauntingly empty.

She coasted past the weeds, the rust, the flaking paint and the boarded-up windows, as forgotten family memories spilled from each gigantic foundation crack. They screamed for attention; searched for proof of their former importance.

Four, maybe five blocks passed and Gina was reunited with emptiness as she found herself in the familiar darkness of the trees surrounded by exit signs. That was it for Lake Timor East. No neon red sign that read "Convicts And Stolen Babies Right Here" with a giant blinking arrow.

Gina drummed her thumbs on the steering wheel. Before losing her courage she gently spun the car around and coasted back for a second sweep.

Lake Timor East.

Waking up some dormant mental math skills, she tallied the homes. Twenty-one cabins seemed habitable, four were maybes and seventeen barely had roofs. Not bad odds.

So . . . twenty-one.

Twenty-one.

Twenty-one.

Okay.

She watched as sharp branches detailed zigzag patterns into the hood and passenger side as she glided her car into the densest collection of bushes she could find.

She lit a cigarette and reclined the seat. Squinting at the gaping structures through the cloudy exhale, her fantasy returned.

She swayed on the porch of the biggest cabin on the block. Her cutoffs were inappropriately short to the point where the pockets peeked out where the denim stopped and her thighs began. She leaned against the large support beam. Her eyes closing during each slow cigarette drag. A family lumbered by. The father seemed irritated as the mother struggled with defiant children. Gina slowly lifted her hand with a friendly, albeit mocking, gesture of friendship. She could hear the children arguing long after she could no longer see them.

The image faded as she tasted filter. Popping open the car's ashtray, she stuffed its tiny remains into the pile of identical corpses. It was a weak similarity, but she turned it into one last sign—she was that tiny filter; trying in vain to stay alive while slowly sinking in a giant pit of similar omissions.

The long term promise of this new life had actually become tangible and the wait had become unbearable. Gina burned to set the wheels in motion. Her heart raced. She stuffed her ponytail into her sweatshirt, pulled the hood over her head and left the safety of her car.

The Plan.

Staying low she crept towards the first collection of homes that looked intact enough to keep out the rain. She stationed herself behind a giant tree and observed house number one. Her knuckles popped white as she gripped the binoculars against her face.

Door to window.

Window to window.

Window to window.

Window to door.

Nothing.

She scanned the yard—no clues, no signs of life—not that she really expected there to be. Paved walkways don't leave footprints and any information the large grass could have ever offered was long gone, thanks to the pounding rain.

Nope.

The doors were the best bet.

Starting to count in her head, she took off running and took the three front steps in a single leap. She jiggled the doorknob. It didn't budge. She jumped off the steps and ran the perimeter.

Five, six, seven, eight . . .

Basement window intact.

Back door locked.

Twenty-three, twenty-four, twenty-five . . .

Stumbling upon a large picnic table, she slid underneath and watched the house for any signs of movement triggered by her entry attempts. Her hand gripped the revolver.

Minutes passed—nothing.

By the time Gina crossed the first four houses off her list she was soaked to the bone, but getting quicker. Getting braver. She pushed the large windowpanes, kicked doors and failed to manipulate plywood-covered windows.

Half an hour passed. She pressed on thoroughly and meticulously. Her confidence mounted while a tiny nagging voice began to whisper that she was wasting her time. No crusty-eyed convicts were here. No abducted babies were here.

She slipped in the mud and took a knee going around the side of the fifth house. Regaining her composure she took the left corner and stopped dead in her tracks as the telltale signs of a forced entry lay in splinter form at the base of an empty back door frame.

"Oh shit."

Gina backed away slowly and stood beside the knee-sized dip in the mud.

Minutes ticked by. Her fingers throbbed around the .38.

THWAK

The wind swung the door open and shut.

THWAK

She regulated her breathing.

Lack of movement invited the chill.

THWAK-THWAK

Her lungs burnt for a cigarette.

She watched the door aggressively bounce off the frame only to come back for more.

She held strong.

She waited.

The rain dripped from her chin and elbows.

Gina wiped the rain from her forehead and "on three" exploded into a sprint. She rolled herself over the fence. Dropping into the neighboring backyard she slid behind a giant tree which allowed a great view of the rebounding door and more than doubled the distance between it and herself. The binoculars made a reappearance.

Back door to basement window.

THWAK

Basement window to back window.

Nothing.

The thick redwood offered mild relief from the downpour and she leaned into it, nearly embracing it.

Her next move remained in limbo. The combination of shelter and the onset of physical fatigue warranted the break. Justification drained the guilt from her body.

She shivered as minutes piled.

Back door to basement window and back again.

Nothing.

The lightning timed itself perfectly with the blinding revelation which sent Gina violently twisting at the waist and frantically checking behind her.

"Stupid," she scolded herself, imagining Kevin Conner smiling at her through the back door window while all her attention remained on the neighboring house. She imagined staring at the other house's swinging back door as he exited this one, walked up right behind her, studied her through his one good eye with a tickle of amusement before he winded up and crushed her skull with a hammer.

And no one would ever be the wiser.

Travis was the only soul who knew where she was. If his secrets didn't leak—no one would ever find out.

Ever.

Not even her daughter.

She was again disturbed by thoughts of betrayal on Travis's part. She could picture Conner crouched atop the tallest cabin in Lake Timor, studying his prey from above. Ready to strike. Yelling through the storm into a cellphone, describing her movements to Travis, who lay safe and warm, miles away in the bed they shared. Under the covers. Listening. Waiting. Anticipating her screams.

Gina looked around the yard. This cabin's back door, basement window and two upper level windows seemed undisturbed.

Gina returned her attention to the house on the other side of the fence with the animated door.

Back door to basement window and back again.

Nothing.

This had to be the house.

The wind picked up and sent the rain sideways, drilling the waterlogged clothes back into every pore of her body.

The storm had finally found her hiding place and punished her for momentarily escaping it's wrath. The increasing cold forced the decision making process. Officially unable to control the violently shaking shivers, Gina needed one more inspiring hit. Closing her eyes she felt the August afternoon sun cover her body as she lay on the sand in front of her beachside property. The feeling of completion was overwhelming, no one would ever fuck with her again; not physically, not mentally, and sure as hell not financially. Just as the cool rim of that particular afternoon's third gin and tonic touched her lips, the daydream was shattered by the thunder, returning her to the volatile present.

The chill climaxed and got the reaction it demanded. Gina raised the revolver, hopped the fence and charged the back door.

Fighting against her waterlogged clothes she picked up the pace, estimating the distance and trying to time the door as the wind continued to pinball it open and shut. Element of surprise, her mind screamed as she bared down for the impact, shouldering the door as it swung back towards the frame. The door flew open and smashed against the door stopper as momentum carried her inside—the barrel of the gun swept the kitchen left to right as she charged the staircase. During "treetime" she concluded that Conner would be holed-up on the second floor to utilize the birds-eye view of the street. Her heart raced. Lighting provided a split second layout as the top of the staircase greeted her with a long hallway—two doors on the left and one on the right. First left was closed, first right was ajar and far left wide open. The gun's barrel guided her as she charged through the open doorway at the end of the hall.

The .38 scanned everywhere. Nothing. Back into the hallway. Kicking open the ajar door revealed a toilet and small shower. "Fuck," she yelled as she spun 180 degrees back into the hallway and forced open the closed door. Charging in, Gina ran straight into a bed post and her ribs bounced back from the impact—the pain not even registering. A quick scan revealed an empty master bedroom. Another burst of energy floated her down the stairs back into the kitchen.

THWAK-THWAK-THWAK.

The door continued to protest her arrival. Left. Right. Nothing. The closet. Nothing. Gina spun through the kitchen and into the living room. Behind the couch, behind the chair, the front closet. Nothing. She stared at the second staircase. The one that led to the basement. "The basement—these rich assholes dug basements for their cabins?"

Halfway down the staircase she felt her balance shift and turned her stumble into a leap as she landed at the bottom of the staircase smashing into the wall with another bout of unregistered pain as she used the momentum to spin into the den. The gun threatened a fridge, a couch, a wicker chair and settled on a single door. One last burst of adrenaline sent her careening through the door into the tiny furnace room. "Fuck." She spun back out into the den, wiped the sweat/rain combination from her eyes with the back of her gun hand and began pacing. Conner wasn't here. She was wrong. No. No. She crept back up the stairs.

Something was wrong. The ever-important element of surprise was long gone, but she must have missed something. Something.

Think.

Think.

Think.

Attic.

The tiny trap door in the upstairs ceiling seemed as undisturbed as the rest of the cabin but she knew she was right. She had to be right. Conner had to be up there. Charging back into the master bedroom sent Gina into the same bedpost a second time. While her rib cage ignored it before, this time around the pain from her knee smacking solid pine shot straight to her brain as she collapsed to the floor. Gritting her teeth she lifted her battered body and slid the large chair into the hallway. She stared at the door to the attic.

This made perfect sense. Conner must be somehow entering and exiting from the roof, and he must have heard her by now, and he's either waiting for her, or he's escaping.

These two options motivated one final dramatic entrance as Gina hopped onto the chair, pushed aside the large cover then jumped straight up, sending her head, shoulders and arms into the opening as her chest hit the side of the frame, knocking the wind from her. As her legs dangled comically in the hallway, her elbows supported her bodyweight as she moved the gun back and forth with her wrist, fully knowing that if she was forced to take a shot she would have to let go of the opening, aim and fire while free-falling back into the hallway, but as her eyes darted left and right she was met with nothing but darkness and moldy insulation. There was no floor, only pink padding which irritated the small amount of exposed flesh in between her sleeves and gloves. Left to right. Empty. Nothing. The fire in her shoulders became unbearable as her elbows shook, continuing to support her bodyweight. Admitting defeat on every level Gina relaxed and lowered herself out of the hole, dropping down into the chair.

The shock, the knee pain, the rib pain and the burning shoulders all presented themselves at once as she sat blankly in the chair in the middle of the hallway. She listened. She heard nothing but the rain and the door.

THWAK-THWAK

Dragging the chair had cut deep grooves in the hardwood

floor, her eyes followed the winding grooves back into the bedroom where she saw and cursed the bed's solid wooden frame. As a soggy Gina sat stewing in the giant chair, reasons not to run downstairs and shoot the goddamn door off it's hinges were rapidly disappearing. Something had to absorb her spite. It wouldn't be Conner. She was wrong. Travis was wrong. There were no abducted children in Lake Timor, no gimpy-eyed convicts, either. She could no longer even tap into the beachside daydreams that spawned this aggressive raid in the first place.

Slowly soaking through the old chair Gina was forced to return her thoughts to the current series of setbacks she currently called life.

Every.

Horrible.

Repetitive.

Mundane.

Moment.

The shock of her failure couldn't even produce tears.

In her mind she was back at her apartment.

Back at the Correctional Facility.

Back at the grocery store, waiting in the express line with milk and diapers.

Back—

—Hell no.

She shot forward and returned down the stairs to the main level and resumed pacing.

She wasn't going out like that.

There was, like, fifteen or sixteen more options here. Fifteen or sixteen more cabins. Fifteen or sixteen more places to hide.

Maybe Conner went from cabin to cabin searching for food.

Hell-damn-yes.

This made complete sense.

He looted each cabin. He kicked in the doors of the

better-looking ones, scoured the place for food and moved on.

Gina turned and dropped to her knees beside the couch searching for signs of recent use.

Okay, it was strategy time. She peeled the drenched sweatshirt from her body and let it drop. Her T-shirt was just as soaked but weighed a lot less. Gina emptied her pockets. The binoculars and the gun rested safely on the coffee table while she forced open the sandwich bag keeping her cigarettes dry and fumbled with the lighter.

Even without the thirty pounds of wet hooded sweatshirt the remaining damp clothes began to take their toll as she slumped into the large musty chair and continued to inhale. The lightning illuminated the giant swirling dust storm—the unforeseen effects of her sudden laziness.

Blinking into the wallpapered emptiness around her, Gina gave her mind dangerous permission to once again slink into the unknown. Had she carelessly missed an obvious hiding place? She felt she was being watched. All her senses told her to shoulder check—just in case—but she refused to give in. Remaining motionless, she continued staring straight ahead and closed her eyes.

She could feel Conner slowly creep out of the kitchen.

He was tiptoeing up behind.

Arms crossed.

Hugging a giant sledgehammer. The large square mallet floated on the end of the handle above his shoulder creating the illusion of a second head.

No one knew where she was.

If nothing else, he could just knock her out and dump her in the windowless furnace room and board-up the door. She would wake up and slowly starve to death. Her stomach eating itself for eight-to-ten days before finally giving up the fight.

They would never find her body. At least not before the rats and insects did.

Gina's eye's remained clamped shut as she stole a quick drag.

She could totally feel his presence. Right behind her. He was bending over now, smelling her hair. Breathing in the scent of his prey.

She remained motionless while her mind dared him—no, begged him to do it.

She felt her hair move with the motion of Conner raising the giant hammer.

She refused to flinch.

The hammer cut the air as it descended towards her skull but stopped on a dime inches above the top of her ponytail as a repressed detail suddenly surfaced and stopped the vision dead in it's tracks.

An ax.

Conner used an ax to kill those two people.

The scumbag used an ax to kill his own parents. Not a hammer.

An ax.

With her eyes still shut, the vision continued.

Realizing his mistake as well, Conner brought the hammer up to his face and studied it before sinking back into the kitchen's shadows, only to reemerge seconds later caressing a giant ax.

Gina remained defiantly still.

Conner bounced the tip of the ax inches above the back of her skull, getting the spot just right, before committing to it's violent course. Satisfied, a smile crept across his face. The ax vaulted into action then cut the air as it plummeted towards her skull. The second before her brain repainted the living room Gina's eyes shot open and caught Conner's reflection in the front window.

Once again it wasn't Conner.

It was her boyfriend.

It was Travis.

She wondered if the crack CSI team would be able to

conclude she was actually in the house by a pair of dried ass marks in the furniture.

The cigarette was, unsurprisingly, almost done.

Fifteen more cabins.

Maybe sixteen?

Seemed plausible.

With lighter in hand, she readied herself for the follow up smoke.

She snapped the flame to life.

Her arm swayed to the rhythm of the silence.

The flame's tiny orange dot multiplied on the reflective objects in the darkness around her.

She waved it right.

Tiny reflections danced right.

She waved it left.

Tiny reflections danced left.

Her thumb went to work on the lighter: roll-release-roll-release-roll-release. Gina watched as the reflections pulsed. Her head fell back and she exhaled at the ceiling as she realized she was losing interest and hope all over again.

Fifteen more cabins? Maybe sixteen?

Her smoke burned down to the filter. Gina managed a slight smile as she snubbed it out on her T-shirt.

The chill found her again. Bringing a follow up smoke to her lips, the lighter performed its intended job—no longer a tool for amusement.

She entertained the thought of trying the taps in the shower, seeing if the water was still functional. As she continued to smoke away the shivers she seriously considered risking all the wealth and fame in exchange for a scalding shower, but the idea was aborted as quickly as it appeared while she ran though the checklist: No towel, no dry clothes and if she had learned anything from the horror movies Hannah downloaded, it was that bathing yourself while a sociopathic killer was on the loose led to an immediate death.

Smoke billowed out her nostrils as she imagined herself running from the house wrapped only in a towel as Conner chased her through the kitchen, across the town's only road, and screaming barefoot into the deep dark woods. Seriously? How stupid would you have to be?

And yet here she was.

Her life had finally reached B-Movie status.

While Gina was far from an expert in hydro management, she was pretty confident hot water was a result of some sort of hot water heater, which needed a certain amount of electricity, which, after connecting the dots, meant there would be no warm, pre-death lather. She was, however, surprisingly thirsty.

She dripped across the floor to the kitchen, stood in front of the sink and triumphantly twisted both the hot and cold taps simultaneously.

RRRRRRRRMMMMMMMMMMMM

The entire faucet structure shook as it was rudely awakened years after retirement. It rattled and roared but refused to produce results.

THWAK-THWAK-THWAK

Upstaged, the door tried unsuccessfully to reclaim her attention.

Gina looked down at the shaking apparatus and lifted the cigarette to her lips again as she peered out the kitchen window overlooking the back yard and the neighboring back yard with the tree she had foolishly hid behind.

"The Hidey-tree," she now called it with an eye roll.

The humor and another drag signaled the night's end.

RMMMMMMMMMMMMMMMMMMMM

The pipes begged for relief as the horrible sound continued to scratch her ear drums raw. She was sure they were bleeding by now.

The aftermath of the failed water-drive continued to reverberate through her skull long after twisting the taps shut.

Fifteen or sixteen more cabins? She felt the desire to continue The Plan slowly fading again.

This is stupid.

Fifteen or sixteen more cabins?

Sure.

But not tonight.

Not—THWAK-THWAK-FORCHRISTSAKE!!

Gina spun around and strode into the living room. She snatched the two important objects off the coffee table, returned to the kitchen, stopped the door's never-ending journey with her foot and aimed the .38 at the top hinge.

This was going to be spectacular.

Her finger massaged the trigger as she began the countdown.

"Five, four."

The white curtain moved in the window of the cabin across the back fence.

She froze.

A familiar looking orange orb flared mid-window..

Her filter dropped with her jaw.

The dot flickered a second time, then disappeared. Someone in the window was using a lighter.

The curtain sagged back into its proper hanging position.

Gina dove to the floor. The revolver rattled against the hardwood as she spiderwalked backwards on her hands and feet until her back hit the wall. She aimed the .38 at the backyard. The wind and rain disappeared and reappeared as the door resumed slamming open and shut. Fuck, fuck, fuck, fuck, fuck, fuck. Was it him? Was it Conner? Did he see her now? Had he seen her before, when she was in the backyard? When she was behind the tree? Was he on his way over? Oh fuck, he's on his way over right now. He's walking through the rain, stalking forward, step after step after step. The fence didn't even slow him down, he busted right through it. Sent lumber flying. He's dragging an ax across the wet grass.

He's got Travis's maniacal look on his face.

You're going to die.

You're going to die.

You've got a gun.

Gina's mind ruptured into action and she threw herself forward, diving back-first against the cabinet beneath the sink. She flung open its doors. Nothing. No wrench, no hammer.

No ax.

Gina crawled across the kitchen floor. She reached up and yanked the drawers out one after another.

They crashed to the floor and coughed up their contents, littering the kitchen with rusty cutlery and blunt cooking utensils. Gina frantically sorted through the gritty pile until she came upon the prize. A cleaver. Stained and dirty brown—but a cleaver. Now armed with something to shoot with and something to chop with, she jumped up and threw the taps back open, sending another dose of RRMMMMMM through the house before she dropped to the ground and slid herself from the kitchen and into the living room. The taps made sure there was no way Conner could track her by sound. The smallest things she could do to level the playing field had literally become a matter of life and death. Scratching across the floor on her hands and knees Gina got her footing and raised her body just enough to land an impressive shoulder-block to the couch, knocking it over. It boomed as it toppled backwards to the floor and sent a mushroom cloud of dust into the air. Gina gathered another bout of momentum, bared down and shot herself shoulder-first into the giant reclining chair, sending it crashing into the front door ,blocking the main entry. She dropped behind the tipped couch, her back against the wall beside the front window; cleaver in one hand, revolver in the other. She methodically alternated the .38 from the back door to the front door to the back door to the front door.

Repeat.

She was sure her heart was going to explode.

No one knows where you are.

If he tries the front door the recliner won't stop him, but it will slow him down, the sound of door-hitting-chair will be enough warning to give me a clear shot and if he comes bursting through the back door he's a dead man. He won't expect it from this angle. The first thing he'll see is the staircases and as he's glancing up I'll take the shot. BANG. Game over.

Her confidence began to sizzle again.

She waited squatting until her legs shook, then she knelt. When her knees gave out, she sat.

How much time passed? Minutes? Hours? She had no scope, no point of reference.

Maybe he didn't see her.

Maybe it wasn't him.

Maybe her mind was playing tricks on her.

Maybe she would survive tonight.

Too much time has passed.

Another gut-check moved her from behind the couch and back to her feet as she hunched her way into the kitchen and positioned herself underneath the window above the sink. She slowly raised herself from the floor and peered out into the backyard at the backing cabin.

Nothing.

No mysterious floating disc of fire. No moving curtain.

Nothing.

Options were weighted.

Gina slid herself across the floor, grabbed the puddle of sweatshirt and stretched the drenched fabric back over her body. It was time to take this to the next level. More options were weighed. Maybe Conner's game-plan was identical. Maybe he was outside in the rain, positioned behind the infamous tree waiting to pick her off once curiosity got the better of her and she decided to sneak a peak; her broken spirits cut down by an ax to the brain the second she stuck her head out the back door.

Or was it the front door?

The decision process had begun to get ugly and she decided to take back the precious element of surprise and crawled over to the cracked, yet somehow still intact side window in the living room.

She knelt and quickly peered outside.

Nothing.

Dropping back to the floor she used the mental picture she captured to guide her hands as she reached up and released the clasps, slid the window up, took a breath, chucked the cleaver across the room, tossed the revolver out the window then followed it, rolling her body back outside into the rain.

Hitting the ground on her hands and knees, she snapped the revolver back into her hand and aimed it at the desolation around her.

Thunder exploded as Gina spun around the side of the house barreling barrel-first into the front yard. The .38 scanned everywhere as the rain did everything in it's power to slow her down.

The street was empty. The wind screeched but nothing moved—anything easily manipulated by harsh weather was violently carried away long ago.

Standing in the front yard she slammed her eyes shut, tried to filter out the storm and strained to hear a child's cries—the child's cries—a little girl begging for her mama, something to force Gina into immediate confrontation, to force the fear and caution out of her brain, but she came up empty. Gina wiped the rain from her eyes and slowly returned to the side of the cabin. She gathered herself for another encounter, and before her brain could stop her body, she charged around the other corner, screaming silently into the front lines of the backyard. She was sure she was reaching cardiac arrest as she tore across the cement and over the patchy yellow grass with the gun primed for release. The patio set was her cue to spin her body around 180 degrees and prepare to release the six shots of lead death at any movement near the still noisy back door. She backpedaled until spine met lumber and the collision with the back fence knocked her to the dirt. The gun scanned the area as she held her breath. Everything was as she left it.

Part of her was relieved. Another part of her wished Conner was just entering the back door with a giant red target on the back of his head. One bullet would have entered the base of his skull and exited out of his misshapen eye. Done. But it was not meant to be. Crouching in the mud, throbbing spine parallel against the fence, Gina felt a difficult degree of comfort at how absolutely ready she was to take the shot. For the past two days she had imagined putting a bullet into Conner so many times the image now seemed more reality based than the daydream it was, but she had often asked herself if she would be "woman enough" to actually pull the trigger, to actually snuff out a life, if, and when, the opportunity presented itself. She asked herself this somewhat rhetorically, as she already knew the answer, but deeply searching inward seemed like something a normal person would do and going through those motions made her feel slightly more human.

It was time for the checkmate.

Carefully, she fed her binoculars into an opening in the fence and studied the back side of new odds-on-favorite cabin. She focused on the back door first.

The small window was smashed from the outside in.

Bingo.

She scanned the second floor windows. Plywood covered two and something hung from inside the house covering the third.

Fucking Bingo.

The inward smile found its way out as she continued to search the cabin's perimeter for more signs of life when she stumbled upon something she somehow missed during her initial sweep of the neighborhood. It was something that shouldn't have seemed odd, but the inability to remember another like it in all of Lake Timor, East or West, made this structure seem suspiciously out of place. Gina lowered the binoculars and examined the back of the tiny one car garage stuffed in the corner of the driveway.

It actually belonged to the neighboring cabin, but its placement beside the cabin-in-question was way too much of a coincidence.

The garage took the guesswork out of her next move. Gina circled the block, ran across the front yards and crept beside the freestanding single car garage. Finally returning the gun into its soggy denim holster she sucked air as the cold steel slid against her abdomen before she dropped to her stomach and peered around the corner to the front of the sad little structure.

It looked like it was a high-end model of those do-it-yourself garage kits which upon completion, forever require you to exit your car and physically raise the door before driving in. It struck her weird that some millionaire wouldn't have found a better way. To drive the point of this oddity, Gina quickly scanned the rest of the street. Not one other garage on either side of the block.

These people dug basements but couldn't build garages?

The door was shut and level to the ground but where the locking mechanism should have been, there was only holes and bent metal. Gina followed the trail of damaged and twisted shrapnel which revealed a large padlock still in the locked position shining through the mud.

B.I.N.G. fucking O.

She slowly reached around the corner, scraped her hand against the bottom of the door and struggled to lift it. Clearly a two-hand job—it didn't budge. She inched her upper torso around the corner positioning both hands firmly on the base and ignoring the pain from her battered spine and tired muscles, she pushed up. After repositioning her body a few times mid-push, it finally gave and the rusted rollers creaked to life. She guided the door up, cringing with each squeak, until the space between the door's rubber bottom and the cement was Gina-sized.

Without hesitation, she slid herself into the garage and came face-to-face with tire treads as she let gravity do its job and softly glided the door back down; the outline of the car's side faded into nothing as the door once again rested flush on the cement, cutting out any light the stormy night sky offered.

The darkness stripped her of her senses and she scrambled with her lighter, scraping her thumb raw on it's rough trigger. The flame finally caught life and illuminated the entire corridor. The two-door hatchback took up a good eight-five percent of the small hanger. Scratch that: the two door hatch back with the broken back window took up a good eighty-five percent of the small hanger. Holding the lighter firmly above her head, Gina slowly rose to her feet and peeked inside the car. The driver's side back window had been smashed and the aftermath sparkled across the seat. On the passenger's side sat a dirty milk crate containing an equally-as-dirty blanket. The seatbelt was carefully weaved through the crate's plastic handles and clipped securely into place.

This latest discovery threw Gina for a loop.

She stood and pondered and processed the crate's purpose until the sight of Conner meticulously stressing over the safety of transported dairy almost made her laugh out loud.

Almost.

BABY AMBER.

The thunder sent her dropping to the floor and the lighter spinning into the sudden blackness.

OH CHRIST—BABY AMBER.

Gina sprawled across the grainy garage floor. Her hands scraped the cement in search of the lighter. Fingernails cracked and bent. The panic was overwhelming as the horrible images tore holes in the hiding places of her deepest parental fears.

FUCK ME—IT'S A GHETTO BABYSEAT!

Her fingers brushed back and forth between the bottom of the car and the wall as her mind screamed for escape. Her palms were covered with a dampness thicker than rainwater and she knew they were scraped bloody. How many times had she circled the car? The lighter was gone. Keep it together—that poor child—digging a shoulder into the car's side, she tightly felt her way around the vehicle. Tire to door, to door, to trunk, to door, to door, until her nails clawed at the driver's side door handle. She popped it up and tore it open as the interior light pierced the darkness. She pulled the gun from her waist and slid into the seat. Her relief was short lived. She looked sideways at the filthy, buckled-in milk crate and sailed a bloody fist into the side of it out of pure anger. Her knuckles protested as the crate didn't budge. She finally examined her hands, which were, as she expected: scraped bloody. Large black pieces of dirt had already lodged themselves into some of the deeper wounds. Gina couldn't stop staring at the horrible little milk crate and as tears threatened, she brought the backs of her hands up to her eyes. Somehow looking away from the crate proved harder than staring into it. Her finger tips slid gently along the top fold of its dirty cotton contents. Suddenly the interior light seemed ridiculously bright. She was positive the single light was bleeding through the four walls of this tragic poor-excuse for a garage. The light emitting from this two-door hatch back was somehow cutting through the walls as well as the storm. Gina was positive its unearthly glow could be seen for miles.

Three wise men were already on their way.

Feeling a rare strain of milk crate induced nausea, she slid out of the car and away from the plastic baby holder and peered under the vehicle where she finally located the missing lighter. Shoving it in her pocket she forced herself to stare at the milk crate one last time; making sure she had a solid mental picture to revisit, just in case the slightest amount of hesitation reared its ugly head, just before putting a bullet into Kevin Conner's chest.

CHAPTER VIII

BING

Gina stood at the front desk as the pimply-faced teenager working the late night shift lumbered around the corner. Despite the limping, the bruises, and her black spy suit that dripped rainwater right through her backpack and pooled on the floor by her feet, she did her best to act casual. The teenager eyed her curiously as she dug her hand into her jean pocket and produced a haggard wad of cash which he carefully used his fingertips to remove from the blood-encrusted palm of her hand. The kid slowly began unfolding and smoothing out her cash as Gina smiled warmly at him. Any adult would have called the police, a doctor, or an exorcist—or at least inquired about her sorry state, but his only concern was finding ways to glance at Gina's chest without making it obvious. Stretching dry clothes over her wet body seconds before spilling into the motel's check-in was a great idea in theory, but as her hair matted against her face and clung to her shoulders, the fresh T-shirt looked just as painted-on as the black one which currently drained from her backpack. Once again, her body was cutting some serious corners for her and she made no attempt to cover up. Not being able to stare directly at her girl parts was slowly killing this guy. He happily handed her a key and finally abandoned all reservations. Openly gawking at the one-girl wet T-shirt contest he muttered, "Uh, seven." Gina smiled sweetly and sent the screen door swinging as she walked down the long alcove and slid the key into the seventh door.

The steam from the shower fogged up every window and

mirror in the tiny room and probably caused a mildew problem which would never be resolved, but she didn't care. Gina had never felt a warmth this wonderful before in all of her life.

She pressed her open palm against the plastic wall and studied how the bright neon green and black lanyard weaved around her knuckles and between her fingers and of course, the bronze treasure that dangled from it: the key to Conner's car.

Once again, she had changed the game.

When she noticed—then stole the key from the ignition, good or bad, she had stranded Kevin Conner at Lake Timor. The risk was huge. If he noticed it missing, the jig would be up and he would be ready and waiting.

The hot water shattered against her skull and ran down her back as she took a swig of Jack Daniels, careful not to get any water into the bottle as she drank.

Drinking in the shower—another first.

Leaning forward against the smooth tile wall, she let the spray attack her lower back—closing her eyes as the water pressure did it's thing.

She thought about the fat kid seven doors down. She had already given him a story to tell for the rest of his virgin life; she should invite him into her room and really blow his mind. She figured the mental image of deflowering the random underage fat kid would be humorous, but it played out more malicious than she expected. She chalked it up to her apparent fixation with people whose workdays begin when everyone else is getting ready for bed.

Back to getting wasted in the shower.

The combination of exhaustion and hunger now worked to her advantage- the buzz came quickly and powerful. She twisted the taps, stumbled through the stained shower door and somehow maneuvered a towel around herself. The motel room's floor was impossibly uneven.

Amused by her squinty smile, she wiped her hands across

the mirror clearing a space just large enough for further self-admiration. She at least looked somewhat human again. After scrolling through her limited mental thesaurus she landed on the word "sexy." She stumbled forward and pulled open the curtains hoping maybe, just maybe, the desk clerk would be passing by and see her in this advanced state of undress, but the windows were just as steamed as the mirrors.

Her confidence peaked in gulps as she tried to cut through both sets of fog and prepare for the following night.

In a matter of hours it would be Judgment Day for Conner.

Tick tock.

Tick tock.

Again, Gina wiped a section of the mirror clean. She bounced up and down on her toes with one fist properly curled and ready for action and the other tilted sideways—respectful of the bottle it held. She scowled her heavyweight champion scowl into the mirror. "We gonna get it on 'cause we don't get along," she whispered then laughed as she tipped the bottle again, causing her to hack and choke.

She began a new game and kicked at her wet clothing. It took all her concentration to push the soaking heap into the bathroom but as she spread her black camouflage attire across the curtain rod she saw the gun on the side of the sink, snatched it and returned to the mirror for Act Two with her newest prop.

She practiced her fiercest snarl a few times then snapped the gun up and pointed it at her reflection.

Macho slogans poured from her mouth as fast as JD poured into it.

"Don't think I won't do it—bitch."

"Don't . . . even . . . try."

"All right, we'll do it the hard way—which knee do you want it in, asshole?"

Something was missing.

She ran to the bedside table and returned with a cigarette in her mouth.

She ran lines a second time with smoke escaping from her nostrils after each threat.

Fucking awesome.

She attempted another swig but the bottle hit her front teeth. Gina steadied herself and raised it to the lamp, examining its remains with a level of intense concentration usually reserved for ancient artifacts and UFO sightings.

The bottle was two-thirds empty.

"Goodness," she exclaimed in a tone more proud than surprised.

Gina closed her eyes and she was right back in the dark garage, filthy and wet and endlessly searching on her hands and knees.

Her eyes fluttered open and although the room was blurry and uneven, the realization came quickly:

I'm safe.

I'm warm.

I'm clean.

I'm drunk.

I'm alive.

She stumbled back and tried to sit on the side of the bed but only caught half of it and teetered off the side, slapping at the bedside table on her way down. She knocked over the touch lamp and sent Hannah's MP3 player, the gun, and Ryen's picture down to the floor along with her. Laying in a heap, Gina laughed into a fit of hiccups. Her status was officially train wreck, yet she had never felt such complete control. Tomorrow night she would reinvent herself as the most famous girl in the world and if she played her cards right, she would never have to do real work again.

Conner was trapped and Conner was screwed and she had the power and all the moves—and a gun.

She reached under the bed, unplugged the sideways lamp and pulled the pillows to the floor. It took half a dozen tries but she managed to slip the MP3's ear buds into place before leaning her daughter's picture against the baseboard. Technology seemed impossibly futuristic as NLX somehow pounded the piano keys through the tiny wires and into her ears. Gina traced the outline of Ryen's tiny face with her broken fingernail. She turned onto her back, outstretched her arms above her head and ran the back of her hands against the bedside table. There was something symbolic about sleeping underneath The Bible which she guessed was inevitably inside.

She knew it was in there but felt no need to remove it.

She didn't need God's Words.

She had never asked for his help before and he had never offered for free.

Her ticket to celebrityhood was a fish in a barrel, a forty minute drive away.

She knew this was the final night for what she would later refer to as the Old Gina and she was proud that she did it alone. She felt like she was shedding her skin.

She let her hands slide back down the face of the bedside table and rest on the floor. Keeping her eyes open suddenly became splitting atoms and along with it came the realization that she was about to pass out on the dirty floor of a one-star motel, draped only in a towel. Her paranoid-damaged mind had finally let go and all that was left was her breathing.

Gina had never felt such peace.

It was everywhere and everything.

The dreams rose to the surface in no time at all.

***

It was an afternoon of black dresses and white facial tissues.

Gina had spent the morning debating whether to make the effort or to just bail on the whole thing. She really didn't want to face her co-workers. Not yet. But on the flip-side, Officer Claire always wore a smile and always made her laugh. He was a good man, one of the few she respected. One of Gina's best memories from her time at the correctional facility was the afternoon she and Claire managed to share a quick cigarette in the staff washroom while he explained to her the O Face, (when a dying person lays there with their mouth open—a perfect O) and the Q Face, (when said person finally dies and their tongue rolls out). He then scolded her for laughing into a loud coughing fit, risking the entire operation. That moment alone was worth the trip to pay her respects.

Arriving late, all eyes slid to Gina as she crossed the graveyard and joined the regularly scheduled service already in progress. She didn't know the majority of the crowd, however, she purposely didn't migrate to the large group of colleagues. Standing by herself she respectfully bowed her head while her peers studied her from afar. She knew what was said about her. She knew her bedroom was a popular lunchroom topic. It was hypocritical to hold their gossip against them, however, these were the people she worked alongside every day and not one of them had made the effort to contact her after the attack. After the scare. Not one phone call after they collectively dropped the ball and forced the SORT Team to come in and clean up their mess. Gina knew the story of her unfortunate situation would have zigzagged at the speed of light from room to room through the entire facility. Word of mouth. What's the stupid cliché?

Bad news travels fast?

The story would jump from person to person with identical initial reactions: immediate shock which fell to sadness which drained to relief and that's when the jokes would have returned. The thought of Gina underneath a group of strange men was a mental image they already had. When you jump into bed with a co-worker, you risk certain workplace labels and Gina found that out the hard way. Lunchroom gossip? She was just as guilty as the rest of them and would be fooling herself to think that Gina French was off limits for behind the back ridicule. One day she walked in

and the room snapped silent. The entire table looked at the
floor and began dropping awkward conversation fragments
as Gina replaced the coffee filter and began brewing a fresh
pot of terrible-tasting, but complementary coffee. She turned
to face the table, but no one had the balls to even look at her.
They were busted. Gina noted that sleeping with one co-
worker had somehow made her the official whore of the
workplace. One.

Now, separated only by the closed casket of a mutual
friend, she stood defiantly across from them, wondering how
long it took for one of them to cut the tension and use her
nightmares, as a punchline. It wouldn't have taken very long
for someone to fill in the blanks when the "easy girl" was
almost raped. The priest began his "Ashes to ashes" speech
when Gina decided she had had enough and turned to make
her exit. The last thing Officer Jim Claire deserved was
having his funeral upstaged by the Traveling Slut Display.

***

Ignoring the unusually sticky sweat running down her
face, she kicked her light jog into a sprint as she rounded the
corner. The rain, like her hangover, had finally broken, but
more dark clouds loomed in the distance. The foreshadowing
was beautiful. Her heart pounded inside her chest as she kept
the pace. Her sneakers splashed mud up her legs but she
slammed through every single puddle in her path. The run
was therapeutic and necessary. The smell of her alcohol-
laced sweat turned her stomach but she kept on. Hannah's
MP3 player set the pace as Axl Rose motivated her with his
menacing thoughts. Her lungs burned as she spotted a
convenience store in the distance and decided it would serve
as the finish line. The guitar solo tore into her eardrums as
she forced out the pain. She turned it on one last time and
snapped the sprint into a full on run. Every muscle bulged
and the storefront grew as she cut the distance. Her legs
shook and the familiar burn in her back returned. Gina
pumped her arms, ignoring the pain as she dangerously

reached the point where she was two, maybe three strides away from a full-on body failure when she slapped the wheelchair ramp with her hand, signifying the end of her painful journey. Bent over with her hands on her knees and gasping for breath, Gina felt her body burn with pride.

Tonight.

It ends tonight.

Inside the One-Stop she loaded up and left with bottled water, dry cigarettes, a steaming cup of coffee and a surprise purchase. Just for Kevin Conner. She began her slow walk back to the motel and the thickness of the day's inevitable events were lost in her new found clarity.

It was going to end tonight.

Tonight.

Her cigarette hand rubbed her abs. She was a machine. She was an unstoppable machine and after tonight the world would finally be forced to agree with her.

She thought about her last night in her old life.

Sleeping on the floor in a towel. Drunk to the 10s.

A fitting metamorphosis.

That tiny area between the bed and wall was her cocoon.

Yesterday she was a caterpillar.

Today she was a butterfly.

There was no doubt in her mind—no second thoughts—it would all play out in a matter of hours, then she would be free.

Free of her old life.

Free of her old habits.

Gina's mind was no longer a fractured collage of horrible events.

The bills were gone.

The job was gone.

The custody battle was over.

The failed relationships were gone.

The judging family was gone.

The rape attempt was gone.

The only thing that finally punctured her newfound outlook was the news report she caught on the tiny television in the motel office during checkout.

Baby Amber's parents pleaded to the camera. The sad desperation in their voices was annoyingly heartbreaking, but the vacancy in their eyes was the real story. It was their dead eyes that stuck.

If the child was still alive, Gina would reunite a family. Give a young couple reason to live again. Reason to get out of bed.

Then there was Conner. He too, was coming home tonight. She would organize a city-wide toast. Flood downtown with civilians raising their glasses the exact moment the electric chair's switch would be flipped.

They would cheer for her.

Obnoxious and outspoken—and God, they would cheer for her.

She didn't break her stride as she plucked the cigarette from her mouth and tossed it aside without even glancing at it.

Cigarettes tasted like the past.

New Gina was above nicotine.

New Gina was above everything.

New Gina was above everyone.

Rebirth was a forty minute drive away.

Tonight.

***

The car scraped back into last night's makeshift parking spot. During the entire drive the windshield wipers remained useful for a few minutes then annoyingly squeaked along the dry glass as the rain momentarily let up. Fearing her wrath, even the storm was reluctant to commit.

It was Go Time.

Gina tossed the backpack into the hatch, stepped out of the car and wrapped her hand around the gun.

Conner's surprise remained snug in her pocket.

She silently crept from cabin to cabin, past the tiny garage until she stood in the backyard of the summer-home with the possessed curtains and the inviting orange orb.

This was it.

She watched in silence.

The back window.

The side window.

No movement.

Nothing.

She wondered what kind of a monster takes a baby hostage and demands nothing? Who destroys a family "just in case?" or "just because?" The images inside of her head were gruesome. A baby laying on the cold floor, its cries of hunger and neglect unanswered.

Christ.

I should have acted last night, I should have—

No.

Gina stopped herself—the Old Gina wallowed in should-haves.

New Gina regretted nothing.

She dropped the binoculars in the grass. It was time to end this dance. The music was over.

She stalked up to the back door, slowly pushed it open with her foot and entered the back room, gun first.

Cigarette butts and empty ravioli cans littered the damp dining table.

Milk cartons sprawled everywhere and the odor of sour milk attacked her nostrils.

The stench would have made Old Gina flinch.

Everything had been disturbed.

Lived in.

Every drawer was removed and lay on the floor. Every cupboard was open.

There was something else in the air, mixing with the sour milk—what was that?

Urine?

Gina pulled the afternoon's last minute purchase from her pocket and death-gripped the pepper-spray.

She stepped around the garbage and took to the stairs. She felt cat-like as she floated up the steps without a single life-risking creak.

As she slithered to the top she heard it.

Breathing.

Inhaling and exhaling.

Deep slumber.

Something moved.

Someone was here.

Conner was here.

Gina quickened her steps and after the first creak in the hallway sold her out- she broke into a run. The door was only five steps away and ajar.

Her eyes bulged as she planted her left foot and shot herself forward.

Wonder if the whore's clean?

She pounded the sole of her right foot into the carpet and threw herself at the door.

WONDER IF THE WHORE'S CLEAN?

BAM

The door shot open, and she charged through the frame.

There he was.

Conner sat straight up and before he even had time to focus his eyes the momentum carried Gina onto the bed where she brought her sneaker up and buried it square into his nose. Even through the thick heel of her running shoe she felt the cartilage crumble. Conner's head snapped back and Gina rolled on top of him and they both spilled off the bed. Just before they hit the hardwood Gina swung the pepper-spray from her side and planted the base of the canister right above his eye. The air left Conner's body as they connected with the floor. He grabbed for her hair; she elbowed him in the nose, then threw her body backwards as she extended her arm and unleashed a small blast of pepper-spray inches from his face. Her back smashed against the wall and her legs remained on top of his stomach as he rolled over and scoured his eyes. His screams of pain and surprise were elating. She kicked at the back of his head as she pushed herself away.

She needed room to strike. She jumped to her feet as Conner got one arm on the bed and tried to lift himself. Gina cut him off with another snap sidekick to the temple. As Conner turned to cover his head from the possibility of a second blow she triggered the pepper-spray inches from his face a second time. His screams came louder he sent his legs flailing, managing to connect with her thigh. It was a push more than a kick, but it sent Gina to her hands and knees, where she dodged the follow-up strike, his sock whizzing right by her left ear. Back to her feet, she shot herself forward. Conner was sitting up against the wall—his arms like a giant X, trying to protect his face, but Gina saw the opening and pistol-whipped him, the handle of the gun soaring right between his hands and connecting with his forehead. The sound of the blow was somewhat anticlimactic but she knew it felt worse than it sounded. His hands scrambled to his skull, leaving his nose exposed and Gina relentlessly drove a stiff knee into something that was once two nostrils and an arch. The impact shuddered his whole body and he screamed. Gina tried for another knee but he managed to block that one with his hands.

Wonder if the whore's clean?

She abandoned his head and went for the obvious, driving her sneaker between his legs. Despite the solid crotch-shot and the moan it produced, Conner's hands remained on his face so Gina continued the assault on his genitals. Two, three, four more kicks found their marks, followed up with a horrible heel stomp for good measure. Conner finally brought his knees up and swung one hand forward in her direction. Gina couldn't have been any more ready. She smashed the butt of the gun into the top of his hand as it flailed in her direction, stopping it dead in its tracks and snapping it down at the wrist. As his hand retreated he desperately flung his other palm onto the bed and tried to pull himself up a second time leaving his face wide open. Gina's attack was primal.

Wonder if the whore's clean?

Another lunging heel strike connected under his nose. She brought her foot back and swung the toe forward, burying the tip of her sneaker into the bloody mess in the middle of his face. Conner's head snapped back and his skull bounced off the wall as he managed to blink his bloodshot eyes open for the first time since the first pepper-spray attack. Gina turned sideways, grabbed the windowsill for support and stomped her heel into the screaming mess on the floor in front of her. The blows rained down. Ribcage-forehead-knee-forehead-forehead-ribcage-ribcage.

Wonder if the whore's clean?

Wrist-elbow-ribcage-shoulder-forehead-ribcage-ribcage-ribcage.

She snarled as she felt one of her blows sink deeper into his side than seemed possible. Conner's head popped forward as Gina shifted and kicked him in the nose. She gave it everything she had. The gurgling sound was barely audible as she collapsed forward on top of him and pounded the base of the pepper-spray into his forehead as they both crashed to the floor again. One hand remained limp by his side as his other flailed aimlessly in the air, gently patting her on the back and head—streaking her blonde hair red. His eyes glazed. His blood was everywhere. His nose was missing. His words were gibberish.

Gina got to her feet, jumped back and surveyed the damage.

He didn't have a chance, not a Goddamn chance. How long did that take? Thirty seconds? Forty-five? Didn't even use the gun.

Conner tried to sit up, but fell backwards. His arm swayed above his head like he was conducting some sort of invisible symphony on the ceiling before returning to his puffy eyes. His other arm hung lifeless by his side. Blood caked the side of the bed and the wall.

For the first time she became aware of her surroundings and spun a quick 360.

More cigarette butts. Empty tuna cans. Musty sheets.

No child.

He moaned.

Gina cocked her gun and held it on him as she steadily retreated out the bedroom. Standing in the hallway she looked at the other two doors. The bathroom was wide open, the other was shut. She turned back to Conner who had managed to turn onto his side and was now clutching his shoulder with his one, still functional arm. Amazingly, he was determined to get a leg underneath himself. Gina shook the gun forward at him and yelled "Hey," but Conner continued to try and rise. She yelled a second time, but he seemed unaware of her presence. He sputtered blood and coughed as it ran down the front of his shirt. He managed to get his weight on one knee and was shakily working on the second one as he leaned his back against the wall for support and began to pull himself onto the bed, his hand clawing at the pillow. Gina looked down the hall at the closed door then back at Conner.

GODDAMMIT!

She rushed back into the room and sent a half-assed kick just under his neck, pounding the back of his head into the wall, sending him sprawling forward onto his stomach. She pulled the top cover off the bed and tossed them over the broken killer.

"Ahhh-ah-muhhh."

His muffled whimpers and unrecognizable dialect angered her.

Wonder if the whore's clean?

She sneered and jumped knees first onto the pile of blankets and hammered the gun down into the quivering mass. She had no idea what part of the anatomy the butt was connecting with, but it didn't matter—a solid shot was a solid shot and he couldn't take too many more solid shots.

Wonder if the whore's clean?

Gina lost all control of herself and of time itself. Panting and sweating, the carnage came to a halt. She climbed backwards off the mess of saturated fabric and limbs.

The muffled moans sounded inhuman.

Gina charged out of the room and down the hall. She flung the door open.

Two chairs and a couch.

No bed.

No child.

She spun back down the hallway and stuck her head in the bathroom. She didn't even let mental images worse than the PG-14 "Baby Amber floating face down in the bathtub" fully conjure before she yanked the plastic curtain aside and stared at the dry cracks.

Strike Two.

Gina's anger boiled.

She charged back to into the bedroom and screamed at the bloody-sheet-and-limbs-cocktail:

"WHERE THE FUCK IS THE KID?"

The pile stirred and moaned and sputtered.

FUCK.

Gina sent a light kick at what had to be his head, spun around and bolted down the stairs. She punted milk cartons and cans of cigarette butts aside, sending them brilliantly scattering as she charged through the kitchen and into the living room.

Nothing.

The closet.

Empty.

FUCK.

She heard some movement above her. Shuffling followed by a thud.

"STAY THE FUCK DOWN—I SWEAR TO GOD I'M

GOING TO COME UP THERE AND SHOOT YOU IN THE FUCKING KNEES!" she screamed.

The dragging sounds continued.

CHRIST!

Think!

She ran back and forth across the main level as her mind scrambled through the most horrible worst case scenarios she could come up with:

The oven.

Empty.

The fridge.

Empty.

The ice box.

Empty.

FUCK.

The dragging sound from the second floor produced another thump just above her.

"YOUR FUCKING KNEECAPS—I SWEAR TO GOD!" she screamed.

Thump.

FUCK

Thinkthinkthink.

Thump.

FUCK ME.

Gina leaped over the mess in the kitchen and charged up the stairs. She swung the revolver around the corner and pointed it where she left Conner, but the bloody skin/flannel combo was on its feet, stumbling toward her. The sudden change of events didn't even have time to register when the shot rang out and Gina felt part of her stomach dislodge.

The impact sent her entire torso twisting and smashed her spine-first into the door frame. That was when she saw the blood splatter and skin on the wall. She slowly looked down into a hole in her sweatshirt and saw the dark void just under her ribcage. Blood pulsed from the wound and down her pant leg. The pain hadn't even registered when another shot rang out and splintered the door frame inches above her head. She looked up unable to move as Conner, still charging, still draped in a white blanket like a welfare kid on Halloween, shouldered into her stomach, forcing her spine back into the doorknob before momentum spilled them both into the hallway then down the staircase. The world rotated two or three times and not even the sudden SMACK of the kitchen floor fully brought her back to reality. She couldn't look away from her side.

Through the blood and the muscle she thought she saw bone.

Gina fought through the shock and tried to stand but her head jerked to a stop and Conner brought her back to the floor face-first by her ponytail. Her cheek exploded as it met the hardwood.

You're going to die up there.

The pain was everywhere—her side, her neck, her knee, her back; it unified and attacked her brain. Fighting through the cobwebs she focused on survival. She could see the can of pepper-spray spinning on the floor just out of reach. She also saw a large moving object out of the corner of her other eye. Although her body refused to respond, her peripheral vision was trying very hard to keep her alive. Everything turned slow and murky. The pain was so blinding she was unaware if she still gripped the revolver, but as Conner came into her vision she played the only card she had. Gina swung her arm at the Conner-sized blur Relief washed through her as she recognized the sudden flash of silver at the end of her hand. Conner collapsed on top of her as the barrel of .38 jammed right into the deformed corner of his eye but her vision immediately blurred as the red-hot barrel of his gun burned deep into her eyebrow.

The sound of the pepper-spray's revolutions got slower and slower until coming to a complete stop.

Gina's right hand shook as the .38 hovered inches in front of Conner's eye.

The smell of burnt flesh—her own burnt flesh—turned

her stomach as the imprint from the smoldering barrel of Conner's gun blistered her forehead.

Her side tingled and itched.

She struggled for words, "just . . . just . . . just . . . "

Years of chain-smoking had perfected her multitasking abilities and now they were keeping her alive. The world tilted and bent. She squinted through the shock and used her elbow to press the gritty rag into the large gape in her side while her other hand kept her revolver aimed at Conner's irregular eye.

The Plan had taken a rather unfortunate turn. Her entire existence had now become an intense counting game.

Inhale.

Squeeze.

Exhale.

Squeeze.

Inhale.

Squeeze.

Exhale.

Squeeze.

Grinding dirt particles into her open wound sent panic scraping at her brain.

No matter how tightly she sandwiched the stained cloth into wound, she knew she was bleeding to death.

Inhale, squeeze, exhale.

Gina's mind kept the rhythm steady while her eyes did their best not to dwell on the silver blur hanging inches from her face. When she adjusted her eyesight and focused on the barrel of Conner's gun, the face of the man with his finger on the trigger distorted in the distance. It had to be one or the other.

DAMMIT.

Once again she caught herself focused on the weapon and not its operator.

KEEP.

FOCUSED.

Inhale, squeeze, exhale.

As they sat across the small table from each other, Gina wondered if Conner's distorted face would be the last thing she ever saw.

Thanks to her attack, his face was even more distorted than usual.

His head tilted up, as if studying something on the ceiling, but his eyes looked down at Gina with spooky clarity. Conner's game plan was identical. One hand kept his gun on Gina's eyebrow as his free hand pressed a washcloth against his crushed nose. His bright red irritated eyes streamed tears down his cheeks every time he gently urged the cloth, but neither gravity nor compression could stop the blood that trickled from his collapsed nostrils. Both of their do-it-yourself medical emergency kits were failing as blood dripped freely through the fabric squares, pooled onto the table and collected underneath their chairs.

Through clenched teeth she heard Conner mutter something about The Lord.

It seemed like an eternity had passed since their post-stair-tumble standoff began, which had escalated into a dark fog of confusion filled with shouting and stumbling. The present standoff was much less dramatic. Both sat waiting for the other to make the first move; hoping it would be a stupid one.

How the fuck did he get a gun? How did he—

Inhale, squeeze, exhale.

THUMP

Although the table was small, to keep the weapons close to each other's heads they had to lean forward. Conner seemed unfazed by the awkward angle of his spine, but the pressure on Gina's lower back was relentless. Her splintered chair was not level with the ground and as she shifted her weight, desperately trying to remove the strain from her lower lumbar, the chair violently tilted, sending a hot knife of pain sliding up her spine. Conner's agony seemed to be unchair related, attacking his entire body in random bursts. Gina waited patiently for these moments. Anything to keep her mind from puking up images of yellowish puss filling the cavity in her side with poison.

Thoughts of her body trying to heal itself over the filthy rag.

Every time Conner's body tensed she stole a glance at the floor beneath her own chair, keeping track of how quickly and how large the blood puddle was becoming. Her only hope was to slow the bleeding. How much time did she have before she bled out? It was impossible to eyeball; no way to guesstimate liters as the dark circle expanded.

Conner blinked down at her as the gash in his forehead seeped into his eye.

Inhale.

Was it washing out the pepper-spray?

Squeeze. Exhale.

THUMP

Gina's chair shifted and the tiny impact of the fourth leg hitting the ground shook another moan from her gut. Conner wheezed and forced out a cough as blood and spittle arced onto the table. Gina bared down on the rag as Conner readjusted the cloth on his nose.

It was officially a waiting game.

It was now a clock-race between Gina's bullet-torn side and Conner's shoe-removed nose and unknown internal damage.

Another coughing fit sprayed more bloody saliva onto the table. The memory of Gina's foot stomping, then sinking into his side sent a shiver of courage through her.

That had to have seriously tore something up on the inside.

But was Conner's unseen trauma more deadly than the hole blown out of her skin?

That was the million dollar question.

Inhale—hurry up—squeeze—and die—exhale.

Who would bleed to death first?

With every blink, his eye seems to gain more focus.

The silence bore on.

How long had they sat here, guns primed at each other's heads?

Both sat at the table. Both beat to shit. Both pointing guns at each other's faces. Over and over the adrenaline attacked, peaked, sustained, and decayed.

Both made a habit of sliding their finger up and down the triggers, keeping the blood circulating.

Staying ready.

Gina tried to keep above the unrelenting waves of panic but as the minutes silently ticked by they crashed in higher and stronger.

You're going to die up there.

She ached for nicotine's calming effect.

Risk it. Pull the trigger. End this now.

There was no way Conner would not have the reflexes to pull his trigger as his head came off—and vice versa.

The chair shifted and Gina's body responded in a flash of pain.

Inhale—Goddammit—squeeze, exhale.

Conner's eyes were terrified and terrifying at the same time. Blood poured through the cloth, through his fingers, and down his forearm. It dripped off his elbow and onto the table.

Checkmate.

Gina focused on Conner's nose, hoping to summon dormant telepathic powers. She tried to use her mind to accelerate the flow of blood from his face. Drain it from his brain. Her focused attack on his nose was never predetermined but in the heat of the moment she took great pride in kicking it beyond recognition. She wondered what was left of it, how much of it actually hung between the rag and Conner's face?

God, it was bleeding a lot.

She watched the blood trickle down his arm and collect at his elbow, timing the seconds between drops.

Gina's victory was cut short as she realized somewhere during the new counting game she had lost concentration and relaxed her elbow. She panicked and winced as she forced deeply into the open wound. She silently cursed herself. Her mind raced. How long had she stopped applying pressure? How long had she lost more blood than necessary? This stand-off was going to come down to a photo finish and how much life had she just leaked during her carelessness? She had to keep it together.

She had to slow her bleeding and wait for Conner to die.

Gina searched for words. "Just, let's—let's just—"

She studied his eyes as she frantically corrected her posture. He was having problems of his own.

Conner flustered with the dishrag against his nose. His bloodshot eyes blinked streaks of crimson.

He's fading.

He can't last much longer.

His breathing became shorter and the desperation of his intake echoed throughout the kitchen.

Each breath seemed to send his body into a spasm.

Each one harder to control than the last.

He quickly glanced at the back door, then back to Gina.

He's going down.

I have this one.

Gina clenched her teeth and pressed the towel deep into her side.

The pain blinded her. It whited out all thoughts of incurable infections.

Her brain searched for the missing part of her body.

It itched more than it pulsed.

If she could pull anything positive from the crater he put in her side, it was an overpowering distraction from her burning shoulder as she struggled to keep her revolver level with Conner's abnormal eye.

The last thing he needs is a bullet in there as well.

She fought back a smile.

Her confidence sparked.

She bared down harder on the dark cloth, wringing out some of its collected blood and imagining the flow slowing.

Slowing, slowing, slooooooowing, stopping.

She imagined the rag fitting perfectly into the wound. A perfect seal. Its contents no longer escaping.

Inhale, exhale.

Conner sucked in and shook as his gun dropped past Gina's eye line and bobbed just below her mouth before slowly climbing back up to her forehead.

She kept stealing glances at the floor.

Her puddle wasn't growing. She was positive.

I stopped the bleeding.

I'm winning.

I'm going to survive this.

Gina could feel the hospital's immaculate silver nozzles expelling disinfectant and cool water into her wound; washing out all the neon yellow venom. The hole being sewn closed. The stitches sterile and clean. The large bandage properly holding her insides inside.

She could be minutes away from medical attention. Infections take days before becoming lethal.

The burning in her shoulder retreated and her revolver steadied.

Conner had slowly, and by the look in his eyes, extremely painfully, slid the soiled cloth past his face and now held the inside of his elbow firmly against what was once his nose.

Conner's body's language started to betray his confident stare.

The blinking slowed down.

A calm vacancy began.

Gina smiled.

She watched Conner react to her defiant smirk. The intense hatred momentarily returned to his eyes but it had no longevity. In a matter of seconds they went vacant again.

Unoccupied.

He was fighting to keep the game going.

He shakily pushed the gun forward another two inches towards her forehead.

Gina didn't flinch.

Gina's tiny smirk didn't falter.

The gun shook.

She watched as Conner's eyes floated towards the ceiling then snapped back—ceiling—back, over and over.

Inhale—he's losing it—exhale—he's on fumes.

She ignored her missing side.

She ignored the pain yo-yo-ing up and down her vertebrae.

Conner's body shook as he desperately played his final card and tried to take back control.

His teeth gritted, he let out a breathless cry and somehow lifted himself slightly from his chair. He returned the barrel of his gun back against Gina's forehead.

Inhale. OHSHITOHSHITOHSHIT.

Gina tensed her trigger finger and closed her eyes as she felt the barrel of his gun somehow slide perfectly into the slight indent previously burnt into her flesh.

OHSHITOHSHIT

She shut off all other senses using only her ears, waiting for the BANG so she could instantaneously return the favor.

OHSHIT—

hugggffffffff

Suddenly the cool pressure of the steel in her skull was gone.

Suddenly her mind screamed for oxygen and she gravelly inhaled as her eyes shot open.

The effort it took for Conner to touch his gun to her forehead had apparently become unbearable. He had slumped back into his chair. Defeated. His gun bobbed barely a foot above the table.

It now pointed at her chest.

SWAT IT AWAY

Conner's eye's fluttered

SWAT IT.

THUNK

The sound of his gun's handle hitting the table snapped Conner back to earth.

His arm steadied and the weapon rose level with Gina's throat, shook, then slowly declined back down until it finally rested on the table.

His initial target had been a surefire death sentence but it had downgraded from her eyebrow to just below her breast.

Even now, gun resting on the table, his hand shook to keep it upright.

The desperation crept into his face.

Gina kept her eyes locked on his

Drop. Dead.

Another patch of collected blood spilled from the arm crook, covering his blood-geyser nose. She followed its journey as it cascaded straight down into his lap.

How much damage had she done to this child-stealing asshole?

Gina remembered the initial assault.

The heel to the nose, the pepper-spray, the knees, the unforgiving flurry of a maniacal pistol-whipping.

The unforgiving flurry of a maniacal pistol-whipping.

She liked that.

When they made *Gina French, The Movie* she imagined how the film editors would shoot the scenes separately but splice together the footage of the Gina/Conner beat-down with the scene of Conner chopping his parents. Judging them through his crusty eye. Showing them no mercy, no remorse.

Inhale—that's good film—exhale.

Her breathing had finally caught rhythm. Quick short gasps through her teeth kept her chair steady and caused no ill effects on her side or lower back.

Mental clarity had almost returned.

She swallowed the shoulder burn and held the gun steady at his face.

Stealing another glance below, the blood puddle seemed untouched.

Conner coughed up another helping of dark crimson mass.

His gun continued to shake and point at her abdomen.

Her slight trace of a smirk continued to mock.

He wasn't going to shoot.

He was no longer physically able to do so.

Any second, he's going to collapse.

Conner squinted through glazed eyes.

Slowly, he sunk further in his chair.

His limp wrist tilted his gun sideways.

His eyes blinked shut, slowly reopened and rolled towards the back door, then back to Gina.

Tiny slits.

He. Is. Done.

Now it was her turn.

Gina leaned forward and stared deeply into his eyes.

She was unable to make the comparison—unable to measure his under-chair puddle of blood against her own, but the large dark smears across the tabletop were impressive.

The babynapping America's Most Wanted escapee was done.

Conner followed her eyes as she looked him over.

Gina brought her eyes back to his; her smile a little wider.

Confidence mounting.

Fantasies of sterile surgical instruments deep inside her wound stoked her billowing courage. Keeping the rag fused into her side, Gina held her breath and slowly leaned to the right.

THUMP

Her chair repositioned but she was prepared. She kept

leaning until Conner's legs came into view. His chair seemed to be floating atop a lake of blood. The liquid-black oval nearly doubled the size of the one pooling beneath her.

Gina returned upright and searched his eyes.

Vacant.

Her smile widened. Teeth peeked through.

Keep him busy.

Keep him distracted until he bleeds out.

Keep his thoughts from retaliation.

Keep him from panicking and doing something frantic.

Something desperate.

Conner quickly glanced at the back door, then back to Gina.

Fighting through the pain in her lower back she once again multi-tasked. Her eyes and gun remained locked on Conner as she slowly bent at the waist, dropping her head low enough to allow the fingers from her left hand to trace the burnt ring above her eye. She did so without relieving any of the pressure from the elbow/rag/open-wound homemade lifesaving devise.

Conner studied her tiny movements intensely; his gun shuddering back to the upright position.

Satisfied with the quality and depth of her branding, Gina's fingers slid down her face and gently massaged her cheek as the pain mentally snapped her back in time when Conner had snatched her hair and forced an awkward meeting between her face and the floor.

Was her jaw broken? She slowly opened and closed it.

Nope, but she counted loose teeth by pushing them forwards and backwards with her tongue.

Inhale—three—exhale.

Not surprisingly, she tasted blood.

Gina's eyes dropped to the floor then rose back to Conner.

Her blood-puddle now seemed like a tiny afterthought.

Conner's eyes no longer looked like squinty slits. Conner's eyes looked shut.

Okay girl, slowly lower your arm and use your gun to swat his away.

Inhale. Exhale.

Gina's revolver slowly began its slow decent.

Inhale—Conner's nose—exhale.

Inhale—Conner's mouth—exhale.

Inhale—Conner's chin—exh—

FUFFFFFFF

Conner's eyes opened as his arm suddenly slipped off his face. Stringy blood dripped between his arm and nose. Gina shot forward, jamming her revolver inches from his eye. Conner's eyes went wild with panic, but no triggers were pulled. Conner quickly pushed his arm back into his nose then hunched forward, propping his elbow on the table and trying his best to angle his arm so the gun resumed pointing in the general direction of Gina's face.

SHITSHITSHITSHIT

Finally someone spoke.

"I don't have th—kid."

Conner's stained pupils washed clean by anger.

Gina said nothing.

"I don't hhhhhhh—the kid," he repeated.

Gina said nothing.

Conner tried for a third time but the wet coughing fit took over as he shook his head back and forth. The bloody arm crossing his nose swayed along.

He looked like a fucked-up elephant.

Conner wheezed, choked and caught his breath. It came shallow and sharp and as he gulped for oxygen, his arm slightly separated from his face splattering a collected heap of blood onto the table. His gun-hand wavered back down to the table.

He desperately waited for Gina's reaction.

He got none.

Gina said nothing.

Her tight smirk more surprised than arrogant.

Conner's eyebrow's dropped.

"YOU BITCH—bi—bitch," he trailed off as he sandwiched his shaking arm back against his almost-nose.

Gina said nothing.

Conner's bright red eyes slanted and bore into Gina as he fought to raise his elbow off the table and returned his gun to her face.

The hairs stood on the back of her neck.

OH SHIT.

The smirk faded.

Conner shakily sat straight in his chair. His arm clenched against his nose. His gun drifted back to Gina's forehead.

Just keep him talking; keep him from pulling the trigger.

She matched the seriousness of his stare and carefully spoke:

"Where. Is. The. Child?"

"I don't . . . " He shuddered the rest of his statement away as Gina shook her head.

Not good enough.

Gina was once again aware of the stabbing pain in her side—she could sense another wave of agony building.

She tried to speak with her initial clarity but the blinding pain stole her breath mid-delivery.

"You. Are. Going. to bleed—ta—death any second. Ughhhh. Give the family—ughh."

Her anger flared at how desperate and rushed it sounded.

Conner took a second to digest the demand.

His eyes blinked.

FUCK.

She watched the wheels begin to turn.

She was positive he had dissected the tone and processed her desperation.

She was sure he now knew the life-threatening severity of the gunshot wound in her side.

How bad her spine was.

How much blood, she too, was losing.

She could tell he was thinking he may have a chance, after all.

That maybe he could outlast her.

Gina's tone had betrayed her.

She breathed panic back into her lungs and her mind screamed to pull the trigger.

Take the chance.

He is onto you.

Pull.

The.

Trigger.

Conner surfaced another hearty helping of inner blood all over the table as he shook his elephant-head and continued his denial.

"Don't—have the kid. Stupid bitch."

Conner's body language and breathless words hadn't changed but Gina could no longer stop the fear from seeping into every pore.

You're going to die up there.

Gina stared inside the gun's barrel as it crept back up and hovered inches from her face. She imagined hearing the crack and watching the bullet exit the gun before it drilled through her skull.

I won't even feel it.

Her side was splattered on the upstairs wall and her head was about to be splattered against the kitchen's wilted sunflower wallpaper.

How long would she be aware of her situation after the bullet tore through her skull?

Would she die seeing her brain emptied all over the dated cupboards?

Her thoughts and memories crudely stuck to the fridge like child's art work?

Would Travis even report her missing?

Pull.

The.

Trigger.

Gina's return to silence seemed to infuriate Conner and he sputtered out his first demand:

"Guns down."

Conner took a huge breath and continued:

"Guns down, we both walk."

Gina blinked.

What the fuck did he just say? Is he bargaining with me?

The past week and a half surged through her injuries and obliterated the pain in her side, back and shoulder.

Naked anger festered.

We both walk?

The incident.

The job.

The responsibilities.

The risks.

The money.

The lies.

The family.

The handicapped boyfriend.

The Plan.

The daughter.

The drive.

The search.

The fame.

The fight.

The struggle.

The gunshot.

YOU.

SHOT.

ME.

Gina blinked.

Mouth agape.

We both walk?

She was officially fuming.

We both walk?

She had risked everything she had, everything, and found and pounded an escaped killing machine; a Death-Row superstar into a broken, quivering helpless two-dimensional—thing. Something no longer human, no longer worthy of basic human emotion and interaction, not worthy of pity. She reduced something that was once so proud and feared, into whatever mess currently sat swaying and dying in front of her—dying while begging to be spared.

She violently stomped out his true colors.

She did this.

Alone.

Gina French.

Not the police.

Not Travis.

Gina fucking French.

Guns down, we both walk?

Gina gave herself to the anger.

The consistent flashes of pain attacking her spine no longer registered as she steadied her revolver and forced it forward towards his eye. She shook her head back and forth. Gina slowly opened her mouth as wide as it would go, stared into his eyes and gently over-enunciated the word "No."

This was the moment.

There was absolutely no turning back.

Guns down, we both walk?

No chance in hell.

No fucking chance in hell.

Gina took one big breath. Her lungs were raw, but she forced through it and repeated her counteroffer.

"No."

Not getting the deal he was hoping for, Conner clenched his eyes as he shook, cycling more blood from inside his stomach, out his mouth, and down the outside of his shirt.

The angle of his gun floated just left of her head.

SWAT IT AWAY, PULL THE TRIGGER, BLOW HIS HEAD OFF.

Conner blinked and swayed the gun back at her nose.

What is the matter with you? ANOTHER opportunity lost!

His words still floated in the air.

Guns down, we both walk?

The chair shifted and she cringed for another spine-spasm which never came. Her legs had become tingly and numb.

Conner looked lost as he gasped for air and waited for something from her.

How long had they been sitting there?

Their eyes never unlocked.

Should she have pulled the trigger then?

Risked it all early on?

No.

Guns down. We both walk.

No.

This was how it was going to end.

This was how it had to end.

Conner silently stared on. The shaking became worse and the gun that floated inches from Gina's face began to violently rattle.

Pull.

The.

Trigger.

Conner's eyes were hollow and broken but above everything else—

Desperate.

Desperate and what else?

What else did she see?

Desperate and pathetic.

She leaned forward into Conner's shaking gun, locked eyes and sneered in a whispered tone:

"NO."

Conner clenched his eyes and winced as his body trembled.

Pull the—

Conner's eyes flashed open and he managed an angry scream.

Blood slid off his tongue and splattered the table.

Standing her ground, she sneered as his yelp trailed off.

"It's over, Conner. I—"

"I SAW THEM!" Conner screamed.

The sentence was cut off by a wet coughing fit.

More blood leaked from his mouth and nose as he hacked.

Just shut up and die already.

Conner tried again. This time it escaped as whisper, but he got it all out.

"I saw them, all . . . holding you . . . down"

Gina's jaw painfully dropped.

THUD

Wonder if the whore's clean?

Anger became shock and shock burst back into anger. Gina became unglued.

That was his closer?

That was what he was waiting to throw in her face?

That was his saving grace?

That he saw what happened to her during the riot?

That he saw what almost happened to her during the riot?

That he saw them holding her down?

That he only watched?

That he didn't join in?

Was that the point of that statement?

That he only *saw* them?

That he did nothing while a group of monsters held her down?

THUD

Hold the bitch down.

Because he walked away when she was being traumatized?

THUD

Fuck the shoes.

Because he did nothing while a handful of the absolute worst human beings this rotting planet ever produced took turns beating on and undressing her?

That was why she should put her gun down and let him walk out of here?

Give him back his car keys and let him drive right out of Lake Timor, because he didn't raise his hand?

This selfish asshole killed his parents, walked away from a gang rape and wanted—wanted what? A pat on the back?

Is this really happening?

Is this seriously fucking happening?

Did he just say that?

"I saw them holding you down?"

The kettle came to a violent boil.

"FUCK YOU!" she unleashed into his face.

Gina's nostrils flared.

Her side flared.

She released the saturated rag from under her arm and sat straight up. The pain from the now-exposed bullet wound sent sparkly white spots dancing underneath her eyelids but her anger was now firmly in the driver's seat.

Conner steadied himself in preparation for the bullet, but the shots came from her mouth.

"You worthless piece of shit. You did—NOTHING? Nothing, Conner? You want applause for that?"

She felt blood release from her side.

"You expect me to—to what? Let you walk—walk out because you didn't, what? Get in line?"

Conner braced himself and pushed his gun forward into her forehead.

Gina shook with anger.

"You did nothing while they tried to ra—take me? That's your ticket out? You want my forgiveness? Because you didn't want to partake?"

THUD

Wonder if the whore's clean?

"You want absolution?"

Another gush of blood expelled from her side.

Gina kicked back and stood up, her spine clenched as the chair slid through the blood-puddle and dented the fridge.

Ignoring the giant leak in her side, she clutched the gun with both hands. Conner struggled to get to his feet, knocking over his chair and keeping the handgun raised. This forced him to separate his arm from his face and slap his palm down into the blood-smeared tabletop to steady himself. The removal exposed the blood-encrusted saggy flesh between his eyes and mouth.

Gina's hate continued to bluster. "You chose freedom over getting off and you want a medal?" She adjusted her stance to keep her balance. "Any idiot would choose free— ffffreeee—" Gina staggered from pain and trailed off. Each heartbeat, every pump of blood sent waves of pain crashing through her entire body. She could feel the warmth leaving her side and running down her pant leg.

"Ohhhhhhhh, wait, I think I get it now, you didn't get involved," dropping to a whisper she continued, "cause you're a homo?"

Conner's almost-nostrils flared. He sharply slid the table to the side, sending it crashing into the wall.

His gun remained at her face.

Gina had found the button.

That four letter word brought him back from the dead.

Stringy blood oozed and hung from Conner's mouth and pulpy-nose-thing. He forced himself forward. Gina slipped her left hand back to the hole in her side, stepped in, and met him halfway. Standing face to face, both pressed their weapons into each other's foreheads as the random screaming resumed.

Conner sneered through gritted teeth as his body teetered.

"YOU STUP—"

Gina cut him off.

Her words rang surprisingly clear.

"I have nothing you want."

She steadied herself as Conner regrouped.

"Homo."

Their faces were now less than two feet apart. The barrel of Gina's .38 planted deeply into the deformity at the side of his eye. The barrel of Conner's gun pushed up on Gina's left eyebrow—forcing her eye eerily wide while the other squinted in pain.

Pull.

The.

SCREW THAT.

Her tone dropped to a whisper.

"I. Have. Nothing. YOU. Want. You homo—THAT'S why you did nothing."

Conner opened his mouth but Gina cut him off again.

"Nothing."

Conner gurgled and forced another seemingly impossible volume of crimson mess from his nose and mouth and drew breath into his body. His chest heaved. Conner shook his head and pushed the gun harder into her eyebrow. Gina didn't budge. "YOU—" Conner started, but again Gina cut him off.

"Naaaaaaaaaaaa-THING!" she whispered into his face. Her eyes stabbed at him with disgust. She leaned into him, her mouth over-enunciating every syllable. "You watched, you wished you were under that pile, you wished you were—one jealous—homo!"

Conner exploded and lost his footing. He took a desperate step back, trying to steady himself as Gina jammed the barrel of her gun deeper into his eye, forcing him off balance. Conner kept his eye locked into Gina's as he faltered backwards and out of control; somehow placing one foot shakily behind the other as they careened towards the wall.

This is it. The impact of his back hitting the wall is going to cause the guns to fire.

He's about to hollow out your skull.

Take. The. Shot. Before. He. Does.

It felt like they were standing stationary and it was the wall that soared towards them.

Two Feet.

Take the shot.

Take the shot.

One Foot.

Taketheshot.

Taketheshot.

Inches.

Taketheshottaketheshottaketheshottaketheshot.

FUCK.

Gina clenched her eyes and waited for the sound of his, hers—someone's—gun exploding as Conner's back crashed into the wall and she crashed into him. The impact of his skull hitting the cabinet sent the barrel of his gun sliding up Gina's sweat-soaked forehead. The sticky bottom of its handle jutted into her eye as the weapon now pointed safely at the ceiling. Conner's head bounced forward off of the cupboard door. The barrel of Gina's gun sliced across his slippery features as she leaned forward, colliding her forehead with his face. Conner shrieked as his nose took one more for the team. She snapped her left hand to the top of her head and grabbed the barrel as she brought her forehead sailing back into his once-upon-a-nose for a follow up attack. A wet smack rang above their screams. Her second head-butt sent his skull back into the wall as Gina leaned back and popped her right arm into the small space between their faces, burying the butt of her gun into his nose cavity. The collision of metal and broken cartilage was finally too much and all resistance disappeared. Gina's left arm suddenly snapped straight up above her head. Conner's gun firmly inside her curled fingers.

He let go of his gun.

The game's climax mounted. With his gun safely above

their heads, Gina quickly rotated her slippery gun out of his nose-hole so she could shoot him in the brain. The barrel had just touched down on his hairline when an unimaginable pain jigsawed through her entire body. Gina's world flashed white-hot as her lungs wailed and her body thrashed, sending both guns scattering in different directions across the kitchen floor.

His fingers were inside of her.

The bastard had stuck three fingers deep into the hole in her side.

Gina had no time to think, only react, and she threw herself backwards, but Conner held on and they toppled to the floor. The impact changed nothing. Conner landed on top of her, his fingers scratching deeper in the wound as Gina's hands slapped and clawed at his arm, leaving herself wide open. With his free hand Conner grabbed her throat and forced all of his weight onto her chest. Her screams suddenly cut silent. Face-to-face, Conner's chin rested on her shoulder as his busted nose emptied into her hair. Gina's body continued to flail underneath him, her lungs scraped for air as her mind tried to shut itself off, protecting her from the streaking pain. His unseen fingers curled—forcing her eyes open and in one last defiant self-preserving act, she turned and bit into his ear. Her teeth sank through the thin flesh. She felt her top and bottom rows connect as the skin separated between them. Conner removed his fingers from her side and let go of her throat as both of his hands rushed to his ear. Gina sucked oxygen, half swallowed the piece of ear but choked it back up. She swung her arms, legs, elbows, and knees trying to slide out from underneath him. Her upper torso slipped free but as she rolled to her side Conner's thick arm wrapped around her neck. Her nails pierced his fleshly forearm and tried to pry it back. He tensed up. Her lungs shrunk. Her fingers scraped deeper and deeper. Conner slid his other hand down her side where she intercepted it before his fingers could invade her gunshot wound a second time. They lay on the floor, holding hands by her side as she clawed deeper and deeper at the arm across her throat. There was no air. Everything was sticky with blood. Gina was positive her nails had tore away his forearm's flesh and were directly scraping bone, but his grip remained.

Conner drew breath and bared down, forcing his forearm deeper into her throat.

Her legs kicked. She made contact with a chair. She sent a milk carton spinning.

Gina's eyes bulged.

You're gonna die up there.

The room started to pixilate.

Her lungs combusted.

OHSHITOHSHIT

The blackness emptied from under her eyelids.

AIR.

Gina screamed in her head as the hand guarding her gunshot wound let go of Conner's invading fingers and snapped to her throat. Her movements were somehow lightning quick and she managed to force a tiny separation before Conner could react. Gina violently twisted her neck and gulped at the air but Conner answered quickly: his free hand shot up and clenched his wrist, reinforcing the death grip on her neck as his tattered forearm flattened her throat. Gina could feel everything under her chin being crushed and compacted. Again, her breath was cut off. This time there was no escape. Gina's nails searched through the wet skin hanging from his forearm and resumed their desperate excavation, but all her strength was gone. Blood vessels burst in her eyes. Conner swung one leg around her waist and brought his thigh down against the missing part of her side. Pain ripped through her body as her throat released a tiny croaking sound. Another blow from his leg sent her eyes rolling up as her body trembled, about to give up the fight.

Don'tcloseyoureyesdon'tcloseyoureyes.

Conner leaned back and Gina felt her throat collapsing into itself.

Conner smashed his leg into her side a third time and the pain no longer registered.

She was going down.

Everything sparkled and danced.

Her fingernail gouges became gentler and gentler as she used her remaining energy to focus on a milk carton inches from her face.

You're gonna die up there.

She fought to read the label over and over.

FOCUS.

2 Litres. 3.25% Whole Milk

2 Litres. 3.25% Whole Milk

FOCUS.

FOCUS.

A fog filled the kitchen. Everything drifted out of focus and multicolored lights danced behind her eyes.

It was dazzling. Beautiful. One giant Christmas Tree. She had seen this before.

The haze thickened.

Gina struggled to read through it.

2 Litres. Whole Mi—

The multicolored lights were spellbinding.

Red. Green. Yellow.

2 Litres. 5%

Her body let go and her mind took her away.

CHAPTER IX

THE CHILL IN the steps cut through her jeans.
She removed the brand new half-pack of cigarettes from her pocket and quietly tore the cellophane with a minimal amount of crinkling. The cold stung her hands as she slid the carton open and stared at the ten familiar strangers.

She stared and stared.

Boney-M radiated from inside the house as she imagined the rest of the family descending upon the recently produced snack-plate which would be presented on the basement coffee table; an impressive collection of crackers and cheese lined symmetrically between the fireplace and the Christmas Tree.

Santa themed napkins would be passed around.

If someone were to take a snapshot (and there would be many) it would look ripped from the mind of Norman Rockwell.

And as much as Gina hated the idea of families all around the world still blindly following some sort of December 24th Template, passed down from the housekeeping magazines of the 1950s, she secretly despised herself even more for being unable to rise above it. Christmas brought a warmth even she couldn't resist. Christmas mornings and shiny wrapping paper and terrible FM radio holiday songs brought a sense of belonging. These were some of the few genuinely good childhood memories that the pressures and complexities of adult life had not managed to erase.

Torn paper revealed plastic ponies and dolls; years later, cassette tapes and skirts.

These were the moments she still cherished.

153

Life was hard. Bad decisions and bad people seemed to control her actions no matter how much she forced change.

But her misery was her cross.

She wore her bad luck like a badge of honor.

Her life would have broken anyone else.

Easily broken anyone else.

She was convinced that she was the only girl—no, the only person period in the world who had the fortitude to stubbornly keep getting back up, no matter how many times life violently knocked her back down.

She was a soldier.

She was allowed one day off from the fight.

The struggle could be put on hold for twenty-four hours.

Just half.

Her fingers raced against time and the atmosphere as she drew the first cigarette from the half-pack. Her thumb stung as it rolled the jagged lighter-wheel; the flame popped to life and ignited the smoke.

She clutched it between her lips and repositioned the blanket around her body, better utilizing its warmth.

Her hands jutted into her pockets.

After each intake she tasted guilt, but after the fourth drag the colorful patches of the Christmas lights bouncing off the backyard snow distracted her from the inevitable negative self-reflection.

Just half.

The rare calmness made her uneasy at first, but she eventually accepted it completely.

What was the countdown now? Was Christmas Day ten minutes away? Five? It had to be getting really close to midnight—the food replenishment was a dead giveaway. Like clockwork, Dad would help Mom proudly bring out the carefully prepared tray of goodies right at the buzzer. Minutes before everyone was allowed to open one gift from under the tree. Another tradition that nostalgia somehow kept alive all these years.

As her secondhand smoke wavered into the brisk night air she marveled at the irony.

Fifteen, twenty years ago her heart would have been racing as she watched the minutes tick down. She would be under the tree, frantically crawling over her brothers while debating the famous French last second change as she studied her gifts. She had one shot of choosing the single best gift—the others would have to wait until morning. Which would it be? The large one with the giant red bow? The tiny green one? The misshapen one from Grandma? Grandma had yet to sell out and get her a single practical Christmas gift. She hated the word "practical". She vowed at an early age she would never become "practical".

Gina's ears began to sting from the cold so she weaved a corner of the blanket into a makeshift hood and snuggled even deeper into it.

Unnoticed, the smoke burnt past the halfway mark.

The white snow sparkled under the moon as it cut into the night. The blinking reflections continued to calm her.

She heard the last song on the Boney M CD end and the sudden silence added to the moment.

She was long past the reasonable time allotted for a bathroom break. Any second they would realize she was missing and come looking for her.

She would return inside and curl on the floor by the fire. Her dad would excuse himself and return with two fresh cups of coffee. Both secretly laced with Bailey's. This was a pretty recent tradition she secretly shared with her father, but one she really looked forward to. She could remember back when Mom was still somewhat functional, she would scold her sons, frowning upon alcohol consumption on Christmas Eve. Christmas Day was fair game, but for whatever reason, Christmas Eve was off limits. When she had arrived that afternoon Gina had discreetly slipped the bottle into her father's jacket pocket as they hugged right in front of Mom. Openly disrespecting her mother's and his wife's decade old rule seemed unnecessary and cruel.

Silence.

In seconds she would be back inside. She would sit by the fire and drink her laced coffee. She would laugh, eat crackers and festive cheese while the family grave-robbed stories from Christmas's past. In minutes it would be midnight. It would be Christmas Day. A round of hugs would be concluded with a small-scale gift exchange.

Eventually, one by one, everyone would retire to their respected rooms until Gina remained alone. There she would sit in yuletide solitude watching the fire as the embers faded. Most years she stayed awake all night keeping the fire going strong into Christmas morning.

She had yet to decide if that was tonight's game plan.

Tomorrow, Christmas Day would spiral out of control as it always did. By mid-afternoon all the presents would be open, the grandmas and fiancés would arrive and Gina would smile as another Christmas would roll into December 26th and she would be sucked up by the returning routine of her disjointed life.

But none of that mattered now.

The smoke burnt to the filter as she took in the last few seconds of this amazing moment.

The silence, the snow.

The peace.

She couldn't remember the last time she felt peace like this.

But she knew, life, as it always did, was somehow about to become even more complicated.

She heard her family stirring and knew her time was officially up.

She flicked he cigarette butt deep into the yard and estimated where it would have disappeared into the snow.

Her secret hidden until spring.

She stuffed the half-pack deep into her jean pocket and slid a handful of breath mints under her tongue.

She stood, readjusted the blanket into an overcoat and slid her hands under her shirt.

Although she dreaded it, even time was now working against her and very soon she would have to make her announcement.

Any day now, she would be showing.

TRAVIS

CHAPTER X

THE NIGHTMARES DODGED the medication.

Oddly enough, what burned his brain awake wasn't the actual act of murder itself, but the feeling of the knife as it separated the skin. Travis relived the sensation as the knife slid smoothly, point first into the neck. Even with a blade that sharp there was an initial resistance before the skin popped and the weapon sunk to the handle. He twisted the blade deeper. The poor bastard never saw it coming. Travis had been thorough; he had preplanned every detail. It was without flaw. Just like he imagined, he crept through the dark, snuck up from behind and grabbed him. He positioned himself so the anticipated release of blood would spray forward and away, but much to his disappointment the blood pulsed from the wound and spewed warmth over his forearm and glove.

A minor setback.

Travis held steady.

He had planned for a struggle and there was one.

DIE.

Arms flailed and a pathetic gargle rose from his victim's belly but seemed to exit out his new orifice. Travis spun the knife once more for good measure. It caught on something deep inside. The jugular? The spine? Whatever it was, the knife refused to rotate. After what seemed like forever, the violent body spasms surfaced, peaked, and were suddenly gone. The bastard was dead. It was done.

Travis slowly let go and listened to the sickening hissing-

almost whisper-like wheeze the knife made as the body fell forward and free from the blade. The dead bastard landed in an awkward jumble of arms and legs behind the dumpster. It was easier to look at now because it was no longer a human being; it was a faceless mass, a sexless lump of flesh. A stiff. A cadaver. He had to call it something and settled on the word corpse, and the corpse lay face down in the filth as the rest of its life emptied and pooled. Travis looked down at his blood covered hand, then at the knife. Tiny pieces of flesh stuck between the serrations. One by one Travis's fingers uncurled and the knife fell to the ground. No dramatic bounce, no ominous clang. He glanced up the alley, then down the alley—it was empty. No witnesses, no screams.

The crime went undetected.

Travis grabbed a handful of discarded newspaper and wiped the top layer of blood off his sleeve before he slowly removed his gloves, inverting them in the process. Lastly, Travis wiped the blade against the Weekend Extra, slid it back into his sleeve and retreated into the shadows. Into the silence. He lost himself, randomly darting past the rats and over the sewer grates. Past the homeless and the tragic. Away from the sensation of the knife struggling to pierce flesh which suddenly caught vomit in his throat.

***

Travis snapped awake.

In an attempt to move his body faster than his brain, he flung himself from the bed and stared into the tiny mirror. The guilt became tears and he did everything he could to muffle his sobs. How long can your body function without sleep? He had no idea, but he was slowly finding out—the nightmare had come within minutes, as it always did. He had accepted the fact that he would be forced to relive these events over and over and over and over again, night after night after night. Travis had no excuses—the punishment was justifiable but it was his body itself that refused to accept the unofficial sentence—and again he silently asked himself:

how long can you live, how long can you function without sleep? An intense surge of claustrophobia brought him to his knees and he broke into prayer for the fifth time today, begging God for some sort of comfort, but the instant the knife punctured one of His creation's flesh, Travis knew God stopped listening. He knew damn well.

He was on his own now.

As he knelt in the darkness he swore he could feel the warm gurgle of blood pour over his hand. He fought not to open his eyes.

Just in case.

In case.

I'm still there, still in the alley.

Travis felt the vision taking shape and realized, even on his hands and knees, fatigue was sending him away and the nightmare was priming to return. It had reset itself, looped back to the beginning and patiently waited for its cue to begin all over again. He forced his eyes open and slapped himself awake. Staring at the ground he shakily rolled himself back onto the bed and lay on top of the covers. It was cold tonight. The chill would keep him awake. Keep him safe. He ran his hands over his body. He had no way to gage how much weight he had lost in the last nine days.

Nine days?

He was a rail. His skin sunk between his ribs and his tattoo seemed shrunken and warped. New bruises covered old ones. His thoughts crept to happier times; the mornings he lay in the sun studying Gina's scars and bruises while she slept. Her body rising and falling, silent, naked and beautiful. Times had changed and now he was forced to play this game alone. He ran a single finger along the stitches in his eyebrow, dropped his hand, pulled up his pant leg and studied the large scars that jigsawed his repaired knee.

Travis wiped his sleeve across his face and prepared himself for another long night of the routine; sitting cross-legged on top of the covers, staying awake by shivering in the dark and focusing all his thoughts on the large pipe which exited the wall beside the sink and jutted into the roof.

He had endured eight nights of this.

Tonight would be Night Number Nine.

Nine. Nine. Nine. Nine. Nine. Nine. Nine.

His back ached.

His eyes dropped.

The pipe went dark.

The dream crept forward.

***

Across the street and through the front window, Travis watched as the bartender passed the bastard another pint. There he stood, all smug in his grass-stained soccer uniform. His grins and nods dripped arrogance. The guy had all night to change, but he, like the rest of the team, chose to remain in the sweat soaked jerseys long after Saturday night's victory became Sunday morning. They wore them religiously. Win or lose, their post game celebration played out like clockwork and part of the ritual was the need to remain as a unit.

Look at him.

Look at the bastard.

"Mister Smug."

He had no idea he was being watched. How long had it been now? Two months? Ten weeks? Travis had two folders brimming with notes and observations stuffed into his glove box. The meticulous documenting had stopped when he realized the pages were identical. The bastard was smug, but he was routine. This Saturday, like last Saturday and every Saturday before, Mr. Smug sat in the bar and drank with his teammates, even the Saturdays his presence could be better spent somewhere else—with someone else. Regardless, Saturday was the night. Travis continued to watch. Mr. Smug laughed and tipped his mug. He would pay the tab and his life would end and he was oblivious to it all. Next Saturday night, one of the soccer clones would have one less person to pass to.

Travis watched him raise his glass and the team followed suit. He wondered if the forwards and the keeper knew what kind of a monster they played alongside each and every weekend.

They couldn't know. They'd kick him off the team so fast.

Mr. Smug's double life enraged Travis as he squeezed the steering wheel. His heart raced. He was going to do this.

Now.

Closing time approached. For whatever reason, Mr. Smug would always be one of the first to leave before the 2 A.M. mass exodus. Travis watched the digital clock in his dashboard. The red LED flipped to 1:52 and suddenly there he was, there was the bastard, standing and shaking hands. He tipped the last of his beer down his throat, and gestured for his jacket. Travis watched his target exit the bar and begin south-just as he had last Saturday, and the Saturdays before. The bastard would leave early, leave alone, and take a shortcut through the alley. His car waiting patiently in the free lot, three blocks down.

The noise from the pub briefly echoed into the night as the door swung open and cut back to a dull hum as it swung shut behind him.

It was time.

At home Travis had practiced with the small section of wire. He wrapped it around the palms of his thick electrical gloves and squeezed the length so straight, so tight, that his skin stung through the leather. His plan was perfect. He would wait in the alley and as Mr. Smug swaggered by, lost in thoughts of drunk driving, Travis would emerge from the shadows, slip the wire over his head, drop it to his neck and before the bastard had time to react, Travis would press his fists together and pull and pull. The wire would dig into his neck and cut off his air. Mr. Smug would fight, but Travis would be ready and ride him to the ground if he had to. Travis had the element of surprise and the bastard would be tipsy. He couldn't wait to see the flow of red stain the lime

165

green and white of his stupid little soccer jersey. Week after week he had scrutinized every detail of the execution, but tonight, for whatever reason, as he stood in his kitchen preparing for another Saturday night stakeout, he couldn't pull his eyes from the knife set that hung magnetically to the silver bar above the sink. Especially the smallest of the bunch. The last one on the left. As he slipped the carefully rolled wire into his pocket and stretched on his gloves, his attention remained on the tiny blade.

He had to hold it.

The handle felt smooth and familiar. Travis held it up to his face—the jagged edges danced in the light. Suddenly the wire and the strangulation seemed destined to fail. It had taken one entire month to formulate the attack and now it unraveled in seconds. Variables taunted him. What if Mr. Smug was quicker and stronger than Travis anticipated? What if he fought off the wire? What if he rolled forward and sent Travis to the ground? Sent his skull splitting against the pavement?

This was real. This was big and Travis could not screw this up. He could not fail.

The knife was definitely the way to go—how did he not see that until now?

One shot—right in the side of the neck.

POW

Then all he had to do was cover the bastard's mouth if he screamed. Cover his mouth and physically stop him if he tried to run towards the street.

Quick.

Flawless.

The last knife on the left was smooth and tiny and beautiful and there it sat on his dashboard. Itching and ready.

Mr. Smug stood in front of the pub, seemingly enjoying the night. His pauses were unnecessarily dramatic as he zipped his jacket and stretched, arms extending above his head.

Travis had conditioned himself to hate everything about this guy:

The receding hairline he chose to ignore.

His stupid four-leaf clover calf tattoo.

The way he waved his hands when one of his stories was climaxing.

The way he would laugh at his own punchline and look around the table making sure everyone else was as equally dizzy from his wit.

If only his teammates knew.

He would die very soon but the real tragedy was that he would die without his sins being exposed.

Without tearing them kicking and screaming out of the darkness and into the light.

He would be buried in his illusions.

He would die as a normal, tax paying, voting, outstanding citizen.

He would die as a volunteer who donated his time and helped those in need.

He would die as a loyal friend, a mentoring brother, a loving son.

He would die as a model employee.

He would die as a father.

Above all—he would die a sinner.

His offenses unforgivable, even in the eyes of the Lord.

Travis snatched the knife, slid from his car and began the two block loop which, if timed perfectly, would intercept Mr. Smug in the second alley of his now infamous shortcut.

The knife ready and steady.

The walk began.

***

Travis slumped forward and lurched himself awake. Sitting cross-legged had saved him from deep slumber once again. He swatted away the pending exhaustion as he squinted into the darkness and let his vision slowly focus. The two gray blobs merged and the image sharpened.

Travis stared at the pipe.

He shook his head in anger. How long was he out? Maybe five minutes? Maybe? The only thing more horrific than the nightmare itself was the fact that each time he slept, it got longer. Each time the scene started a little earlier. There was no escape—and even if he could escape it, it would follow him. It was in his head.

Travis stood and began to pace: thus started the second half of his nine-day-strong nightly routine:

I'm going to Hell.

I'm going to Hell.

I'm going to Hell.

Back and forth, back and forth. The cold floor stung his bare feet. His eyelids slowed with every blink.

I'm going to burn in hell for what I've done.

Gina French.

He gave her a gun and a map and sent her out the door.

Then he never heard back.

For four days he barely ate. For six days his cell phone remained glued to his hand.

He waited to get the call from her.

He waited to get the call about her.

For one day shy of a week he barely slept—but it wasn't like it was now—it was a different kind of "no sleep".

Not knowing kept him awake then. Knowing kept him awake now.

But waiting for that call seemed like a lifetime ago. In reality, how long has it been? Four, five months now? The seasons had changed twice since the call finally came. Two seasons missed and discarded. Two seasons and six days eerily foretelling his future.

For six days he didn't get the call.

Not knowing was a Hell all of its own. Willing the phone to ring was exhausting in itself, trumped only by the sudden onslaught of unimportant, unrelated calls that rained down by the dozen and threatened to tie up the line. Family members, the bank, nosy telemarketers, all wasting your time, all absorbing your slowly rising ire.

What if she called while I was negotiating my long distance rates?

Time wasting scum. All of them.

By the fourth day without contact Travis stopped checking the call display, punching the Talk button milliseconds into the initial ring.

By the fifth day he abandoned his strict rehab schedule and sat on the couch with the familiar bag of ice on his knee and the phone in his hand.

It was on the fifth day when the negative thoughts broke down all the walls.

It was on the fifth day he felt insanity whispering at him from the darkness behind the television.

Maybe she didn't find Conner.

Maybe she did.

Maybe he marched a bed-sharing coworker through the rain and to her death.

Maybe Conner found her.

She would die for my greed.

No, she would die for their greed.

She knew the risks. This was the only option. Truly the only option.

Even bouncing around inside his own head, Travis could not make that statement sound legit in any way, shape or form. He needed to direct his anger and most days it landed on the prison facility. And rightfully so. Instead of comforted as the survivors they were, they were silently and unofficially accused of collaboration and abandoned by the system that placed them in that horrible situation in the first place. Low wages, inadequate staffing, and rushed training slowly matured into an ugly eruption which they took the brunt of.

Which Officer Claire took the brunt of—

Which Gina took the brunt of—

A decent beating was nothing to call home about; scars would heal. What didn't kill you made you stronger, right?

They beat on her and undressed her and then you gave her a loaded gun and sent her on a suicide mission.

Her death is on your shoulders now, its yours and yours alone. No one will share your guilt, there's no one you can talk to about this, there is nowhere to go to escape this.

You sent her to her death.

Baby Ryen.

Travis frantically rubbed his face with the back of his fists. Christ.

Baby Ryen. I orphaned her child. Her baby will grow up without a mother; Social Services will take Ryen and despite the tiny veins of ice water she inherited from her mother, she will grow up lonely and insecure, bouncing around Foster Care, never knowing how hard her mother tried to forge a decent life for her, using her own screwed-up life as an example of what not to do. By the time she's a teenager she will be so consumed with hate she'll turn to drugs and sex and her life will nose-dive into the dirt. Despite Gina's single goal, the cycle will repeat itself. A teenage pregnancy will force immediate life changes, a downward spiral—what's the cliché? A leopard can't change its spots? And that kid will grow up and have a crack-baby and that baby will grow up and have another crack baby and so on and so on.

And it will be—

All.

My.

Fault.

Travis began nervously tapping his thumb against his eyebrow.

And here's the best part: outside of the bedroom, you truly don't know anything about Gina French. Nothing.

You can close your eyes and remember the birthmark on the inside of her thigh, the deep scar on the arch of her back, her muscular legs and how the morning light looks as it bounces off her flat abdomen just above her panty-line. Sure, you can close your eyes and recreate Gina physically. You could sculpt her body out of papier-mâché—but when she's clothed, what do you really know about Gina French? You pieced together her past by splicing Gina's odd comment or story between lovemaking and random rumors from random coworkers. Gina French was someone so obviously broken she was willing to jump in and play the lead role in your production of "Killer On The Run"—a plan you yourself didn't have the balls to carry out. Oh, that's right, hide behind the knee injury, Travis, hide behind the knee, you coward!

Ryen.

I orphaned her child.

Travis once watched as Gina carried her daughter from the couch to the playpen and marveled at Ryen's immediate flare of anger brought on by the unexpected change of location. The violent all-out defiance that flashed across her tiny face was identical to the frightening one her mother displayed from time to time.

This finally flipped a positive switch in Travis's head.

Gina French was a fighter. Gina French would not lay down and die for anyone.

Gina French was someone who would scratch and kick and bite and cry and bleed and break until she got her way. This was her one shot and Gina French would fight for her daughter.

The thoughts of Ryen crying for her dead mother trembled his hands. Travis leapt into problem solving mode. Worst case scenario: Gina doesn't come back and Ryen is legally awarded to her parents or one of her brothers or Hannah.

Day Five was spent striving for justification. A brief power-outage left his couch-side digital clock blinking 12:00. It was symbolic. Travis never reset the clock. It would be Day Five for the rest of his life. He let the bag of ice slide off his knee as he squeezed the phone with both hands.

Baby Ryen.

What about baby Ryen's biological father?

The birth father question had been asked once and Travis still wore the mental scars of the over-the-top response Gina had dropped on him. She literally detonated right in front of his eyes. Like the wild beast protecting her young that she was, Gina had gone National Geographic on his inquiry. Her face tensed and contorted. She cleared her throat and leaned into him. The lingering cigarette smell Travis had never particularly minded suddenly classified as a stench. Gina stared into his eyes and snarled that she would be rotting in the grave before ever—ever—letting that smug bastard have full custody of their daughter.

And that was the first thing Gina French reiterated to Travis after she finally returned home from her trip to Lake Timor.

RING

It was a happier memory, but not by much.

Travis stood at the bottom of the steps and caught his reflection in a puddle. He was losing weight and his beard was growing in patches. The reflection wasn't crisp enough to see the puffy rings around his bloodshot eyes but he knew they were there. He felt them pulse. He had no idea how many more visits he had in him; each one left him a little more dead on the inside.

But at least he could walk out these doors, which was something that Gina could no longer do.

The house was beautiful. Moving the suitcases and baby furniture was another thankless, exhausting job, but the possibility of a good deed erasing the smallest fraction of his guilt was worth the dedication. And surprise, surprise, it didn't alleviate shit.

Nothing could ever repay his debt.

His shaky hand brought the take-out Styrofoam cup to his mouth as he swallowed the last cold mouthful of his coffee and headed up the stairs.

Travis quietly closed the giant double doors behind him, dragged himself up the winding staircase and sheepishly poked his head into the largest room at the top.

***

Hannah sat on the edge of the bed and smiled warmly at him as Ryen bounced and happily cooed on her knee. It was Tuesday, so the Home Care Aide was there doing her thing in the corner of the room, rummaging through a tabletop full of gauze and bandages and charts. She nodded politely at Travis.

And there, in the opposite corner, propped up in the wheelchair, was Gina French.

Travis spent most of his days trying to force the word deteriorating from his mind, but that's exactly what Gina was doing. Slowly deteriorating.

Her once proud, tight skin and muscle now hung miserably off her slim frame. Gina looked weathered. He could barely look her in the eyes and when he managed the courage—Christ, did that ever pile on the guilt.

Ryen cooed at her mother and Gina's icy glaze didn't flinch as Hannah began the heartbreaking act of placing Ryen on Gina's lap and strapping the child into the special safety harness. Of all the routine things Travis had to endure this was by far the absolute worst. Watching Hannah balance Ryen on her mother's lap while moving Gina's lifeless hands to the small child's face once sent him speed-walking to the bathroom where he immediately flushed the toilet, praying the sounds of his stomach emptying into the bowl would be masked by the running water.

He tried to look away, but could still see the scene play out in the corner of his eye. Hannah held Gina's wrist and stroked Ryen's hair with her mom's limp hand while the child giggled and squirmed. The Home Care Aide was right there, spotting Hannah and Ryen; both arms outstretched and ready to catch the child should she fall.

This was the only quality Mother/Daughter time Gina's condition would allow.

And this was permanent.

Forever and forever.

Amen.

Gina barely rolled her eyes down at Ryen who playfully clapped and squealed up at her mother, oblivious to the levity of the situation. As horrible as this was it was only going to get worse as Ryen got older. Never would Mom be able to kneel down on the floor and play dolls with her daughter. She would never help her shop for pretty dresses. She would never pat her shoulders and smooth her hair before her first date. Never hug her after her first broken heart.

Ryen's wedding would have to be wheelchair accessible.

This scene would eventually replay itself with her grandchildren and her great grandchildren.

Even brushing her child's inherited blonde hair would never be done without assistance.

Travis felt his rushed lunch slowly start to rumble and rise. Clenching his eyes, he breathed it back down.

If he was ever going to survive, he had to toughen up.

His cell phone rang and he quickly silenced it without answering it. Just answering the phone filled him with guilt. He had planned for weeks to chuck that thing into the abyss—nothing reminded him more of the hell his life had become than his ringtone.

CHAPTER XI

FOR SIX DAYS he begged the phone to ring. For six days he was sure she was dead. Six days—no contact? She was dead. Her brains had been blown out, or worse: Conner had her captive and was slowly torturing her for her intrusion. Gina was paying for all of Conner's lost years. Like all the others, he probably blamed the system and now Gina was responsible for them all. Making her accept the pain as her punishment. Conner was sick and angry and violent and Travis had spent nearly all of the sixth day imagining all the sick games Conner could be playing with his girlfriend at that very moment. Gina would be begging for death, but there would be more games to be played. By day six Travis's leg had become so inflamed he couldn't even pace. As the sun dipped below the city line it finally became time to act. He tried to lift himself off the couch and his knee screamed in retaliation. Travis couldn't even remember the last time he bothered with his rehab exercises or even bent it. It had been half a day since he stumbled down the hall to pee and now he was paying for it. He swayed on one leg towards the counter. Towards his car keys. The logistics of driving with an unbendable leg no longer mattered. Travis needed to move. He could see his keys and every step became more painful.

They're just across the room. Move your broken ass.

Tears streamed down his face as the pain threatened to rip his kneecap clean off. He kept his focus on the keys and inched forward. How could it hurt more now? Weeks after the attack?

MOVE YOU SON OF A BITCH.

Travis bit down and remembered the doctors lancing bucketfuls of yellow and white puss from the infection. Now that was pain. This was nothing. This was—

THUD

Travis teetered off-balance and came crashing to the floor a solid five feet from the counter. He lay on the tile screaming with useless rage. This was not going to happen. It was time to come clean. It was time to call the police and go get the remains of Gina's body. Begin funeral arrangements. Begin life after Gina. Start coping with the guilt. Start owning up to—

RING

This was the call.

Travis used his elbows and pulled himself back towards the couch. The pain suddenly invisible. It had taken him a good two minutes to hobble four feet and fall, yet somehow he crawled back, snatched the phone off the couch and answered it before the third ring.

He knew this was the dividing line: there was Travis Green before this phone call and Travis Green after this phone call.

They had found her.

Her tiny body was shattered.

Her back was broken.

Her fucking back was broken.

She had succeeded. Travis had been correct. Kevin Conner had fled to Lake Timor and now Gina French's back was fucking broken.

They found her on a cabin floor deep in Lake Timor East. Kevin Conner had led them to her. Conner, the child abductor and parental murderer had the balls to call the police from Gina's cell phone no less, as he sped away from what was now being referred to as the crime scene.

They managed to record thirteen seconds of the twenty-one second conversation. It was studied and played ad-nauseam by the so called audio experts who dissected it and its ever important ambient noise and came up with, "he called from inside a car." Beautiful. The conversation ended when the wind suddenly crackled the line to sheer static followed by a large smacking sound. The experts put their overpaid heads together and concluded that Conner chucked the phone out of the car's window as he sped down the highway.

When the police and paramedics got there she was dead. Gina French was dead.

But somehow they brought her back.

Conner nearly killed her only to turn around and save her life with that phone call.

The police and rescue workers stormed into the cabin and found Gina on her back underneath a thick blanket. They frantically forced air into her, and being the fighter she was, her lungs responded immediately. Once they got the elastic strap of the oxygen mask around the back of her blood-crusted hair they rushed into the second phase and located the wounds. They frantically cut away her clothes with giant scissors and began smearing off the blood. As they cut free her pullover and T-shirt they found a crudely applied butterfly bandage on her side. It had managed to slow the bleeding and in the big picture, it saved her life. The shoddy first aid kit's contents had been scattered all over the floor but the large footprints that weaved in and out of the large pool of blood underneath Gina French seemed to be made after she had become immobile. It was a head-scratcher for the department, but for whatever reason, it seemed like their perp had blown a hole in her side, then bandaged her up and phoned the authorities. It seemed Kevin Conner had wanted Gina to live.

Perhaps he wanted Gina to owe him her life.

And now she did.

It had taken twenty seconds to get Gina breathing, another fifteen to apply the oxygen mask and cut away her clothing, as they reached the one minute mark they finally noticed the position of her body. Something wasn't right. Something was broken. Be it her neck or her spine— something wasn't right.

X-Rays would later conform that Gina's spine had been snapped.

Snapped.

The headlines varied from: "ALTERCATION GONE HORRIBLY AWRY" to "FORMER PRISON GUARD UNSUCCESSFULLY TAKES LAW INTO OWN HANDS", but they all verbally painted a picture of the heroic policemen and paramedics bringing the foolish prison guard back from the dead against the blood spattered backdrop of an abandoned cabin in the middle of nowhere.

They went public with the results of the blood samples. Again, the sheer volume of blood smeared throughout the cabin seemed almost comically impossible to come from just two human beings. Swabs were taken and tested from everywhere: the bed, the floor beside the bed, the hallway, the stairs, the two chairs, the tabletop, the walls, the fridge, and of course the kitchen floor and the blanket. All the blood samples came back containing only two types. Gina French and Kevin Conner's.

And for the second time in as many weeks, Gina (whose name was originally withheld from the public) had a short stay in the hospital, labeled as a "victim" before her motivations were revealed to be financial. The authorities scolded and shook their heads at the local prison guard's decision to withhold valuable information about Conner's whereabouts and decision to pursue the criminal on her own. Charges were threatened. The public was reminded about the obvious dangers and the media immediately soured on her, painting her as an undereducated simpleton offering her body up for sacrifice in exchange for the quick cash-grab. Overnight she became the symbol for both greed and stupidity.

The second Conner was brought to justice and baby Amber was returned, the name Gina French would inevitably become the punch line of the entire saga.

The name Gina French would cause head-shaking and choruses of "what was that stupid little girl thinking?" for as long as people told the story.

And now, there sat Gina French. Unable to do anything else, she sat and waited. Waited for what? For nothing, for everything. How does one prepare for a new life without?

Travis watched as Ryen yawned and lost interest with the lack of interaction from her mother. Hannah used a diaper change as an excuse and the baby was unfastened and removed from Gina's lap. The Care Aide returned to her charts.

Gina's eyes followed Ryen out of the room then floated back to Travis, but only for a second before they dropped back down and observed the floor.

The humility hung thick. Not surprisingly, Gina didn't talk much. When she did, her whispers were barely audible. It was her silence that spoke the loudest. The verbal void silently painted the picture of unimaginable suffering.

Defeat.

Entrapment.

Hopelessness.

Kevin Conner killed her by saving her life.

Today's Home Care Aide filled the large house with a Soothing Songs CD. Violins hummed over bubbling brooks. Birds chirped along with the sitars. The Aides insisted on the compilations and their positive energy, but as soon as they were off shift, Hannah would replace the gentle lark/cricket duets with her homemade "Best Of 60's Gold" and everyone sat in silence watching the snow melt as The Shirelles asked if we'd still love them tomorrow. Thank God the snow eventually shrank into puddles. Between outside and inside there was way too much white. Often, the soothing music and the endless white walls and eggshell furniture had the opposite intended effect and made the house seem bleak.

Travis could recall a few intoxicated instances where the old Gina French would meticulously fantasize about her dream home, the one she was going to design and have built after winning the lottery. It looked nothing like this, but in all fairness, this one was free. Her father, the respected member of the force, called in some favours and managed to set his crippled daughter up in a showhome overlooking the city. Obviously his daughter needed constant care and through more legal papers and government relief for such a bizarre situation, the Home Care Aid positions were funded, ensuring a qualified helper remained in the house from morning to midnight, when Hannah or Travis would tag in and stay throughout the night. Gina's life had become a series of mundane routines—every choice made for her by someone else. An initial visit from Gina's family ended very negatively and Gina had asked that they not return. So now Gina's entire life was left up to Hannah, himself and five faceless, revolving nurses.

Hannah and Ryen returned and Travis began another of his mental games he played to quicken the time; he studied Hannah. He watched her fluff the pillows and try to get Gina to interact with her daughter. She hummed while she fed her roommate; her smile never crushed by the odds. Being a BFF was one thing, but to willingly shoulder it all, out of love, not guilt, was something Travis couldn't fathom. Though he continued to watch, the game always concluded with the sad realization that Hannah was simply a better human being than Travis was on every level.

The worst part is—Travis's mind trailed off.

In the last week and a half, Travis caught himself starting pretty much every mental thought with "The worst part is". Even if he wanted to grab a pen and paper and formulate a list of everything wrong at this point and award a champion, it would be situational. The most recent "worst part" was the revelation that he spent most of his days in the immaculate house not comforting his former coworker and lover, but instead, slowly pondering, planning—mentally scheming ways to remove himself from this entire situation and alleviate his guilt with a single miraculous action.

Travis went through the motions; helping Gina eat, moving her from the chair to the bed, then back to her chair. He made sure she had enough pillows, the windows were closed, and she drank lots of water, but his mind was always elsewhere. Somewhere free and free of responsibility. Somewhere away from all of this.

As Hannah signed up for extra shifts at the restaurant and the Aides busied themselves with more of the paperwork and charts, at least once a day Travis found himself alone with Gina for a two or three hour block at a time.

It was these intimate moments that instantly elevated to the very top of Travis's unwritten "the worst part is" list.

***

The game had changed and so had their moments alone.

The former relations were intense physical collisions, deprived of dialog—now there was no touching, no caressing, no exploring, but the dialog was suddenly endless.

With an audience, Gina acted mentally shut off. The glazed look in her eyes never flickered. Not as Hannah fed her, as Ryen reached for her, or as the Aides emptied her catheter bag. Nothing. But in these moments of privacy between herself and her former puppet master- the former puppet talked.

Travis had to lean in close to hear her.

The whispers were cold, breathy and hate-filled.

The commands oozed with a reminder of unpayable debt.

Gina would get Travis to do things that Hannah and the Aides dismissed.

Today it was dying her hair.

Travis grimaced at the deep purplish finger-sized bruises still etched into Gina's neck as he covered her shoulders with a giant vinyl sheet and prepared a basin of warm water. Her whispers continued as they listened to that particular day's

Home Care Aide clunk pots and pans together on the floor beneath them, busy with lunch prep. Travis slipped on the rubber gloves and removed the bottle of dye. Today, Gina's thoughts were more random, more paranoid than usual but Travis said nothing as he concentrated on his task at hand. Washing her hair usually shut her up, so Travis took his time. He sponged the warm water on her scalp and watched as it trickled down her once healthy head of natural blonde hair. Gina quietly moaned, enjoying the sensation; one of the few sensations left to enjoy. Travis carefully pulled back all her damp hair. Hannah would be pissed right off, as Gina had asked her first and Hannah flat out refused, promising to dye her hair back to its original bright luster on Saturday, but Gina was adamant about it and Travis decided he would much rather take Hannah's spite than Gina's. For whatever reason, watching Hannah try to act angry kind of made her kind of sexy. Travis smiled a secret smile behind Gina's back as he squeezed pure black out of the small tube and began working it into Gina's hair.

The dye ran through his fingers and dripped down her hair. Gina sighed as Travis meticulously massaged the thick black into her scalp. Travis worked slowly. He sometimes pinched an individual strand between his thumb and forefinger and slid it through, watching the color change as it glided along. Travis kept one eye on the clock as he basked in the wonderful silence.

"Travis," she suddenly croaked.

Dammit.

Too much time had passed and Gina had figured out his game. The Aide would have lunch ready any minute and Travis hadn't been given today's sermon. Gina usually stretched the hushed tales of her unending suffering, and his responsibility for it all, throughout their entire time together, but today Travis had massaged his way through a good forty minutes of silence. Unearthing his hidden agenda filled her eyes with a sudden intensity.

The tirade began, but because of the time restraints Travis received it in point form:

The boredom, the humility, the helplessness—all because of Travis and his stupid fucking Plan.

Travis's scalp massage became less enthusiastic as he willingly stood there and absorbed her ill-will. He eagerly awaited the day he would finally numb to the verbal onslaught of accusations, but it wouldn't come that day, that week, or that month.

Each cascade of guilt, as repetitive as it was, just expanded the giant pit in his stomach.

Which was no comparison to the obvious one in Gina's soul.

Travis emptied the last of the bottle directly onto the top of her head and began streaking it down towards the remaining blonde patches. He stood in front of her now, and refused to make eye contact. He focused instead on the circular burn in her forehead and imagined how the new hair color, or lack there of, would accent the sunken color of her eyes—or lack there of.

Gina's tirade slowly began to lose momentum and Travis knew what was coming. Some days the boredom was stressed, other days her humiliation would take center stage, but no matter what she decided to dwell on, on any given day—it's unsettling conclusion always remained the same. Predictability was just one more stark contrast between the old Gina and new Gina. His hands reached the bottom of her locks that hung around her neck as she started to sob. The vision of his own hands encompassing her neck and squeezing the sorrow from her body once and for all had never been so tempting.

Hannah wore a mask, she had to—no one wanted a future like this one. Gina was now a drain on himself, Hannah and society. What kind of a life could she offer her daughter? In these moments of isolation Gina begged for death more times than not, and today, Travis almost felt up to the chore.

Gina made him accountable because he was accountable. This was his punishment.

He would take her abuse. He would take and take and take and take, while watching the clock with the corner of his eye, counting down the minutes until the care provider or Hannah would return and Gina would retreat back into silence; watching and stewing with her lips locked shut.

Thankfully, that time was now. The Aide yelled from the kitchen below that lunch was ready. Travis anticipated the hired help's reaction to Gina's new doo.

It wouldn't be positive.

Travis drew some fresh water and kept reminding himself that at the end of these horrible, horrible interactions, he would effortlessly open the front door and exit into the rest of the world.

While Gina French remained in the chair.

Her sobbing made it harder to wash away the black residue but he did his best. He dabbed her hair with the back of the towel but let her tears drip free. He rolled her to the mirror and crouched down, placing his head on the back of her chair so both their faces appeared in the mirror as the masterpiece was revealed. Gina sniffled, ignored her hair and focused into her own eyes—as if using this opportunity to fine-tune her icy stare. Figuring out how to take it to the next level.

Travis marveled at how surprisingly well a jet black mane suited her.

Had they done this in their former lives, the simple task of changing her hair color would have been stretched throughout an entire afternoon. Alcohol would have blurred the tiny instructions on the side of the box. They would have giggled and guessed and eye-balled applications in between cigarettes. The afternoon would have ended between dye-stained sheets. Back then, the favors Gina asked for would have been sexual—now, a different place, a different time, different people—her one and only favor was beyond his capabilities as a human being.

CHAPTER XII

ALTHOUGH GINA CONSTANTLY alluded to it, the first time she actually whispered into Travis's ear that Dan had to die he dismissed it as just a new chapter in her ever expanding secret, one-on-one, harmless rants. It was brought up, dropped, then brought up again. She slowly alluded to it more and more. The legal battle over Ryen becoming a losing one and Gina, the relentless fighter, was suddenly unable to lace her own gloves. Each visit unearthed a new story for Travis. An update ready for those moments away from the hired help's eavesdropping ears and away from Hannah's cheery ideas of windy afternoons spent drinking coffee from straws on the balcony. While it started as an idea, a brainstorm to stop the inevitable daughter takeover, it was quickly upgraded into a hard, solid fact.

Dan would legally win his daughter back.

Therefore Dan had to die.

Dan must die.

Everyone thought it, but no one dared verbalize the fact that maybe, just maybe, Ryen would indeed be better off if the arrangement had reversed itself, if Ryen spent her weeks with her biological father and weekends with her broken mother and her supporting cast in the serenity house. It was thought, but never said aloud. Old Gina may have reacted with outrage, but voicing this opinion to New Gina would be suicide, plain and simple.

Once Travis had accidentally bumped into Hannah in the kitchen as they topped up their large white coffee mugs and the muffled conversation finally took place. Hannah joked that offering the custody reversal as an option would cause Gina to break every law of medical science and leap from the wheelchair to strangle them both on the spot. Even as they secretly plotted against Gina's adamant wishes, Hannah constantly glanced over her shoulder at the staircase as if Gina would somehow suddenly appear, clawing her broken body down the stairs to shut them both up. Unbeknownst to Gina, the legal papers she demanded remained on the table, unsigned. Did they really want to go ahead and try to award Hannah custody? The lawyers would laugh in their faces. The Roommate over The Father? The writing had been on the wall for a while now. Even when her spine was functional, her life was still a mess, and now that Gina required more care and attention than the infant in question, nothing would stop Dan from reclaiming his daughter. And why not? Dan's recent promotion and engagement were well documented and he had worked hard to create an ideal lifestyle suitable for his, or any child. Dan's situation now had more advantages than Gina could have countered back when she was a fully-functional, blue-collared, self-centered, nicotine addicted, alcoholic.

But easing Gina's pain was everyone's 24/7 job and those closest to her played their parts to delay the inevitable. It was like a game of chess where the pieces sadly kept moving long after checkmate was declared.

But sometimes new information is introduced too late for normal measures to step in and stop something already in motion. Sometimes you have to jump away and play both sides. Sometimes when the full story emerges, you are forced into the role of a double agent.

Watching the blinking light from the coffee maker bounce off of Hannah's soft features as she mulled over the stack of legal paperwork, Travis realized that he was now a double agent.

Travis was trapped. Even when he left the house he never

truly left the house. Its events and conversations followed him home and kept him up at night. Gina had caught on that she was about to enter a battle for her child she had no chance of ever winning and that was when she played her full hand. She craftily let her secrets bleed one afternoon while the Aide disappeared for an excruciatingly long grocery run. Gina's facade immediately dropped as the door closed and the tears cascaded as she smeared her fears all over Travis.

Dan was not who he appeared to be.

Of course he's not, Travis initially thought, already bored. Gina continued to conveniently repackage Dan as somewhat of a monster. Straight from left field Gina swore he struck her on more than one occasion. Dan's anger would flare and he would knock her down with the back of his hand. Was that fact or fiction? He had no idea, but Travis had a hard time imagining Gina taking her medicine and not retaliating. The Gina he knew would have immediately picked herself up off the floor and killed the fucker on the spot. The stories continued. The yelling fits. Dan's erupting road rage. Travis sensed that Gina could see that her brainwashing was not working and quickly built her story into a blistering climax: One Saturday morning Dan lost his temper and shoved a very pregnant Gina backwards. Her back smashed into the sharp edge of the counter and actually punctured her skin, missing her spine by 2 inches. Gina stressed the time line over and over—"Six months pregnant. Six months." Travis's ears perked a little at that one. He knew the wound well. He always ended his finger's morning tour at the small of her back, where he traced the large scar that ran parallel with her spine. She constantly dismissed and dodged questions about the one obvious flaw she was unable to fix, but now she couldn't tell him enough about it.

Dan had shoved her. Hard.

She hit the counter and collapsed, her legs went numb and she cried and screamed and held the squirming baby inside her tummy as she felt the back of her shirt saturate.

After the hospital stitched her up and confirmed the unborn's safety, she used the bedside phone to call Dan, who sat just down the hall, and hysterically broke it off with him. She hissed into the phone that he could slap her around and do whatever it took to make him feel like a man but if he ever did anything again that endangered their child, unborn or not—make no mistake about it, she would kill him. Dan, realizing he had in fact crossed the line, repented and slithered away. Three months later the legal people got involved and Dan, the abuser, got to see his daughter every second weekend.

Gina was spent. She sobbed uncontrollably as Travis silently nodded and let his mind work out the details.

Was any of this even true?

The story kind of checked out. Again, the part of her little sob story that immediately stirred up doubt was the chapter where Gina portrayed herself as an cowardly little bitch who refused to stand up for herself while Dan beat her like a drum. But now, with a mind as damaged as her body, Gina was convinced that to protect Ryen, Dan had to die.

Travis listened and listened, almost amused by her request. He stole a glimpse of himself in the mirror.

No, I'm not a murderer, I just set up scenarios where other people kill each other. The playmaker.

This fact was never left out while he tried to reason with that thing that motionlessly berated him from the wheelchair.

He wasn't a killer, and he dug his heels in deep. Weeks passed; the conversation was constant and increasingly desperate as every day passed. Travis dreaded the visits and began drinking before—then during them.

I'm not a killer.

glug

I'm not a killer.

Sometimes, whenever Hannah or the Home Care Aide momentarily left the room, Gina fired angry information at him so quickly it sounded like she was rapping. Travis would not budge. One afternoon the insults burned hotter and the alcohol sparked his dormant courage. Mid-sentence he grabbed the handles and spun the wheelchair around facing Gina to the wall.

The second he realized what he had done, his heart stopped. The look of absolute shock on her face as he dismissed her from his sight pulsed through his brain.

Gina went silent for eight days.

Travis came everyday and stayed all day, firing off apology after apology, but nothing he said could get her to talk or even look at him. Suddenly he missed her brainwashing. He cried at her feet. Her forgiveness became his only alcohol-fueled reason to get up every morning. On the eighth day she finally broke. As he sat in front of her on the edge of the bed, blubbering with his face in his hands, Gina suddenly spoke his name. Travis's puffy red eyes emerged as his fingers slowly parted.

Did he imagine it? He waited and the name finally came second time.

"Travis."

This time he saw her lips move and her dead-eyes penetrated into his.

He shot forward off the bed and knelt at her feet slipping her hands inside his own.

"Gina, I'msosorryI'msosorryIcan'tbelieveIdidthat—"

"Travis."

"ThankyouIamsosorry—thankyouIwillnever—"

"Travis. Look at me."

He eagerly wiped his tears with the back of his hands before quickly replacing them over top of Gina's.

Gina spoke with an unsettling calmness and clarity.

"You did this to me, Travis. You are responsible, cope with that however you see fit, but Travis, I will not be discarded. I will not be left alone. It's either you or my Ryen. If you want this all to go away, all you have to do is tie up that one loose end and you can walk out the front fucking door and never look back. You have my word."

Travis's black and white existence suddenly exploded into vibrant colors.

Travis stumbled to his feet and ran out the room, down the stairs, and out the front door as the brilliant sunlight immediately seemed to be his and his alone. This was his only exit from the hell he had made for himself. One horrible future sin would alleviate him from one horrible former sin. Was the exchange worth it? Would the guilt of murder be worse than the ongoing guilt of tearing someone's life away?

He had no idea.

He had no options.

And he was suddenly very excited to commit murder.

***

Days became weeks and her bile ate them both alive.

Gina drown him in her constant misery and dangled the rope of freedom inches from his fingers. Every character flaw of Dan's, no matter how irrelevant, was driven into Travis's skull and he welcomed it. He let Gina's stories scrape away his common sense. He let her scrub his brain with paint thinner until only the hate remained. The hate and the promise of escape.

Dan and Travis.

Travis and Dan.

Two grown men with nothing in common except for fucking Gina fucking French.

Ever since Gina's ultimatum was delivered, the air seemed crisper. Travis could repay his debt to Gina in full with one swift action. If it was done correctly, no one would know. He would walk away from this mess and as she put it, "never look back." He would move on, move away, and start a new life. Over time he would slowly forget about Gina French. Hannah would be awarded custody of Ryen. Ryen would remain with her mother. Ryen would grow up in a safe and secure environment without the possibility of being raised by a soccer playing asshole with a history of violence against women.

An alleged history of violence against women.

Travis quickly buried the doubt. He had to. Guilty or not, with Dan dead, everyone got what they wanted.

It was the only way.

The image of a Dan shoving pregnant Gina into the counter top ran through his mind on a loop.

WHAM

Crumple

Blood

WHAM

Cumple

Blood

Over and over, day after day.

Then he began to stalk Dan. By the second weekend he had Dan's Saturday night routine memorized:

7:20 out the door.

7:45 arrive at Soccer Center.

8:15 game begins.

9:30 exit Soccer Center with team.

9:45 arrive at the local Irish pub.

Even on the weekends he had Ryen, his Saturday nights belonged to the team.

The pub was all windows and Travis could easily watch Dan throughout the evening in his various degrees of drunk. Dan was an animated drinker, always playing little pranks on his teammates, little shenanigans. Yes, *shenanigans*. Travis liked that word. It conjured up images of spiteful little creatures looming in the shadows waiting to play evil tricks on you.

He had some serious fucking shenanigans for a certain woman-beating drunk.

Travis had promised her it would happen this Saturday night, but a last minute uneasy gut feeling prolonged the execution for another seven days. The Sunday morning look of disappointment on Gina's face was stifling, but their secret club continued. When the Aides and Hannah lingered, Gina silently watched the world go by through her empty eyes, but when she and Travis were alone, her dialog flowed effortlessly. Quick and sharp. Threats were now promises. Promises of better days in exchange for one quick service. Travis now began watering his meals down with alcohol and on more than one occasion he was asked to fetch something and immediately stumbled into the doorway.

Busted.

Travis began to hate Hannah's little judgmental looks. Her furrowed brow and her pursed little lips. She had no idea how he, and he alone, was about to change everyone's destiny. She would never understand Gina's sick little utopian vision and how to get them all there. No, she just made the best of a bad situation and marched along oblivious to the bigger picture.

Sorry honey, sometimes "everything happens for a reason" no longer cuts it, sometimes you have to force change. Sometimes you have to get off your ass and do something unpleasant and uncomfortable to trigger necessary progress. Sometimes you have to do a little more than try to change people for the better with your annoying little facial expressions, little girl. Sorry, not everyone can be everything to everybody like P.L.H.—"perfect little Hannah".

Her ability to handle horrible situations with unfaltering positivity slowly made Travis loathe her as well.

The list ran long.

***

Another two weeks passed. Two weeks. Two weeks of Saturday night study sessions and silent visits.

One afternoon Gina became violently ill and the nurse injected a mild sedative and "sent the bitch into slumberland", giving him the afternoon off.

As he drunkenly navigated down the front steps, he felt a sense of freedom that was almost more intoxicating than the

$33.50 of alcohol he had already poured down his throat that particular day.

Travis began to walk. No fixed destination, he just walked. Up and down the streets. His feet zigzagged underneath him and he was sure he wore his public drunkenness like a hat, but he didn't care. Actually, he didn't care about anything at that moment. He felt like he was breathing fresh air for the very first time. The sun on his skin provided a warmth he somehow never experienced before. The downtown lights and sounds spiraled around him and he soaked it all in. People whizzed by, consumed by conversations, talking on cell phones, steaming coffees in hand. Shopping bags hung at their sides. One man flagged a cab. A woman leaned against a light post as she inspected the sole of one of her shoes. There was nothing spectacular about this particular woman, but Travis remained glued to the site of her worried face and her loose heel. He studied the disapproving lines in her forehead as the defiant heel refused to remain stationary. The old Travis would have scanned from her face, to her chest, to her ass, to her legs and been on to the next one, but today he saw absolute beauty in the subtle features. Her hands looked smooth, the whiteness of her teeth were dazzling. Strands of hair toppled forward and obstructed her view. She stroked them back behind her ear as Travis's little world glowed.

Maybe this was the message.

Maybe this was God's lesson.

This was His plan.

Travis felt such a complete love for this unnamed woman, but unlike every other woman he ever secretly studied in public, visions of a sexual encounter did not play out in his mind. Travis wanted to take this woman's pain away. He wanted to hold her and be held. Nothing more.

He laughed at how lame comparing broken souls would be, but he marveled at how freeing the slightest chuckle made him feel.

Maybe this was God's reward.

"Everything happens for a reason." Travis was so sick of hearing Hannah say that. She used it more as an excuse than as a creed, but now even that sentiment seemed crystal clear in his drunken haze.

Bad things happen each and every day.

Maybe Gina French needed Travis to do a bad thing.

Maybe God needed Travis to do a bad thing.

Everything happens for a reason.

Travis was a good person surrounded by horrible people. He couldn't even remember how it all began anymore. It felt like he awoke from a deep sleep and everything was different, everything was better, and he didn't dare risk closing his eyes again.

The woman admitted defeat and continued on shakily, taking baby steps and trying to put as little weight on her broken footwear as possible.

Travis watched her walk away and was stunned at how beautiful her jeans were. A perfect collage of blue and white. Denim. How had he never noticed how wonderful denim was?

Someone or something had removed his blinders and lifted him above the haze that clouded and jaded the population.

Travis felt graduated.

Elevated.

This moment was his promise and Saturday would be his test.

This. Saturday. Night.

It was time.

Time to move on and move past.

Time to start again, start over. Escape from Gina French's stuffy room and escape from Gina fucking French. He would do what needed to be done this Saturday night and then Sunday morning, he would say his goodbye to Gina. The daydream was magnificent. He would say goodbye, kiss her on the forehead, then triumphantly fling open the drapes, flooding her dungeon with blinding natural light, sending the cockroaches scattering.

It would be a bittersweet moment of transition.

This. Saturday. Night. Obligations would be fulfilled.

He was no longer doing it because that bitch commanded him to do it, he was doing it because God needed it to be done.

One of his creatures had become flawed beyond repair. Travis would be the cleansing flood.

Everything happens for a reason.

He would be swift, quick, careful, and above everything else- merciful, but make no mistake about it—this Saturday night, Dan was going to die.

The nightmare jumped.

Something is wrong.

Panic turned Travis's legs into stone.

He pressed on through the darkness, trying to hide his bloodstained sleeve as much as possible.

Something is very wrong.

Even under the weight of Gina's demands, Travis had never suffered from an all encompassing feeling of guilt like this before in his life.

No, not guilt.

Dread.

No, not dread, either.

Impending doom?

Travis shot left, then right, spun a complete 360, then shot left a second time. He did everything in his power not to break into a suspicious full on run. Not to struggle the blood drenched shirt from his body. Not to scratched the damp skin off his arm.

Impending doom.

Travis couldn't breathe.

He was supposed to be rewarded for this act, but the clarity had become muddy.

Keep walking

Paranoia shook him.

Someone saw him, he was sure of it.

Leftfootrightfootleftfootrightfoot. Keep going.

Someone saw him kill.

Travis expected to feel a blinding elevation when the knife first bore through Dan's flesh, but he felt nothing. He practically severed another human being's head clean off and he felt nothing.

The alley finally spit Travis out onto a street. Brake lights flared. A dog barked. Was that a siren he heard in the distance?

There was so much blood.

Christ.

He still had the murder weapon up his sleeve. They would find him, find the knife and it would be all over.

Just like it's all over for Mr. Smug.

Leftfootrightfoot—keep going—keep walking

Travis kept moving but had nowhere to go. He was now a murderer, he had killed in exchange for freedom and now his freedom was suffocating him.

There was no sign of approval from God.

He truly believed he would receive one.

Something obvious.

Thunder?

A dove?

Something?

He got nothing.

He was betrayed and abandoned again. He no longer felt God's newfound interest in him; he felt God's fury.

Had he screwed up? Had the message been misinterpreted?

Clearly, he had killed and God wasn't happy.

Travis's head felt on fire. The pressure threatened to burst his eyes from his skull.

Leftfootrightfoot—keep going, keep walking, keep it together.

A young couple walked past him across the street—his eyes shifted from the ground to the sky to them to the ground to the sky to them and he saw they saw the blood; they saw the guilt. Despite the distance and the darkness, he knew they saw everything. They continued on, laughing and poking at each other until the sound of undiluted youthful happiness faded in the distance, but he was sure they knew. Sure they saw.

He felt naked and alone.

He felt guilty and used.

He was already a lot of things he didn't particularly like, and now he was a killer.

He needed to get home and resume drinking.

He needed to get home and drink himself into a Goddamn coma.

A Goddamn coma.

But first he had one house call to make.

He wouldn't get to scatter the roaches, but maybe, just maybe, his reward would be delivered after his ties were forever severed with the paraplegic bitch.

CHAPTER XIII

THE PLAN WAS to sneak inside the house, creep up the stairs and wake her up by whispering in her ear, but as the door at the top of the staircase slowly creaked open, there was Gina French, awake, in her chair.

Waiting.

"Did he suffer?" she asked. A small amount of excitement slipped out with the question.

She was barely a silhouette but her mouthful of repulsive little yellow teeth shone through the darkness.

Travis was too shocked to reply, he just shook his head. A single strand of saliva dripped from his gaping jaw. The seconds he could keep it together ticked themselves down. He forced himself forward and grabbed her shoulders. The action shook the chair causing a sad metallic rattle. Travis looked deep into her eyes and remembered how alive they used to be. Her dead eyes avoided his glare, rolled down, fixed on his bloodstained sleeve and rolled back up to finally connect.

A sick smile crept across her face.

And even before Travis could deliver his closing statements he was struck by the harsh realization that his visitation privileges had not been revoked.

"No, no Gina, you—you said—"

Something deep in her empty eyes shimmered ever so slightly.

"Did you really think that you could just walk away from this? From me?" she whispered with dark amusement.

Travis snapped his eyes shut as his body began shaking.

His grip tightened on her shoulders, fingers sinking into the loose flesh.

Gina's sour breathe shot up his nostrils as her words escaped.

"Look at me, look at what—you did—to me."

Travis shook his head back and forth, unsuccessfully muffling his sobs as the saliva continued to dribble down his chin.

"I trusted you, I listened to you, I slept with you, and I followed you and you took everything."

Travis had nothing, his tank was empty, all he could do was shake his head and take it as she gave it.

"You let me in, you fuck me, you fuck me over, and now you want to just walk on out that door? Ya? Is that the new Plan?"

Gina's eyes squinted into his. Her rotten breath burned Travis's eyes. His stomach contents bubbled and threatened to emerge. Gina continued:

"No matter what you do, no matter what I have you do— I will never leave this chair and that's on your head."

The darkness danced around him, her announcement swirled his perception more than the guilt and alcohol did.

Travis hung his head and caught his breath. The bitch had gone back on her word. Betrayal came crashing down into anger.

His head snapped back up to meet her grimace. "No," he whispered, then followed it up with a louder, sharper "NO." He pushed her shoulders backwards causing the entire chair to move. Its wheels squeaked a quarter rotation and came to a stop. His voice dropped back to a whisper. A forceful whisper.

"Dan is dead. We are done. I can't handle you." Travis stood upright and spun his finger around the bedroom. "I can't handle this anymore."

Black bangs fell into her eyes and she squinted through them at the door. Travis understood her concern; if they woke up Hannah the party would get a whole lot more complicated. Travis stared at the door, listening and waiting. Satisfied by the silence, he turned back to Gina who was already primed with her hate-face back intact.

"You can't handle this anymore? You can't handle this? Anymore?"

Travis matched her angry stare and waited, he knew it was coming, he could see it building to unimaginable heights. Gina's chest heaved as she wound up like an angry record player; the dark vinyl picking up speed, waiting for the stylus to drop.

And drop it did.

"You can't handle this? Well that's fan-fucking-tastic, Travis. You think you can just march me into war and then up and leave when I come back damaged? Do you really think I'm going to let you wash your hands of me while I sit here unable to scratch my nose for the rest of my goddamned life, because of what you did to me? Look at me, Travis, look at me. Really look at me. Guess what, Travis? I can't handle this either! But here's what sucks about being me: you can get up and walk away; you can take a break from this shit! I have to sit here and wither away while strangers chart my bowel movements. This is me now, this is my life, and this is your opportunity to be a fucking man and prove to me that I am more than just a receptacle to you."

The words barely stung Travis. He expected worse. Whatever he was feeling turned to pity.

The house filled with commotion as Gina's outburst simultaneously awoke Ryen and Hannah.

Travis didn't have much time. He dropped his voice to a whisper and delivered his final remarks.

"Be a man? Screw you Gina French. Tonight I killed for you, I killed for your daughter, I killed, period. I did what I promised I would do and Dan's dead and I'm gone."

He wanted to gently push her back another few inches for dramatic purposes, but instead he pinched the rogue inky hair from her eyes and tucked it back behind her ear. They heard Hannah on the steps calling from below. He stared right back at Gina, knowing she had all of five seconds for a rebuttal. If nothing else, he owed her the last words, and unlike her last rant—this one didn't disappoint.

Gina swallowed and returned her voice to a whisper, and with crystal clear monotone barked:

"You can turn around and leave this room, leave this house and never come back, but you will never escape this. After all those time you were inside me, now I'm inside you."

Her smile was sincere as Travis backed away and slung a spare blanket around his shoulders. The door popped and Hannah panted into the room with Ryen in her arms.

Before she could even ask, Gina cut her off with whispers, "It's okay, we calmed down, sorry about that. We—"

Travis quickly tagged in, "I'm sorry, we didn't mean to wake you. It's late. Things got heated—I've been drinking—it's over."

Hannah's look of disgust landed on Travis as he sheepishly sunk deeper into the blood concealing blanket. Hannah looked back at Gina and gently bounced Ryen back to sleep in her arms. "You refused last night, and you refused earlier tonight, how about now? Are you ready to lie down, in bed, out of that chair, yet?"

Gina nodded. Travis offered his help, but Hannah dismissed him and left the room to put Ryen back in her crib. Travis watched her leave and noted how attractive Hannah was in her oversized T-shirt and white socks. He imagined taking Hannah right there on Gina's bed, while she sat there watching, three feet away in her wheelchair, unable to stop them. The lurid fantasy was spawned more from his desire to lash out at Gina, than it was from lust for her roommate, but Travis felt a little relieved that some of his swagger had seemed to return. He felt the smallest amount of hope that can only come with a sense of closure. Yes, he had wronged Gina French, but he had made it up to her by carrying out the most horrendous favor ever to be asked. Despite what she said, it was, indeed, over.

Weighing his options, he finally chose not to disrobe, sprawl out on the bed and wait for Hannah to return. Instead, Travis acted out his original fantasy and walked down the stairs and out the front door.

***

The days that followed, Travis packed.

He drank and packed.

He wrapped his beer mugs in newspaper which bore headlines about the city's 15th unsolved murder of the year. It had taken surprisingly less time than the thought, but for now anyway, his guilt had subsided. He deserved, no, he earned this fresh start. He had almost justified his actions and wiped his conscience clean when he came across Hannah's missing car keys.

He stood with the keys in his hand. The closest he had ever come to seeing to Hannah get angry was when Gina failed to return the set which contained the remote start as well as the single key to the trunk. It wasn't a huge deal, Hannah wasn't someone who got off on being technologically spoiled, but the winter had been long and the inability to start her vehicle from the balcony was more of an annoyance than anything. Travis still remembered the night said keys vanished; with her ride in the shop, Gina had borrowed her roommate's car for a late night visit and the keys were lost (presumably) when Travis violently removed her jeans. The morning search was eventually abandoned and they giggled in his car the entire drive to the restaurant. Of course reliable Hannah had a spare set ready in the wings, but they would take turns mimicking Hannah's "put out huff" for months.

The memory was as warm as the whiskey which trickled down his throat, even now, with his peanut butter toast.

The contemplation continued as the keys jingled in his hand.

Screw it. He pulled on a jacket and headed outside.

One last chance to be a hero.

It was the time of morning the Aide would be getting Gina ready for the day, and Hannah should be leaving for her Tuesday morning shift at the restaurant.

Perfect.

He could drop the keys off to Hannah, apologize for Saturday night, and avoid the negative bitch.

The drive was somewhat of a blur, but he sobered up enough to pull off the perfect parallel park. He missed the bottom step as he attempted the staircase, but nailed it on his second try. He gently knocked on the door and dangled the keys on the end of his finger. Travis didn't really know what Hannah's reaction would be—he was going to bet on "suppressed excitement", but what he got when the door gently opened five inches and came to a dead stop as the locking chain snapped taught, was immediate shock and horror. Hannah panicked, tried to speak, but instead slammed the door.

Travis stood motionless for what seemed like a lifetime until his finger relaxed and the keys fell to the ground.

He knew she knew.

He knew she knew what he had done and he knew he was fucked.

Travis didn't even remember how he got home. He was pretty sure he drove, but his legs told a different story. Actually his whole body ached.

He stumbled through the front door and grabbed at the bottle which tore down his throat, racing the tears which tore down his cheeks. He gulped and gulped until he coughed up the poignant liquid—spraying alcohol across his kitchen floor. He hacked and hacked until his breath came steadily enough to resume consumption. Packing had become an obvious waste of his limited time; today's new goal was to drink himself to death. Drink himself out of this life once and for all. He had no idea how much time he had. He felt a dramatic flare—he should get the golf clubs from his closet and decimate everything and anything he could, but after his drunk frame bounced off the hallway wall a few odd times, his "one man riot" suddenly seemed too much of an effort, and his idea was hazily abandoned. The wall that jumped out and attacked him on the way to the closet went from antagonist to protagonist as he suddenly needed it for support. He blinked and focused and tipped the large bottle once again. The beautiful liquid sloshed back and forth inside the glass tube until his body rejected another heaping volume. Travis coughed his way back into the living room and flopped on the couch. His eyes struggled to stay open, but he fought the urge to make this officially the shortest day in the history of his life. Instead, Travis decided to watch some home movies—one in particular.

Plugging the red and yellow RCA jacks into the side of the camcorder had become long division in his current state, but his persistence eventually paid off and the images were sent from the camera to the television.

And there she was.

Travis fumbled with the rewind button and watched Gina's home movie backwards. He giggled as she fuzzily dressed herself at an impossibly rapid pace. Finding a satisfactory starting point he took his finger off the button. The playheads corrected themselves and snapped into action.

There was Gina French. Mobile and full of life.

She stood in front of the window, the afternoon sun silhouetting her flawless figure like a burlesque show. Travis held his bottle up to the screen, toasting his former lover.

And current victor.

He had the video memorized:

Her serious/sexy face. The button on her blouse she struggled with until she broke character, laughing momentarily before regaining her faux serious composure and continuing with the impromptu strip tease. How she turned her back to him and arched as she slid her jeans down her legs. Down to her underwear, she pulled the large curtains in front of her as she sexily moved in tune with the music, not caring who may be outside, getting the reverse show for free. The curtains formed two giant triangles, only exposing her shoulders and head above the crumpled fabric, and her legs below.

She held the curtains together with one hand and stretched the other above her head, running it through her long blonde hair as she writhed to the beat of the song. She momentarily lowered herself into a crouching position before slowly dancing her way back up. Suddenly she turned her back to him and ran her free hand up her body and slipped off one bra strap, letting it hang just below her bicep, then spun back around and slipped off the other. Gina paused and smiled as she remained safely behind the curtains while one hand drifted behind her back and the garment fell to her feet. She attempted to kick it at Travis, but its strap caught around her ankle and after shaking it off it, it landed on the floor about a foot away. The video shook as Travis heard his own laughter mix with the song's chorus until she dramatically took another deep breath and resumed her intense look. Topless, but covered, she continued to seductively move, while slowly swaying her hips free from the curtains.

He wondered how many times he had watched this tape. At least two dozen during those horrible six days he waited by the phone. Yup, at least twice a day while she was missing.

Those six days still haunted him; the six days he sat here watching Gina French strip while he was positive she was dead. Each time he watched, he felt worse and worse about himself, but he had to see her. Every time promised to be the last time.

Masturbating to a dead girl.

Travis was pretty sure that was going to cost him big in the afterlife.

But now as the images flickered across his screen, as she teased panty removal, there was nothing sexy about the video.

Same footage, same girl; opposite reaction.

And so the dance continued.

Each time her hips swayed out from behind the curtain her underwear had magically descended an inch or two down her hips and each time it angered him more and more.

Saturday night he had looked at her, really looked at her, as she had commanded him to, and he finally saw her for who she truly was. Now watching the fake Gina French of yesteryear dance across his television, sporting her fake smile, kicked at his already-questionable stomach.

How could he share his bed with this . . . creature? This human cavity of festering misery.

As the scene played out he finally studied her face—not her midsection, and he could see her evil plan already brewing somewhere in there. Her eyes stared directly into the camera as she finally slid her underwear down her legs and stepped free from them, still covered by the curtains.

A demonic whore, he concluded as he jammed his finger on the tiny black button-stopping the tape seconds before Gina let go of the curtains for the big finale. This time he had seen enough. It had done its job.

It was finally time for drama.

Travis ejected the tape, let it drop to the floor, then brought the bottom of the whiskey bottle crashing down over and over, obliterating the defenseless casing. A thin reel of black tape unwound into the kitchen as what was once a three dimensional gray rectangle continued to spit tiny plastic pieces all over the carpet. Satisfied, Travis tipped the bottle back, completely draining what little liquid remained after the majority splashed on himself and his surroundings; an unforeseen side effect of using its container as an instrument of destruction.

Goddamn resourceful, Travis smiled to himself as he scratched the giant scar under his knee, closed his eyes, and waited for the police to knock on his door.

The pins and needles tore through his legs and thankfully took him forward to the present. Travis painfully uncrossed them and slid off the bed. Everything hurt. He was freezing. He smiled. His plan worked and he woke himself up. He saw the pipe. His nightmare flashed in the darkness. He frowned. It seemed like he had barely shut his eyes, like he had only slept two or three minutes, but the dream played quicker this time.

Nine days without sleep?

The tank was still empty.

Present time.

The pipe became blurry again and he blinked away the moisture. No matter how exhausted he was, his memories were vivid.

They bounced vibrantly against the dull gray background of his claustrophobic cell.

There were ten shades of irony that Travis now found himself on the other side of the steel bars.

His failure his only companion.

But it wasn't the isolation that kept him in a permanent state of nausea; it was the thought of a visitor or visitors.

The protective custody wing had the highest fatality rate of all the cell blocks; another reminder of the flawed system he was once a part of.

All the rats and snitches that dimed out their fellow inmates were sent here. The pedophiles and child abusers lived here. The rats, snitches, pedophiles, child abusers, and now, a former prison guard called Protective Custody home.

Well documented are the horror stories of what happens to the poor fucks in Protective Custody should a riot break out. The rioters practically line up single file and march on over.

Left-right-left-right.

Angry and anxious. Violently creative.

Although not the same prison which once employed both himself and the demon whore, people knew people who knew people and by the end of the second day word had spread that he came from the system and a bull's-eye immediately appeared on his head. The hatred in the other inmate's eyes was evident.

An entire table applauded and cat-called as he took his food back to his cell to eat while he still could.

Oh ya, he was going to die.

By the end of the first week he was jumped. Three, maybe four people. The attack lasted less than a minute, but the bigger slap came from the CO that eventually broke it up. He aggressively helped Travis off the ground and ignored his requests to see the prison doctor. He was paraded down the hall for all the inmates to see then ushered face first back into his cell. He could hear the cheers as he stumbled and sprawled onto the floor, clutching his gushing arm, his humility stripped raw. Travis could only watch as the officer sauntered back down the hall, earning respect at Travis's expense.

Travis saw Tuesday's beating coming and managed to cover himself for the most part, walking away with minor bruises and the revelation that it would never be over; the inmates would never stop the beatings and the "better than him" correctional officers would never discourage the inmate's hostile advances.

He was going to die, but he was not going to give them the satisfaction or the opportunity.

His torture would not be made into game or his suffering into a sport.

He was going to die.

The blonde monster outplayed him and his game was over.

As Travis practiced twisting his single bed sheet into a rope, he fought the urge to pray. He was adamant that his final thoughts would not be an insult to The Lord.

His actions were beyond forgiveness.

The one single positive thing that came from the entire experience—the only thing that may fall on the heavily outweighed "Good Deeds" side of the giant scale which will determine where his tattered soul would spend eternity, was when Gina managed to confirm that Conner did indeed have baby Amber. For whatever reason he was keeping Amber safe and alive as some sort of future "Plan B". Travis smiled a deep smile imagining the monumental relief the child's parents must have felt when Gina went public with that information. The family, the police and the public were given a much needed shot of hope.

The future family reunion was cut short by the snapping sound the bed sheet made as Travis yanked it tight.

It was time, but the pad of paper on the floor reminded him of the one final task he promised himself he'd complete.

The pipe loomed above him.

Come on, how bad could hell be?

CONNER

CHAPTER XIV

"**T**HIS AGAIN?" SHE sighed as Conner opened wide and slid the smooth barrel of Gina's .38 revolver inside his own mouth. "What time is it now?"

Ignoring her, he closed his eyes.

"Right. Quarter-Past Faggot."

Conner's hands began to tremble, his teeth clattered against the steel.

"Ticky-ticky-ticky-ticky-ticky." She danced her fingers along an imaginary typewriter.

"Is tonight the night?" she asked with what would have sounded like sincerity to the untrained ear, but Conner knew better; she had no compassion.

She never had.

"Pre-DICT-A-bllllllllle," she slurred into laughter.

Conner cocked the gun.

"All right. Three."

"Two."

He forced the weapon further into his throat and clenched his eyes.

"Two."

"Two . . ."

A smile washed across her face.

"Two and a half."

He gagged on the barrel and coughed out the gun. It slipped from his hand and bounced off the floor.

Conner buried his face in his hands as his mother stood laughing in the corner.

He separated his fingers just enough to peek through. Just enough to get a good look at her.

She stood leaning against the wall in her brown slacks and flower print blouse. Same outfit as yesterday, and the day before, and the day before that.

Was it the outfit she was wearing the night she died? Conner couldn't remember and found that extremely frustrating. She played with a loose button on her sleeve as her laughter slowly coughed itself into nothing.

As annoying as this version of his dead mother was, he silently thanked his lucky stars that Post-Axe-Attack Mother didn't show up tonight. She was the absolute worst of the bunch. Post-Axe-Attack Mom would just accusingly point at him with one bony finger while the large gash in her forehead perpetually bled onto the floor.

That was some spooky shit.

It had been Post-Axe-Attack Mom who had sat silently in the backseat when he pulled the car over and tried to reset his nose the night the blonde whore nearly killed him. It took him almost twenty minutes to build up the courage to just grip the thing as the slightest touch watered his eyes, but once he caught sight of the rear view mirror and his unwanted passenger, he held his breath, stared into her accusing eyes and bent it hard left.

The sound was familiar, comforting, and apparently too much for Mother to handle because once his eyes refocused, she was gone. For the time, anyway.

As much as he analyzed it, and he had spent a good portion of his life analyzing it, his dead mother's appearances were nothing, if not completely random. After years of debate, it appeared that the biggest bonus of being dead was a complete absence of daily planners. Dead Mothers follow no formula. Some days she was with him, then she would suddenly be gone. Sometimes he wouldn't see her for months, and just when he thought she was gone for good— POP, he'd catch a glimpse of her out of the corner of his eye.

Judging him from behind her cigarette.

***

His ear scabs itched and his new hiding place sucked.

An abandoned warehouse offered little-to-no warmth, and paled horribly in comparison to the musty lake-front properties. He continued longing for his former place of residence, which usually transitioned into hating his current place of residence, which always transitioned into hating Gina fucking French.

Conner stood and looked at his dead mother.

Mother looked back.

Mother looked bored.

He hated this warehouse.

Apparently career driven yuppies love to see themselves because everything in the building was reflective, something that forced him to document his ongoing deterioration. Everyday he took note as his thick, lean body wasted away. What little muscle mass remained, sagged from the complete exercise stalemate. Waking up and forcing yourself to do push-ups was a hard sell when you've slept crumpled and contorted under a three-drawer plastic desk. Even now, he could see seven reflections of himself without even turning his head. Seven. Conner rubbed his face in disgust, his always shaved head now bore large patchy sections. Disgusting. Some days it bugged him and he wore a cap, other days he gave up and embraced his newfound ugliness. When he moved left, a dozen carbon copies of himself moved left in time with him. When he moved right—ditto. This was hard on the nerves and took some getting used to, but when he went in for a closer inspection, it was all bad. The amount of damage that blonde bitch inflicted on him was painfully embarrassing. His half ear itched. Her nails excavated bottomless trenches in his wrists and forearms. For over a week he squeezed alarming amounts of yellow from the deep infections. And that was the least of his worries; something inside of his chest was still not right, not by a mile, but it was manageable, and swinging by the local emergency room seemed like a bad idea.

The public wanted him dead.

The police were demanding he return the baby he didn't even have.

The child he never had.

Despite the paranoid secrecy, the self preservation, the random house calls from beyond the grave and the nagging internal injuries, it was the blonde bitch's lies that were the most damning.

Saying her lies had one-upped him was an understatement.

He remembered screaming down the highway, caked in blood; some of it Gina's—most of it his own. He was clearly going into shock. His thumb trembled and misdialed four times before finally connecting to nine-one-on. Conner could only imagine how much confusion this act of kindness would cause over the next few days. Conner looked up at Mother. She played with her button and gave him a sarcastic wink.

He didn't make that life-saving phone call. The unknown ramifications of letting Gina die made that phone call and, like most of his good deed attempts, it spun around and bit him right in the ass.

Now the race was on. It was only a matter of time before the police or the FBI or some redneck search party would find him, and then when they did, they would be harsh and they would be swift. All the charts and graphs in the world wouldn't be able to save his black ass once they realized he was unable to produce the baby. Thanks to the blonde bitch's lies, he was officially stuck—here—hoping beyond hope that someone found that child before rations ran out and he was forced to relocate.

Again.

After his first location change took him from lake front heaven to cityscape hell, Conner spent his initial evenings sitting in the car, letting it idle as he warmed his hands and listened to the radio. Some nights he tapped Gina's gun against the dash in time to the music between the hourly news updates. It was on the second night when the story finally broke and interrupted a particularly fun song to drum along to. They had found her and revived her, but his victory was short-lived as the unexpected Conner-Baby confirmation drained the color from his puffy red face.

The female victim, whose name had yet to be released, confirmed that "escaped murderer Kevin Conner does indeed have baby Amber in his custody, but appears to be taking adequate care of the child," as the infant was reported looking, "healthy and playfully unaware of her situation."

The piece was tagged with baby Amber's parents pleading to Kevin Conner for the child's safe return, which was tagged by the chief of police promising Kevin Conner's day of reckoning was coming sooner than later if he did not turn himself in.

Click.

After that, Conner buried the urge to unnecessarily fire up the noisy car—if he didn't have a death warrant before, Gina fucking French's false confirmation had sealed it.

The moment he broke her spine, he jammed his hands into Gina's pockets in search of anything useful and that's when he found his car keys. His car keys. He remembered the feeling of his hands inside her pockets, flat on her thighs, her body twitching as her brain failed to communicate with its missing parts.

Her thighs were solid. He remembered the other men who tore at her clothes during the riot and shuttered. For a woman, Gina French was unusually built, but even unbeaten, even unbroken, he had no use for her body. Maybe it was the vision of the men swarming her, or maybe it was the fact that his dead mother usually lurked close by in the shadows, but either way, when it came to Gina French, Conner mustered up a stunning round of sexual indifference.

Mother's snapping fingers brought his thoughts out of Gina's pockets and he stuffed his hands into his own.

Jackpot.

Conner slid a cigarette into his mouth and carefully counted the remaining tickets to Tobacco Heaven he had stashed in various hiding places around the office. Six days. Six days remained until he would have to make another run. Again. He would have to balance hunger with the risk of capture, which was an excruciating decision to make, because he really wanted more of those toffee flavored chocolates. He had managed to steal a pretty good supply of already-ready foods before moving in. Conner smiled again as he remembered kicking in the back door of one of those closed-for-the winter Mom and Pop convenience stores.

Great idea, putting plywood over the windows, he laughed to himself, real Homeland Security stuff.

Impenetrable.

He exhaled and remembered the fourth one he looted, Baker's Lodge Convenience. Not a soul around for miles. Product shelves stocked high with paper towels, fly swatters, and suntan lotion, while the food aisles, waiting for summer, sat sad and empty. Not even a can of soup. However, to their credit, it was the Baker family that left their lock box underneath the cash register and when his hand slipped around the handle of the .22 it momentarily took him away from his empty stomach.

He was hungry then and he was hungry now.

Conner's smoke stuck out the corner of his mouth as he pressed his face against the side of a dirty, yet completely reflective, filing cabinet. His arm disappeared inside the slightly ajar second drawer. He stuck out his tongue as his fingers swept the darkness, groping unseen chip bags, energy bars, and warm bottled water.

The sight of him speeding down the highway with the car's backseat stuffed window-high with junk food, caused him to snicker once again and incorrectly inhale. As he coughed, he imagined a high-speed chase with Johnny Law ending in a brilliant collision, complete with a rollover, capped by his car exploding into a billion flaming pieces. The heavens would rain candy. Children would dance as Blue Whales and Pop Rocks pelted their heads.

In his daydreams Conner wasn't afraid of death. In real life, he just couldn't kill himself. Sooner or later he knew he would be forced to make that choice. It was the only conclusion that worked. He wasn't going back to jail. He had been repainted by the ugliest brush—and as a result, he would be killed—probably slowly, for something he didn't do. For a missing child he didn't have. To the entire world he was a country-wide manhunt evading, crazy blonde bitch breaking, serial killing, criminal mastermind, who stole random children and did God-knew what with them; while in reality, he was a baby-less escaped convict who got owned by a piss poor correctional officer with ovaries and a rumored drinking problem.

Conner envisioned the people watching the news, reading the papers, streaming through the vile gossip.

Kevin Conner: Baby Stealer.

No contact. No ransom demands. He's keeping the child alive.

Kevin Conner: Pedophile.

Was suicide a fitting way to end it all? Not much of a Blaze of Glory, but he had to die; he was supposed to die. It had been coming a long, long time now.

I don't want to die a lie.

Kevin Conner's childhood had killed him many times over. He continued to die over and over during his youth, and he really died after splitting his parent's skulls with an ax.

CHAPTER XV

CONNER'S MIND KINDA turned itself off when he was young.

"A defense mechanism," he was told by adults trying to sound smarter than they were.

He removed the smoke from his mouth and slightly bowed. Defense Mechanism. He loved big words and his present situation was somewhat of a conundrum. Conundrum was one of his new "big words" he plucked from the pages of the trashy romance novels he stole while scrounging for food. Magazines were obviously not stocked over the closed winter months, but these romance novels had no expiration dates and broke the boredom. Burning the small paperbacks immediately upon completion was an important discipline—the possible humiliation of being captured while reading Candlelight Temptations was too unbearable to imagine.

He grew to love the feeling of a brand new paperback book.

It's smooth glossy cover.

The smell of its undiscovered chapters.

His heart raced every time he opened a new one for the first time.

Every time he cracked the spine.

The unnecessarily graphic sexual encounters did nothing for him. Sex was never important at any stage of his life; survival had always trumped every other urge. From then to now, that's all his life had ever been: a struggle to survive.

A struggle to stay ahead.

Conner carefully held the tiny cigarette butt to his lips and drew as much of the filter into his lungs as he could. Once the flame tickled his fingers he admitted defeat and flicked it in Mother's direction. It rolled past her feet as she muttered something condescending at him.

He studied Mother.

He remembered how Dead Mom stood beside Real Mom and shook her head as he swung the ax into her skull.

Dad begged; emoting for the first time Conner could remember, but Mom made no attempt to move, to dodge, to block. Her familiar smile never wavered as he brought the weapon above his head and swung it at the part in her outdated hairdo. Had the ax been a large mallet and his mother's head a carnival game, Conner would have rang the bell and won the biggest prize.

Betrayal Of Passion (the first romance novel he read by the dashboard light) set the stage for the distinguished Lady of the house to have a steamy affair with the African American slave only to return to bed with her husband for a second round of sexual ecstasy. The book then quoted Shakespeare's *Othello*, "The robbed that smiles steals something from the thief." He cursed his mother after reading that. Even in death, she had somehow won.

In the old days, every time Mom hit him, all she wanted was a reaction, but he tried as much as his little body could to never react. Although her attacks were physical, she really wanted to break his spirit, not his body.

Well, Mom eventually won. She got her fucking reaction one day in particular.

Eventually he got away. But they found him anyway.

Sort of.

Whenever Conner tried to figure out how and why the ghosts of his dead parents started poking around before he killed them, he would get so stressed his nose would bleed.

He took that as a sign to just accept the enormous continuity error and move forward.

Conner often wondered if his abusive childhood was worse than most. There was no checklist or graph to rate his violent upbringing against, no measuring stick to compare it to. The two weeks he was away he would lay awake at night wondering if his parents were beating each other in his absence.

And speaking of his parents, as if on cue, Mother suddenly moved. Her attention shifted from her blouse button to the door where his Father slowly entered; a folded newspaper under his arm. Much like Real Dad, Dead Dad usually had nothing to say. He grumbled and paced while skimming the obituaries.

With Father, you always knew what to expect.

It was almost funny that even after death, Dad was too lazy to switch up his routine.

For the first few years after Conner snuffed-out his parents only Post-Ax-Attack Mom haunted him on a regular basis, but he knew she wouldn't be able to keep her yap shut for all of eternity so she slowly began to accessorize:

-Silent Post-Ax-Attack Head Trauma Dead Mom
-Condescending Brown Slacks And Flower Print
    Blouse Dead Mom
-Going Out Of The House Sunday Best Fake Dead
    Mom
-Angry Abusive "You Just Wet Your Bed In The
    Middle Of The Night" Nightgown Dead Mom.

It was like she was part of a toy line from Hell.

Father seemed a tad disoriented. His eyes darted around the room until Mother lovingly chimed in, "Go sit your lazy ass on the chair already." Father sulked his way over to his only destination option and sank into its cushiony comfort. Father was just kind of there. He came and went and never got involved. Not even being on the wrong side of a grizzly murder and a postponed trip to the afterlife could reattach him to society.

When Conner was a little boy, when Conner was a bad boy, which was apparently often, Real Dad would punish him as well, but unlike his sociopathic wife, he seemed to get no joy from it, and that was why Conner murdered her first. He thought maybe the hex his mother had over his father would be broken—lifted—and the instant she left the world Dad would suddenly snap out of his trance and they would go outside and play catch or something.

Looking back, Mom couldn't properly cook or clean, but give her credit, that woman could bleed.

The spray from her skull somehow managed to equally coat all four walls of the living room—a testament to his axmanship. He put his foot on his mom's throat and shimmied the ax handle until the blade popped free from her skull. He wiped it across what may or may not have been her flowery blouse with the loose button and he studied his father. Dad, dripping in his wife's warm blood, screamed like nobody's business and embarrassingly fell from his chair. His precious newspaper soaked up some red as Dad continued to crawl away, leaving hand and knee prints on his wife's precious, yet already stained and worn, living room carpet.

Conner shrugged, guessing an afternoon of blood soaked Frisbee was not in the cards after all, and advanced.

Dad began to beg.

Suddenly his dad was full of life and wanted to live; he suddenly wanted to live very badly.

Conner stopped dead in his tracks and studied him. The harsh lines of age sagged under his wide eyes. After a life of not getting involved, poor Dad finally had no choice; he was involved. He screamed and screamed and begged and begged and apologized and repented and prayed and Conner just stood there staring at him like he was some sort of undiscovered species captured and observed for the first time. Something wasn't right. This wasn't his dad. His dad sat in silence reading the paper as his wife struck his son with a belt for breaking a plate.

Who was this guy? So full of moxie.

Conner took another step forward as his dad desperately shifted backwards. Both of them simultaneously slipped on the blood soaked carpet. Dad took an elbow as Conner took a knee and the ax banged into the wall. With nowhere left to go, Dad finally sat on the carpet with his back against the wall and began screaming, "Please-please-please-please-please-please-please-please," until his breath fractioned and his plea became, "pees-pees-pees-pees-pees."

Conner lightly tapped the top of the ax against his own forehead, letting his mother's blood run down his face and dribble off his chin as Dad continued running out of steam, whispering, "easeeaseeaseeaseease."

What was this guy's deal?

Eventually Conner shrugged it off; he came here to kill them both and now he was just stalling. He had planned to raid the house for smokes after the deed was done and watching his dad grovel was dragging on way too long. It was no longer cute.

Conner brought the ax down but Dad blocked the shot by crossing his arms. Conner had aimed for the head but felt the blade strike bone early and not with nearly enough momentum. Dad screamed gargly torment and tried to escape, but the ax was stuck deep in his forearm. With a wet shuck, the ax finally popped out. Dad screamed and screamed.

And screamed.

Such a production.

Dad was wide open for the next shot and it found its mark. Conner swung so hard at Dad's receding hairline that his own feet momentarily left the ground. The blade dug deep into his skull and Conner knew removal was out of the question. That shit was in there deep.

After the second kill the vividness of the situation faded and the following minutes muddled together. Conner was head-to-toe-soaked-crimson and the only quick answer to this mess was to fetch the kitchen's roll of paper towel. Each square instantly exploded red and pulled apart as he ran it across his face. His cheap parents would never pay for the Brand Name paper towel and this got Conner thinking that maybe, just maybe, cleaning up spilled cola wouldn't have been such a big deal if it hadn't taken half a roll of their crappy D-grade paper towel. This revelation caused him to chuckle at his dead parent's expense.

Eventually he managed to wipe the stringy plasma from his eyes, and began the pre-planned looting process. He had snatched a half-bottle of scotch and a quarter carton of smokes when he began to ascend the staircase.

He was curious to see if they had touched any of his stuff in the past fourteen days.

***

All of his daydreams seemed to end with him smoking, which always made him crave another even more. Conner continued to relive the past while he stared at the wall of his chilly, reflective, yuppie office building hideout. He was transfixed on a particularly odd stain about halfway up the empty panel as Mother finally gave up trying to annoy him with her silent stare. Over the years he had eventually trained himself to block her out and although he admired her persistence, eventually even she would admit defeat and storm out of the room. Conner was still confused by the dramatics of these departures. He wondered if she thought leaving in a huff would cause her son to chase after her.

"No, no, please stay and haunt me some more!"

He squinted into the distance to see if Mother was still kicking around and sure enough, he found her pacing back and forth in the hallway. He must have missed the grand exit. Conner smiled and sparked his lighter to life. He studied her as she walked to the end of the hall and back, over and over, seemingly lost in her own daydream.

The nicotine inspired movement and now it was Conner who paced.

It was going to be another cold night. He had blankets, but the nights seemed to be getting colder, not warmer, despite Spring's empty promises. As his lungs filled and emptied, more complex problems reared their ugly heads. Conner poked his finger into his stomach and was saddened by how easily manipulated his droopy skin had become. He began counting days on his fingers. How long could he realistically live off of stolen junk food before becoming violently ill or malnourished? He could feel Type 2 Diabetes just around the corner. Supplies were low. It would be less than a week before he would be forced to make another day trip at night, restocking the filing cabinet. He brainstormed how he could get better food, but he knew it was just a time wasting exercise. After all this, he wasn't going to get busted in the fruit section of the supermarket.

"Notorious serial killer apprehended with an arm full of bananas and a paperback copy of *Romance At Blackstone Castle.*"

There was no way he was going down like that.

No matter how much time he spent on elaborate robbery plans, he knew the little family-owned convenience stores were the only smart way to go. It was chocolate bars and potato chips until one of three things happened:

-he got captured
-he ended his own life
-his slick, fat encrusted heart exploded.

Dammit.

It seemed like he had just lit it, but the cigarette had already burned down to the filter. Conner angrily strode across the room, stuck his upper body into the hallway and flicked the smoldering butt at his pacing Mother who jumped by the sudden appearance of her earthly son.

Another toss, another miss. The butt went rolling past her feet and he smirked at the momentarily surprised look on her face—she was on edge, and that put him on edge.

The lady had ice in her veins. Something was up.

***

He remembered sitting at the kitchen table when he was eleven. The macaroni and cheese tasted unusually good that day and Mom was grumpy as usual. She was explaining how useless her son was while pouring water from the kettle into her mug of instant coffee. When she got to number six on the list she looked up at Conner and accidentally poured the boiling water past the mug and on to her hand. Mother jumped back and screamed and Conner laughed. He saw the look of pain and outrage burst across her face, and that was the last thing he saw for a while.

She snatched the cup of unstirred coffee and splashed it across the table at his face. Instinctively Conner brought his hands up and his long sleeves absorbed most of the scaling water. But not all of it. The pain detonated in his eye as his chair tipped and the back of his head hit the floor—taking him far away from the pain. He awoke an hour later, on the couch with an eye full of ointment. Mother had probably thought her instant retaliation was clever, but in the long run it completely backfired on her. The skin surrounding the eye demanded medical attention which opened all sorts of ugly doors with his public school and Child Services. Looking back, he knew he was damn lucky. That afternoon, although in haste, she began thinking outside the box and had she gotten away with it—who knows where the journey would have taken the two of them. After the antibiotics and fake motherly concern he was given a candy, they returned home and things went back to normal. It was also around that time that he started growing, and it seemed each month as he got bigger, the beatings became less frequent. Conner initially thought it was because he was growing into his body, reducing his clumsy accidents, but by the time he had reached the seventh grade, he stood face to face with his mom and she had backed off completely.

The nicknames homo and faggot were used less and less, eventually disappearing all together.

When the beatings stopped, she must have spent every night laying awake, waiting for the counter strike which never came. Not until years after she was in the clear, or so she thought. It was probably the last thing on her mind when he crept into their yard and pulled the ax from the stump. He was supposed to be safely locked up. Locked away. Out of sight, out of mind.

The back door was unlocked. Man, did that ever piss him off. Two of the most horrible human beings walking the planet felt safe enough to leave their back door unlocked at night. That was the clincher. He remembered walking past the tiny shelf in the kitchen which still housed the same three photos: The wedding photo, the photo of Conner at the beach and the photo of Mom right before she miscarried with his sister. Right before the beatings began to escalate. Right before she started every sentence with the haunting rhyme, "Little queer get over here." He caught his reflection in the hallway mirror and liked what he saw—any smile was rare, but this one stretched from ear to ear.

He looked important.

And he was.

The ax dangled by his leg as he walked.

He was brimming with confidence.

He looked like he was on a mission.

And he was.

He could hear the opening monologue of the late night talk show and he could see the flicker of the television as he neared the living room.

Ah, the memories.

Mother continued to pace the hallway as Conner finished recreating her final earthly moments in his mind.

He walked up to Mother and blocked her route. Smiling, he stared deeply into her eyes. She avoided his glance. Something was definitely up.

Back in the day, when everyone was still alive, Mother would only get all jumpy and nervous like this on Sunday afternoons when her sisters would come over for dinner. The stress of keeping her secrets secret while people invaded the privacy of her House of Deceit was fun to watch play out.

"House of Deceit?"

Conner really liked that line; those romance books were paying off. House of Deceit should have been the title of his autobiography.

Autobiography?

The idea rejuvenated him.

He should write an autobiography; tell his side of the story. Maybe he could call it *Childless—The Story Of Kevin Conner* to really drive home the stupidity of the situation. Or, *The Skinny White Bitch Lies—The Story Of Kevin Conner*.

He could feel the public's ignorance poke at his anger all over again. What bothered him the most was what he was sure people were thinking he was doing with the stolen child. He rarely had interest in sex; pedophilia made his stomach churn. He had no history of any sex-related crime, let alone with children, and as far as he was concerned, pedophilia should be the one exception to the fair trial rule. It should be an eye for an eye when you deal with child molesters. He lost his childhood to abuse, he could not imagine living with the shame of sexual abuse. It turned his stomach. Sexual intercourse between consenting attractive adults itself seemed borderline disgusting, let alone forcing yourself onto a child. Pedophiles have it the worst in prison and there was no way in hell Conner would be locked back up with a giant P on his forehead.

"She. Screwed. Me. Over!"

He again momentarily thought about just coming forward, just giving up—if nothing else at least he would have a chance to clear his name of that stigma and take back some power from that crazy prison-guard bitch, but his sharp survival instincts kept pushing that thought from his mind. If someone took him out before he had a chance to explain himself, he would die as she painted him—a child abductor.

If the stupid baby was never found, his name would never be cleared. The lying bitch had sealed his fate.

People wanted to believe the worst and she was the worst.

Poor little white girl gets busted-up by the baby stealing black man.

He didn't stand a chance.

Out of nowhere the feeling returned.

They were on the floor in Lake Timor. Fighting for their lives.

He stretched her body and twisted her head as Gina's back shuddered under extreme pressure until her spine gave up the fight. The way her body relaxed, then twitched, then relaxed, then twitched again, gave him a sudden rush of confidence.

Maybe he was the worst.

Mother had stopped pacing. She smoothed her slacks with her hands and stared back into Conner's eyes.

His defiant smirk remained. He stepped to her, raised an imaginary ax above his head and slowly brought it down into her skull—reenacting the matricide. The first few times he had the balls to do this she went nuts. It caused Mother to run screaming in circles. It was a milestone. When he really killed Real Mom, she didn't make a sound, when he fake-killed Fake-Mom, she screamed bloody hell. Now, he had done it enough times that it was no longer novel. As the invisible ax came slowly into her head, she looked distracted, walked away and resumed the pacing/button picking.

He was sure it saddened them both that his bag of tricks had become somewhat rusty.

Ever since her nightly you're too weak to actually kill yourself mockery, Mother had been eerily quiet tonight; almost nervous.

It was making her son nervous as well.

This particular version of his dead mother was infamous for never shutting up, but today she seemed to have something else on her mind. Harassing the flesh and blood she gave life to, who in return eventually took hers—took a backseat to something bigger.

After counting and lighting another cigarette he tried to visualize how much work it would be to write an autobiography. It's not like he didn't have the time. Oh, Mother would have a field-day with this one. She would be over his shoulder for the entire duration, pointing out every grammatical error and inconsistency. She would be outraged by his brutal depiction of her. It would probably be more of a headache than it was worth, but if he kept the folded pages in his pocket at all times, even if death came quick and blindly, they would find his memoirs on his corpse and it would clear the pedophile part of his name if nothing else.

Yes, this was something he had to do. Now. Today. Now.

Conner got extremely excited and almost sprinted to the filing cabinet. Within minutes he had his tools: a pencil, paper and motivation. He began scribbling down his random thoughts as quickly as he could. He could rearrange them in the proper order at a later date—but for now it was all quantity over quality. As he scratched explanations onto the back of the three-holed pages pulled from a training binder, he smoked like a chimney. His careful cigarette ration was out the window—at this rate he would be dry by the end of tomorrow, but this new project trumped everything else.

With his pencil overheating he tore into Gina fucking French.

Page after page, his rage coursed from his body, through the pencil, and onto the paper. His heart raced. This was therapeutic on every level. He imagined the white-gloved officials removing this document from his fallen body. Would there would be bullet holes through the actual paper? He worried that his blood might soak the pages, smudging the ink illegible, but it was a risk he had to take.

As long as a lynch mob doesn't soak me in gasoline and start me on fire, it should remain legible.

It appeared his excitement was contagious: Mother was

back in the doorway carefully studying him from across the room. An over the shoulder glance revealed that even Father had lowered the newspaper enough to investigate his son's latest project as well.

***

As Conner returned to his project he was startled to see Jeremy now sitting in front of him.

Jer had an eager look on his face. Jer was nodding him on, begging for inclusion. Conner nodded back; Jeremy was right. Looking at the big picture, the unlucky young man was an extremely important member of the cast. If he was going to spill the entire pot of beans it pretty much had to start with Jeremy. After all, that was the day that set this whole thing in motion. Doing what he thought a real author would do, Conner closed his eyes and bit the end of his pencil as he tried to collect his thoughts. They came in pops like fireworks across a black sky. Not blurry or muddled, but electric, then gone.

He never lied to the police and social workers.

He truly didn't remember.

One moment he was seated at a table in the high school cafeteria—then came the screams. Then he was tackled and held to the floor. Finally he was removing his blood soiled clothes and being told to place them into clear ziplock bags.

Over the next few days random moments dropped back into his brain. Each one appearing more random and confusing than the last. The most perplexing flashback was the one where he looked into his dripping red hand and studied the no longer cylindrically structured can of soup he apparently used to shatter his classmate's face. Through thirty-three student interviews peppered with "Ummmmms" and "Likes", the police report wrote of a 12:10 Tuesday afternoon when a student described as "reserved" by his peers, sat down for lunch, removed a can of tomato soup and a large white bowl from a brown paper bag, then bludgeoned his classmate to death.

Fifteen years-old. Premeditated or spontaneous? Young offender with an adult crime. Murder charges or no murder charges? All these things whirlwinded inches away from Conner as he sat alone on the other side of the door keeping his juvenile detention room tightly locked.

The police. Blah blah blah. Lawyers. Blah blah blah. Teachers. Blah blah blah. Psychiatrists. Blah blah blah. His parents of all people. Blah blah blah.

Why? Over and over. Why?

In less than twenty-four hours Conner grew to hate not only the word, but the letter as well. Why?

Day after day the unwanted guests came and went and all he could do was sit and nod, his mind a million solar systems away thinking about the snapshot in his brain of Jeremy, the kid who, from the neck up, Conner made not look like a kid. His flannel-covered arms both stretched above the mass of blood, hair and shredded skin that once was his freckled face. His corpse making one final giant Y.

A can of tomato soup.

Why?

Miles away lawyers worked for him against him. Conner began sleeping more and longer. Waiting. Then one night Jeremy was standing beside his bed. Right there. Not judging or accusing or asking Why, just there. Two nights later he awoke to find his parents standing at the foot of his bed with Jeremy. It was illogical and impossible. The living mingling with the deceased. All of them apparitions. Ghosts. Specters. Two living, one dead. The claustrophobic sensation of dread began to envelope young Conner. The walls closed. Fifteen years-old.

"I need to get out of here, don't I?" Conner whispered to the spooks. "I need to come home tonight, don't I?"

All three slowly nodded in unison.

"NO-NO-NO-NO-NO!!!" From the doorway Mother began to shriek.

Dread washed over Conner.

"NO-NO-NO-NOOOOO!" Mother gasped as she disappeared from the doorway; her yelling and foot-stomps faded down the hallway. Conner tried to regulate his breathing and precociously began folding the papers. He closed his eyes. "Don't check on her, it's just more motherly mind games," he concluded, despite the sinking feeling in the pit of his stomach.

No, something is different today.

Conner slowly opened his eyes.

All his senses ignited.

Jeremy was now hovering inches from his face, but it wasn't regular "Dead Jeremy', it was "Recently Soup Can Face-Smashed Jeremy" as blood pulsed from the mass of sunken, shredded skin above his neck. Screaming, Conner spun from his chair and backed away from the punctured eye and the swinging jawbone. This was a new and unpopular twist to Dead Jeremy. Conner had adequately distanced himself from the horrific vision but he was unable to look away. Jeremy rubbed his gurgling no-face as a trembling hand tried in vain to massage said eye properly back into its socket. Blood cascaded between his fingers. Conner clenched his eyes shut and snapped them open. Jeremy remained in his scrambled state and continued failing to properly replace his sagging facial features.

Shaking, Conner finally looked away.

Clench. Open.

Jeremy, in any form, was finally gone, but the victory was short lived. A moan erupted in Conner's ear, causing him to spin around. Jeremy had reappeared inches behind him. The pulsing mess of hamburger bent forward, his jaw dangled back and forth. Conner pushed past the awful reminder of his guilt just in time to catch Father rising from his chair. He too was trembling and stared intently at the doorway as his dead wife's repeating screams of "NO!" drowned out Jeremy's moaning and sputtering. In another rare act of movement, Father stuck the newspaper under his arm and walked with a purpose towards the hallway door.

"NO-NO-NO-NO."

Conner slowly turned and at a facially reconstructed, back-to-normal Jeremy, now standing against the far wall. He had assumed the scolded schoolgirl position: arms at his sides, eyes on the floor. Tears dripped as he gently shook his head back and forth.

Conner's blood pressure pounded.

"What's going on, Jeremy?" Conner demanded. Jeremy ignored the question a second and a third time as Conner finished folding his tell-all memoirs and stuffed the pages into his pants. He snatched Gina's gun from the floor.

The "NO-NO-NOs" got louder as he cocked the gun and strode into the hallway.

This was it. They had found him.

It was time for the standoff.

Please, let them shoot to kill.

His finger tensed on the trigger.

"NO-NO-NO-NO," Mother, her blouse a flowery blur, continued screaming at the far end of the hallway as she frantically pounded her fists against the wall by the exit sign. Father kept a safe distance but looked just as distraught as his deceased wife. All three of them knew it was about to be over.

One bullet in Conner's head took away their playground.

Conner heard the footsteps.

Clip-clack

Clip-clack

They started soft, but got louder as they came up the stairs.

"NO-NO-NO-NO."

Conner's arm went limp and the gun dangled loosely at his side. He felt for the pages tucked safely down the front of his jeans. He brought the weapon back up and pointed it at the door. Fuck it. He would take the first one out forcing the backup's shots to be fatal. He smirked at the back of his Dead Mother's head—this was finally goodbye.

The sun had just emerged from behind a dark cloud and brilliantly back-lit the staircase.

Clip-clack-clip-clack

He squinted into the light, licked his lips and kept the gun steady as the footsteps continued their ascension.

Clip-clack-clip-clack-clip-clack

"NO-NO-NO-NO."

Something wasn't right.

There's only one set of footsteps.

Conner's mind raced and justified. The steps got louder and louder. Louder and faster.

Clip-clack-Clip-clack

The police have this place surrounded they have dozens of officers entering from different parts of the building they are repelling from the roof they are climbing up the elevator shaft they are they are they are . . .

Clip-clack-Clip-clack

A silhouette emerged in the doorway. Even back-lit and through the frosted glass, Conner could see the sun screaming through her long blonde hair.

"Jesus Christ, no."

He fell to his knees and put the revolver to his temple.

The door creaked open.

"Honey I'm—home"

Gina French's smirk tore a hole right through his lungs.

"Miss me, boyfriend?"

She casually strode into the hallway, arched her back, raised her shoulders and began rolling her head from side to side, an indication she was about to do something physically demanding.

"NO-NO-NO-NO"

Gina finished her warm up and suddenly dropped her smile. She raised her eyebrows to Conner then spun at the waist, surprising Dead Mother.

"NO-NO—"

Gina's violent backhand snapped Mother's head sideways and she fluttered to the floor.

Conner's finger struggled against the trigger.

Gina replaced her angry stare with one brimming with curiosity and began strolling towards Conner. Gina froze mid stride, rolled her eyes and turned back. She removed an elastic hair tie from her wrist and placed it in her mouth as she used both hands to collect her long hair behind her head. Her toned midriff peeked as she doubled the tie around her ponytail and began savagely kicking at fallen Mother.

His hand trembled and bore the barrel into his temple as he watched Gina methodically stomp his mother into the ground. Just as it was with him in Lake Timor, her muscular legs found their mark every time. Mother would cover one body part and a sneaker would land a shot in a different location, causing Mother to then quickly cover that part, which sent a return blow to the original body part. No kick was ever wasted.

Gina began to work up a sweat, she took a step back and peeled off her sweatshirt, turning it completely inside out, catching a tight sleeve on one of her wrists. A maniacal smile spread across her face as she violently waved her arm in the air until the garment shook free before returning to the task at hand. She resumed stomping. Veins bulged in her tiny, yet muscular arms.

Gina's arrival brought Conner's afterlife party to four. The number seemed staggering.

Mother sobbed as the bitch tired of kicking her.

Gina angrily bit her lip and faked a few more, watching Mother flinch every time as she guarded herself from her attacker's imaginary blows.

Satisfied, Gina slowly returned her attention to Conner. She crinkled her nose and tilted her head in Mother's direction.

Conner held steady on his knees. One arm hung limp as the other firmly pushed the .38 in to the side of his face. Gina resumed her walk down the long hallway. Her smile faded as his welling tears caused her to completely disappear for seconds at a time. Gina French stood tall (one of the benefits of an unbroken spine) as she swaggered forward..

As she got within five feet he closed his eyes and tried one last time to pull the trigger.

He smelled a mixture of perfume and sweat.

Silence.

Darkness.

He felt a soft breathing in his ear.

"Honey," Gina breathlessly whispered.

Conner refused to open his eyes.

"Conner—baby?"

Conner didn't budge.

"Umm . . . let me know if I'm overstepping my boundaries here, boyfriend, but if the gun goes off at this angle, you're going to shoot through one cheek and shatter your teeth before it exits out the other."

Confused, Conner slowly opened his eyes and saw Gina kneeling in front of him, her hands were clasped together, as if in prayer. Her upper lip safely rested on her parallel index fingers. Gina gave him a sympathetic look and used her eyes to point at his shoddy revolver placement.

She was correct. The .38's barrel had slid down the side of his face and was now causing an indent in his cheek between his bottom and top teeth.

Dead Mom continued to lay there and sob. Dead Dad just stood there trying to be invisible.

Conner slowly removed the barrel from his own face and pointed it between Gina's eyes—dead—Gina's eyes?

Dead Gina?

Gina was dead?

Gina French was dead.

She must have had medical complications and died. She must have gotten some sort of infection her fragile body could no longer fight and died.

She must have—

"I'M NOT DEAD!" Gina shrieked inches from his face, her features snapping into an angry snarl.

238

Conner swung the .38 back around, jamming it so hard into his own temple that his perception momentarily tilted.

Gina mockingly winced through gritted teeth.

"You are not going to stay," Conner calmly stated in her direction. His arm flexed; his finger tense on the trigger.

Gina exhaled and sat cross-legged on the floor right in front of Conner, grinning with anticipation.

"Fuck you," Conner whispered. "You are not going to stay."

Gina stuck her palms up and shrugged her shoulders.

"You are not going to stay."

Conner held his breath and snapped his eyes shut. "oooooOOOOOOOOOO," Gina's voice flanged with exaggerated anticipation as if she were cheering on a penalty shot.

"OOOOOOOooooooooo." It dropped as Conner's shaking hand relaxed. Conner's eyes became slits, just wide enough to see Gina breathing in the moment, savoring the predictability. "Fuck you," Conner repeated under his breath. His slits disappeared and the revolver shook against his head once again.

"ooooooooooooOOOOOOOOOOOOOOOOOOOOOooooooo ooooooooo"

Tears streamed down his face.

"ooooooooOOOOOOOOOOOOOOOOooooooooooooOH FOR CHRIST'S SAKE—WE ALL KNOW YOU ARE NOT GOING TO DO IT!" Gina snapped. His hand went limp and the barrel slid two inches south. "That's your problem, the moment is right here—RIGHT HERE, we're living it—RIGHT NOW, but you're just too goddamn scared to make your move."

Gina continued scolding him as she jumped to her feet and slapped the newspaper out of Father's hands. "You and I, I and you—the things we do together—you and I made history before we met, we made history when we met, and we continue making history long after Lake Timor, yet, you just can't seem to embrace the fact that you and I, when we come together, you can't tell me you don't feel it, there's some chemistry there—you and I."

Conner watched Gina—watched the ghost of Gina—watched the Gina his mind gave birth to—Not-Dead Gina—or whatever the hell this thing was, saunter over to a giant reflective section of the hallway wall. She pressed the bottom of her shirt smooth as she turned sideways, stood on her tiptoes and looked herself up and down. She turned her head but never broke eye contact with her reflection as she shouted in Conner's general direction: "You know what your problem is, you know what's holding you back? You have this—this childhood illusion that life will somehow get better ONLY because it can't possibly get any worse—am I nailing this? I am, aren't I? That's how you live your lousy life, am I right, maybe little bit?"

Conner watched as Father collected his paper from the floor and slowly crept out of the hallway, passing right in front of his gun-pressed-to-his-face kneeling son.

"See ya, Pops." Gina continued the primping and verbal unraveling. "Where was I? Oh yeah, your lazy optimism. Your glass ain't half full and your glass ain't half empty—your glass threw its scalding coffee in your fucking eye and it took you years—YEARS to do something about it, but—pay attention, here comes the part where I complement you—when you FINALLY did retaliate, you did it—Balls. Out. I'm talking All-In, I mean hacking your parents into kindling was spectacular—spectacular—and a rare glimpse of the real Kevin Conner, the Kevin Conner that acts—not reacts, to the world—the Kevin Conner that that can Turn On The Crazy when shit needs to get done. THAT is the Kevin Conner I want. That is the Kevin Conner I need, that—God damn, my ass looks fantastic in these jeans—"

Not-Dead Gina, who had turned her back to the reflective panel, spun back and finally looked over at Conner, locked like a statue on his knees with her .38 revolver stuck to his head.

She dramatically searched left, then glanced to her right; convinced no one was listening, she dropped her voice and cupped her hands over her mouth as she loudly whispered while nodding towards the waistline of his pants, "But hey, if you want to die right here, die a coward, I promise not to rewrite too much of your little underwear-diary there, Anne Frank."

Conner's free hand snapped to his zipper, feeling for the folded confession. Gina smiled at her victory. "Although," Gina spread her hands in the air as if reading the imaginary headline aloud, "'You'll Never Find The Brat's Body,' rolls nicely off the tongue, doncha think?"

Conner's eyes returned to the floor. This was stupid, she was nothing but some bile residue that secreted from one of the many cracks in his brain. An oily film plaguing his psychosis—a daydream. A hallucination. She was just another part of his self-diagnosed mental disorder. This Gina French was no more able to physically manipulate a pen on paper any more than Jeremy, Mother, or Father. His papers—the truth, were safely tucked away where—

"Fine." Gina verbally cut off the thoughts as they silently scrolled through his mind. Conner's angry look of invasion rolled Gina's eyes. "As if I don't know what you're thinking—I LIVE IN YOUR HEAD!"

Conner angrily flexed his gun hand and his eyes went tight. A deep growl escaped from his throat.

Disgusted and somewhat visibly bored, Gina turned back to her reflection and fished some lipstick from her jean's pocket before casually addressing Conner over her shoulder.

"Anyway, Great Big C—whatever, call my bluff, maybe I can hold a pen, maybe I can't. I guess we'll see. Pull the trigger."

Conner ran a single finger over the fold of the papers sticking out from the waist of his jeans.

"Do it," she pressured, as the bright red cosmetic glided across her bottom lip.

"Dooooooooo it."

"Do it Rockapella"

"Go get 'em, Mac!"

"Just . . . " Gina's body drooped. "Look, I'm out of lines—just pull the fucking trigger, dammit, I can't wait to showcase my dormant creative writing skills." Gina suddenly stabbed the lipstick forward and slashed a giant letter G followed by a giant letter F across the reflective panel. They snapped their heads towards each other in unison. Conner's shock was legitimate but Gina's, with both hands framing her dropped jaw, was darkly sarcastic. She turned back to her masterpiece and added a perfectly symmetrical exclamation mark after the F before slowly tilting her head back to Conner; half whispering, half mouthing, "It's gonna get so much worse."

CHAPTER XVI

CONNER FELT A hand caress the side of his face.

His body snapped forward and he nearly pulled the trigger by accident.

A second Gina French lovingly wrapped her arms around his neck and shoulders from behind as he continued to watch the first one continue to obsess over her own reflection.

Conner tried to stand but Gina 2 held him in place and whispered, "Hold on, sweetie—you're going to wanna see this."

"THAT right there, THAT is EXACTLY what I'm talking about!" the first Gina, now bouncing up and down on her toes, shouted over her shoulder. "Don't sit there and mope about how none of this is real. How in the hell do you know for a fact that none of this matters?" Gina brought her hands together, massaging an invisible ball. "The mind is a complex series of pockets, in every pocket—there's five more pockets, in every one of those five pockets—POW, five more goddamn pockets, and so and so on. You can retrieve billions of tiny, dormant, negative, unrelated experiences and use them as excuses NOT to act, NOT to move forward, but so far, really, where has that gotten you?" Still bouncing on her toes, she turned back to the reflective panel and tossed a few uppercuts into the air.

"You have multiple internal injuries that haven't healed properly. You have, you know, THE WORLD screaming for your head on a fencepost. You steal a car with some bizarre fucking 'safetycrate', and you don't even have your own gun anymore, do ya hon? That's MY .38! The gun you had hiding under your pillow all those lonely nights up at Lake Timor only had two bullets and one of those bullets tore out my side and the other hit the doorframe. How was I supposed to know you were empty? Oh, the time we wasted sitting at that table in Timor."

As she continued her workout she pulled her hair free from its constricting tie, letting it scatter to her shoulders. Music filled the room and she broke into song. The rhythm slowly built until she abandoned her punches and bounced up and down screaming the lyrics and starting the second verse with a dramatic high hick on the down beat.

"You know why David Bowie is practically a god?"

Gina 2 whispered into Conner's ear, "It's too bad you're not a fan of girl-parts, "cause this show is going to be super-hot."

"I'm not. I-I . . . " Conner trailed off.

The gun in his hand—Gina's gun—slid back up and met his temple.

Feeling her own music, Gina swayed back and forth for the audience.

"You know why his careers spanned over four decades?"

Gina 2 tightened her grip and inched Conner's face forward, forcing him to watch the show. "How long, Conner? How long can you possibly live like this?"

Gina gyrated back and forth to the mirror, rubbing her hands up and down her body.

"Cause the man reinvents himself over and over."

"Quit lying to yourself, you know where this is headed," Gina 2 cooed into his ear, "you know why you will never pull this trigger."

Conner stared forward, his jaw trembling.

Gina was now alternating between singing into a can of tomato soup and giving Conner a quick music history lesson.

"He was a man with incredible depth."

Conner felt Gina 2 relax her grip.

"It's time you and I had a little reunion, Kevin Conner. I could sure use the company. It's tough making new friends, being all cripple and shit."

Dance-Machine Gina started lifting her shirt.

"Over the years he claimed to be gay, then bisexual, then straight—and you think you're confused? Geez"

Conner's breathing became choppy.

Gina 2 lovingly touched his lip with her index finger. "If you pull that trigger right now, you will never know, you will never, ever, know how this all ends—WHY this all ends. Think about it, Kev."

Dancing Gina continued to tease her reflection by lifting her shirt enough to reveal the bottom inch of her bra.

"Bowie knows no limits. *Ziggy Stardust? The Thin White Duke?*"

Conner felt the back of her hand gently caress his patchy beard.

"Look at her. Do you want this twenty-four seven?"

Gina rubbed the tomato soup can on her stomach.

"The man changed popular music."

Conner's eyes burned.

"Maybe your abusive parents deserved to die for what they subjected their own innocent trusting child to. Maybe Jeremy was going to grow up and be the next Hitler. These are all things we just don't know"

Gina rhythmically tapped the can's edge against her navel ring while slapping her thigh with her other hand.

"Some say he straight up invented Glam Rock."

Conner slowly turned his head to where Mother lay.

"Maybe we're permanently connected, you and I. Maybe in Lake Timor we formed an unbreakable bond. Maybe I'm miles away, laying safely in bed—yet somehow invading your thoughts, scratching your memories, awakening you."

Gina danced down into a squatting position as she continued to keep time with her navel ring/soup can/thigh slap drum solo.

"Two Grammy Awards and two BRIT Awards."

Conner leered as Mother openly wept.

Gina 2 continued, "One day your parents appeared in your mind, so you killed them—hoping THAT would erase the fake ones, but that plan—although rewarding—didn't work out so well in the long run."

Gina swayed back up into the standing position.

Conner brought his finger up and felt the never-forgotten sting of the scalding coffee exploding against his face. Hollowing out his ocular cavity. Reducing his vision. Scarring him for life.

Gina 2 gently tapped Conner on the non-gun temple. "But Jeremy appeared up here only AFTER you souped him to death, so . . . "

Gina thrust her hips, dramatically tossed the soup can down the hallway and shot her arms triumphantly in the air.

"See, Bowie never backed down, even when he went all American and most of his UK fans turned on him, he soldiered on"

He rubbed his damaged eye.

Gina 2 pressed her nose into the scabbed over hole bitten out of his ear. Conner could feel her breath entering and exiting as he watched the disturbing mental illness circus continue to perform. Finally, she whispered her million dollar idea:

"You just gotta kill Gina French."

Conner squinted.

"It's anybody's guess what'll happen. Maybe nothing, maybe everything, maybe Mommy will finally love you. Maybe the singing whore will disappear. Hell, maybe I'll disappear. Maybe by getting all gung-ho, you'll end up a little less gung and a lot less ho."

Dancing Gina's arms remained in the air as she violently shook her hips back and forth.

"In 1981 Bowie collaborated with Queen and the result was a number one hit on the UK singles chart . . . "

Conner looked straight ahead and focused his intense hatred at his dead Mothers.

"Maybe all roads lead to Gina fucking French, maybe her death will finally erase us, Mom, Dad, Jeremy, and—and, be it on the run or locked up in jail before you fry—you'll finally be alone, you'll finally have peace."

Gina complemented her hip thrusts with jazz hands.

"The irony is that Queen had originally brought Bowie in to lay down backing tracks on an entirely different song . . . "

Conner's chest heaved as he sneered at his dead Mothers. Saliva seethed from the corner of his mouth. The .38's barrel still pulsed against his temple.

"Peace, Conner, could you imagine? Not sharing your intimate thoughts with three—now five—other people? No more researching psychosis and social isolation and childhood trauma and long term urban environmental effects and abnormalities in perception and dopamine activity suppression?"

Gina was now bringing it home. She jumped up and down and clapped in double-time.

"But the chemistry between Queen and Bowie was undeniable and a random jam session produced arguably the greatest song both Bowie and the guys in Queen would ever create . . . "

As Conner shook with spite, Mother began to discolor, then slowly became transparent.

Gina 2's tone rose to match Conner's furious mood.

"There you go. See? This moment is NOW. It's happening right now, it's real and it's now, don't you dare dismiss it, Kevin Conner. All this—you—the way you are, the way you have become, is all because of the actions of three people; two who should have showered you with love and protected you from the horrors of an uncaring world and Gina fucking French."

Gina thrust out her arms as she belted out more lyrics before addressing Conner again.

"Did you know the remaining members of Queen and Bowie still argue to this day about who came up with the iconic bass line?"

Conner's sweat stung his pulsing eyes but for the first time since she appeared in his holding cell, he had successfully forced dead Mother out of his mind—ON HIS TERMS.

"That's right. Gina French comes along and suddenly things get messy, I mean 'OPEN UP THE SKY—REVELATIONS' MESSY, and you, you—sure, I'll give Round One to you, you uglied me up good, but I'm still alive, I'm still spinning my web, and I'm still out there." Gina 2 pointed to the window, then slowly brought her finger back to Conner's temple. "And now I'm in here."

Gina brought her arms in, giving herself a hug for the big musical finale.

"Even the effing Royal Philharmonic Orchestra covered that song"

Conner turned his head and for the first time stared into the eyes of Gina 2.

"I need you Kevin Conner, I need this. I need you and I. Come visit me Kevin Conner, come visit me. I'm not hard to find. Use some of those brains of yours. You made a lot of people at the juvenile detention center look silly and years later, in the big time? Come on, you spent over a year mapping out an absolutely brilliant get-out-of-jail-free plan, and then had the patience to sit wait another five weeks before someone provided you with a big enough distraction to execute it. God, Conner, you single handedly masterminded your own escape from prison. You can't tell me you can't find the world's most famous quadriplegic's house address? COME ON! OH and I DO NOT want "bitch Conner" again, I want "crazy-as-fuck-ax-swinging-sociopathic-take no prisoners Kevin Conner". That's the Kevin Conner I want to walk right up my front steps and ring my doorbell so we can continue this, "cause I swear on every one of your mother's graves . . . all the fucking anti-psychotic drugs in the world won't get me out of your head."

Gina 2 ended her rant and nodded downwards at her chest; Conner's eyes followed.

Conner jumped to his feet and screamed and spun and waved the revolver in circles as Gina 2 proudly modeled her faded flowered blouse hanging loosely over the waist of her brown slacks.

Her evil little grin threatening laughter as she barked:

"Little queer get over here and get everyone organized, get them down the stairs and into the car, come on, it'll be fun, like a Goddamn parade . . . "

HANNAH

CHAPTER XVII

AS SHE CHARGED up the stairs with the note crumpled in her fist, Hannah suddenly found herself back in the high school hallways, walking proudly beside controversy's sixteen year-old lightning-rod. They spotted Samantha Parkins as she struggled to slide a large glass shelf onto the brackets inside the school's trophy-filled display case. Gina B-lined towards the girl, but instead of helping steady the shelf, Gina slid behind the chubby teen and violently yanked up her shirt, giving the crowd a perfect side view of Samantha's hanging stomach. The laughter was spotty at best as Gina danced back and forth as the large teenager tried to shake her away.

Finally, Gina's fun had been had and she pulled the pleading girl's shirt back down and patted her belly before swaggering two steps back and admiring her work with an open-mouthed smirk. Gina casually led Hannah away by the arm and began to stress about fourth period's English exam. In a rare moment of defiance, Hannah snapped her arm away and demanded an explanation.

Gina became intensely dark and only offered, "She's friends with Emily Pierson, who's been telling everyone I'm a slut because I hooked-up with her ex boyfriend over the summer." Gina's face became a mixture of sadness and acceptance. "I think she wants to fight me." She sighed, giggled at Emily's absurd reaction to her actions, then switched gears and began denouncing the long term merits of Canterbury Tales.

The mental snapshot of Samantha Parkin's raw humiliation never left Hannah.

Without breaking stride she threw open the bedroom door and unloaded.

"You lying—manipulative—bitch"

Hannah's world had become a spinning clusterfuck of colors and borderless shapes since the neglected mailbox emptied its shocking contents that Tuesday evening:

Phone Bill

Junk Mail

Junk Mail

Water & Sewage Bill

Pre-suicide handwritten letter from roommate's incarcerated murderous ex-boyfriend.

She strode right up to the wheelchair and thrust the note into Gina's face.

Gina said nothing, her eyes drifted away from her best friend's open rage and focused on the empty wall. Even with averted eyes, her face told the story; she had clearly been dreading this moment. Dreading it and expecting it. Biting her bottom lip, she continued to look away. Hannah shot her body left, stood in Gina's new sight line, and shook the crumpled letter inches from her face.

"What are you?" Hannah quietly demanded the first time, then immediately shouted it like a reverse echo: "What are you?"

Gina's eyes darted to the hardwood floor.

More silence.

Hannah's hands balled into fists. Her shoulders rose and fell with every furious breath.

Every second of silence multiplied Hannah's anger.

She waited. Gina French wasn't going anywhere.

The large hanging clock endlessly ticked.

Hannah waited.

Gina's teeth slowly released her bottom lip, her mouth opened and her face scrunched up. Gina began to fight back tears as she croaked, "I—oh, Hannah, I . . . "

The words trailed off and the false look of sorrow dripped away, leaving her sunken features blank and unreadable. Gina's lips began a slow upward curl. It started as a sheepish grin; the scolded look of a child, but as the rest of her features joined in, the smile became less guilty. It widened toothy and proud.

Victorious.

Exposed, Gina studied the waist tie of her bleached white robe, then slowly raised her eyes to meet Hannah. Decades of friendship hung dangerously in the air as Gina took a deep breath and finally broke her silence:

"Hannah, baby, I know you can't tell, but I assure you— I'm shrugging my shoulders."

Gina closed her eyes and exhaled loudly through her sick grimace.

The damning confession crumpled in Hannah's fist.

It's all true.

The weight of the situation made the tiny hairs on the back of her neck straighten and the room became hazy.

Hannah's gasp escaped sharp and audible as Gina's eyes suddenly snapped wide. Her lips still pursed with that horrible smile.

She's happy I found out. Look at her, glowing from her sick double victory.

Anger returned Hannah to her mission. Smoothing the paper on her thigh, she shoved it, text-side out, eclipsing Gina's face.

"Read it."

Hannah listened as Gina aggressively forced the air in and out of her nostrils.

Instead of reading it she seemed to be breathing it in.

Yanking back the note revealed Gina's still-present smirk and a matching pair of tightly shut eyes.

"Oh no French, you are reading this." Hannah kicked the wheelchair's footrest to accent her point.

After months of substitute obscurity, Hannah's dreams

of teaching grade school had been derailed a few years back for one single reason: because she was suddenly needed to be there for her best friend Gina durings one of her best friend, Gina's, bigger times of need. Surprise, surprise, Gina French needed her help. Gina had fallen ill and was unable to work and was desperate for cash and Hannah leaped into action, fueled by the usual thankless desire to fix things, to help Gina French after another one of her "setbacks". Four years of university, a three week practicum placement and poof Hannah had willingly dropped it all for Gina French. Waiting tables was guaranteed money and immediate money. The desire to mold the next generation was transplanted from her classroom of twenty-four students to Gina's lone daughter.

Some of Hannah's happiest memories were of those early days; sitting on the floor, the children sitting in a semi-circle as she read to them. Her voice would squeal high then drop low as her eyes widened and her mouth made shapes. Her superiors had praised her storytelling abilities.

The classroom disappeared as Hannah returned to the joyless present. She clenched the note in her hand and looked back up at Gina. Reading a dead murderer's letter of apology to the roommate of his manipulative lover was seconds away from becoming her new career highlight.

Gina's eyes rolled as Hannah rigidly sat on the side of the bed and turned her body sideways so she could hold the single piece of paper up and face-out for Gina to follow along with.

Gina started to say something but Hannah cut her off. In her loudest public speaking voice she began at the top, "Hannah, I am so sorry and I don't have much time, I have no idea how things got so beyond messed up, please . . . "

"Oh for Christsake!"

It was now Gina's turn to cut her off.

Hannah continued to shout the letter at her roommate but Gina brought out her self-taught turrets and drown her out with a barrage of unrelated swears and random noises. Hannah screamed Travis's final thoughts at Gina until tears streamed down her red cheeks and ended salty in her mouth.

Her voice broke.

DAMMIT.

She had promised herself she would stay stronger than Gina, but deep down she knew it was hopeless.

No one is stronger than Gina fucking French.

Falling on her sword, Hannah let the tears fall as she violently crumpled the paper and threw it at Gina. The dam finally broke.

"Who the hell are you? I gave you everything I have and this is what you do? This is how you treat the people who care about you?"

Gina blankly stared back. Her dead eyes seemed somewhat intrigued by the break in the boredom as Hannah's periodless sentences began to trip over themselves.

"I gave up my career for you. After you managed to alienate everyone else in your life. I was there for you after the surgery, when you were all alone and terrified. I slept in the chair beside the hospital bed for nearly a week. I-I moved in with you, I held your hair while your morning sickness made you puke. I practically raised your daughter—my family practically raised your daughter—I . . . Christ, Gina . . . I—who—"

Hannah's small frame shook with raging sobs.

Gina's face contorted into an ugly grimace, but before she could respond, Tuesday evening's Home Care Aide charged into the room cradling baby Ryen. Without flinching, Hannah snatched the child from the lady's arms and sternly shouted at her to leave. The nurse attempted speech a few times, but Hannah repeated her command and thrust her finger at the door.

As the employee produced her cell phone, Hannah's tone dropped to damage control. She delicately balanced Ryen on her hip and gently placed her free hand over the nameless woman's number pad. "Really, it's okay here, the two of us just need to hammer some stuff out tonight, seriously, take the rest of the night off, I won't tell anyone. No one has to know."

The aide dropped deep in thought with a skeptical look, but emerged with an excited pop as she checked the wall clock. The young woman couldn't conceal her smile as she thanked Hannah, said goodbye to Gina, and nodded as she left the room. There was no distrust between the revolving home care staff and their employer's roommate.

Why would there be?

Hannah continued bouncing Ryen quiet on her hip and stared into Gina who stared right back. No one spoke until they heard the back door shut.. The sound of a car's engine signaled their return to "the stuff that needed hammering out."

"Why would you do this?" Hannah demanded, all smiles, in a baby friendly voice which caused Ryen to squeal with delight.

Gina said nothing and looked away.

Silence.

Ryen wanted a repeat performance and began to fuss. Hannah shook her head at Gina who had once again, mysteriously lost the ability to converse.

Ryen's bounce slowed to a stop.

Gina said nothing.

Silence.

"Screw this." With Ryen still on her hip, Hannah turned, stormed out of the room and stomped down the staircase. She snatched a baby bottle from the fridge, turned the sink tap to HOT and let the scalding water pour over the base. Both Hannah and Ryen stared into the darkness of the backyard as the milk slowly warmed. Even mentally miles away, Hannah thoughtlessly squeezed milk on her wrist, checking the temperature before she offered Ryen the nipple. The child's eyes lit up as she eagerly took it into her small

258

mouth. As Ryen gulped her late-night snack, the words Travis scribbled onto the paper slashed holes in Hannah's brain; the haunting words frantically scratched across the stamped, mailed, and delivered suicide note which currently lay crumpled on the upstairs bedroom floor.

Beside the wheelchair of her crippled best friend.

By the lame feet of a hate-riddled lunatic.

It finally began to unwind.

Grade school secrets, high school lab partners, double dating, college, the surgery, the fear, the rehab, the pregnancy, waiting tables, paying bills, the paternity case, the constant stress of being someone else's only lifeline all of it used to make her feel validated, but every once in a while, a small voice in the back of her skull would nag at her.

This happened to be one of those times.

A life spent on the front lines of someone else's battles had made Hannah tired, weathered, and feel more than a little used. Gina was notorious for overcoming life's setbacks, she unflinchingly attacked them all head on, but this latest tragedy? Paralysis?

This is too much—even for her—and now she's lashing out, striking back, embracing the negative. The vile. Can you blame her?

Hannah's boiling anger began to simmer back to better times until she felt a familiar prodding. Her mind unearthed dormant memories. Events better left buried. All those surreal times she had stepped back and watched in horror as Gina's anger exploded and her best friend went on the offense and tore someone down; verbally ripping them apart. "That's just Gina being Gina," over and over she told herself that.. Tonight she saw Gina French in her most intimate, stripped down, naked, form.

It was scary and ugly.

Gina's latest plan unfolded to an absolute tee; her manipulative scheming paid off with not one, but two people Gina felt had scorned her, dead.

Two people are dead and Gina French didn't lift a finger. She couldn't lift a finger.

Hannah had spent her life watching her best friend weave her dark magic—getting teachers and employers to turn on the students and coworkers she disliked, using her body and her charms to get jobs and second chances she didn't deserve; the list went on and on, getting sicker as it got longer. But this was Gina. GINA FRENCH. Through it all, Hannah had remained loyal, watching from the sidelines, standing up for Gina as people questioned their friendship.

"She makes terrible first impressions, that's just the way she is."

"That's just Gina being Gina."

"She's a little intense, I know, but you just have to get to know her."

Gina lived a complex, difficult life, but they fought through it together.

A team. A unit. An unbreakable sisterhood.

Gina's walls were high, thick, and painstakingly untrusting. There was a certain pride she felt because she, and she alone, had managed to scale them. Gina only let one person inside—and it was her. She was Gina French's best friend. She was Gina French's only real friend. People just didn't understand Gina—they didn't "get her."

Ryen shivered in her arms as the room grew cold.

Hannah caught herself automatically spewing rehearsed excuses for her roommate. The speech had been perfected and recited to more people than she could remember. People wondered how she could stand beside and stand up for such a person as Gina French. "You don't understand Gina, I'm her best friend," was always met with confused looks of pity, and now, as she rocked and fed her crippled friend's offspring, the denial finally ended:

She knew they were right all along.

She was never Gina's best friend.

I'm Gina fucking French's disciple.

And she always had been.

A pulsing hatred unlike anything Hannah had ever felt before began to throb.

All those years.

She cursed herself over and over.

She peered outside into the darkness. For the first time she could remember, she moved without a pre-written internal script and let the anger spontaneously motivate her actions and dialog.

With Ryen still happily slurping away, she stormed back upstairs, flew into the bedroom and violently spun the wheelchair around. Gina's body rag-dolled to the right, then left, then came to a sharp stop as the ride ended. Hannah gently placed Ryen in Gina's lap and fastened the custom baby-holder around the infant. Lastly, Hannah flopped Gina's lifeless arms around her daughter as the baby continued to excitedly suck at the milk, oblivious to the dramatic events as they unfolded around her. Hannah bent over, pulled back her hair, and leaned into Gina's neck.

"You don't want to talk to me? Fine. Enjoy this time with your child, you horrible, awful, little bitch. I'm leaving and I'm taking her. I'm taking your child, and for the first time in your life, you will finally get it. All you ever really wanted— you will be alone, all alone to wallow in self-pity and remind yourself how difficult your life is and how none of it was ever your fault. And as you stare at these walls wondering what kind of a woman I raised your daughter to be, I hope you inhale misery each and every second. I hope you rot in this fucking wheelchair as you count down the days until you die, alone and angry, knowing you have no one to blame but yourself. You miserable little waste of a human being. You are no longer my problem."

Hannah stood in all of her tear-streaking-body-shaking glory and slowly backed away as Gina's eyes remained down.

Ryen continued to slurp, unaware her destiny had just been altered.

Hannah stomped down the stairs and hit POWER on the giant stereo in the main living room. Buddy Holly's *Greatest Hits* thundered throughout the house. Returning upstairs, Hannah momentarily stopped in Gina's doorway. Her glare begged Gina to look up and say something—anything that would continue this one-sided fight. Hannah had so much more she would have loved to get off her heaving chest, but Gina's eyes remained locked down at her daughter. Or the floor. Hannah couldn't tell.

Spinning from the doorway in disgust, she pulled her high school graduation gift from the hall closet and tossed it on Gina's bed. As Buddy sang songs of simpler days, Hannah furiously marched in and out of Gina's room stuffing the necessities of a new life into the gaping mouth of the still-tagged suitcase.

Packing became more aggressive as Hannah's insides twisted over the last three years of her life.

Three years?

The diner had been so good and patient with her as she constantly readjusted her work hours to coincide with Gina's needs. They deserved a phone call, but it would have to be an apology instead of a warning.

The song "Everyday" signaled the end of the CD and suddenly the house was filled with nothing but the sound of Hannah breathing as she stood tired and sweaty in the bedroom doorway. Her body still shaking with change. Hannah's disgust was unwavering as she watched Ryen sleep soundly in her mother's evil arms. The long ago emptied bottle had fallen and lay on the floor.

Gina's beady little pupils had sunk into the natural dark pits below her bottom eyelids and remained downward. The coward's refusal to even acknowledge Hannah's presence began as an annoyance but steadily became a giant thumb in Hannah's eye with each passing minute. Removing an already packed scrunchie, Hannah pried the matted hair from her forehead as she went over her mental checklist. She had a bit of cash in her drawer and more in the bank, but the more of Ryen's things she could take the fewer stops she would have to make on her way to wherever she ended up.

She closed her eyes and imagined how freeing her escape would be. All four tires screaming through the darkness— every mile that separated her from this lousy house and this horrible woman would be liberating beyond imagination.

The three wasted years.

I was nothing more to you than your disciple. A toy. Something plastic and two dimensional you left in the drawer until things got screwed up, then you brought me out and smashed me against the sidewalk until you felt better.

Refusing to allow pity to replace her anger, Hannah kept that image fresh as she zipped the suitcase, walked over to the mother/daughter/wheelchair combo and ran her fingers over Ryen's little blonde head. For what had to be the millionth time, Hannah's heart melted for this tiny creature. Gina had gone to great lengths to damage her own life beyond repair and Hannah silently swore she would never, ever let Gina do the same thing to this child. She would not be given the opportunity.

Hannah turned her nose up at Gina who still denied her. You sad, stupid bitch.

This was it. The end of a long, twisted, bumpy, single lane road.

Hannah leaned in close, tucked the random strands of black hair safely behind Gina's ear and carefully chose the final, friendship-severing words; the last thing she would ever mutter to Gina fucking French:

"She's gonna grow up thinking I'm her mother. You will be nothing to her. Not even a suppressed memory."

Gina exhaled loudly as Hannah paused, then finished:

"I will erase you."

Gina's breathing quickened but her eyes never once flickered from her daughter.

It was time to go.

Other loose ends? I'll need to leave a note for the morning Care Aide.

For the first time Hannah realized she was about to become a fugitive, running from the law. A baby kidnapper— not unlike Kevin Conner. The irony tickled her.

The smell of strawberry baby wash filled her nostrils and Ryen's slumbering smile cemented her decision to flee.

She had heard Canada was nice. Fresh air. Free health care. A place where they take care of the sick and the elderly.

Hannah ran down the hall to the study, snatched a single piece of paper from the printer and scribbled a note to the 8AM Aide explaining how a sudden family emergency caused her to leave with Ryen, "but everything is okay and I'll be back Sunday afternoon." Someone would have to fill the night shifts in her absence. Hannah smiled down at the intricate vagueness of it. This note guaranteed her a five day head start, and probably another two before suspicions arose. She scribbled her cell number at the bottom of the page, then checked her phone to make sure the power bars were strong. She wiped her hands on her pant legs and glanced back at Gina.

Oh right.

She had almost forgotten about the bitchy little plan-ruining tattletale. She wasn't really a mute, she was just pretending.

She could tell Gina was currently conjuring up lies big enough to prematurely alert the wrong people. She paced and weighed her options .

I should bust her jaw, take away her last ability to communicate. It would be a fitting finale.

Instead she opted to end the note with a P.S. explaining Gina's angry fits and recent nonsensical tirades. Unsure of Gina's next move, but confident she already had one ready, Hannah chuckled as the pen went back on the paper, secretly continuing to paint Gina as a paranoid, delusional liar, "not responding well to the current medication." She could feel

Gina fuming as she switched up the game, unaware of what was being written, unable to calculate a specific defense to the unseen words on the paper. Hannah turned the note over and went on apologizing profusely for leaving Gina unattended and placed the time at 7:45AM, letting the morning Caregiver think that Gina had only been left unsupervised for a forgivably short fifteen minutes. Much like the recently dismissed young woman, tomorrow morning's Aide would have no reason to doubt or distrust Hannah's words.

Begging for acknowledgment, Hannah gently placed the note face up on the bedside table, right beside Gina's wheelchair. Right there in plain view.

If only Gina French could turn her head.

Hannah closed her eyes and let the scene play out: the confusion of the morning Caregiver finding an empty house and a furious Gina bursting with frantic tales of kidnapping and betrayal which, at first, might come across as slightly believable, until the note was read. A phone call, if they bothered, would clear it all up. Hannah recited the entire conversion in her head, explaining about her Uncle in critical condition and the hospital's request to quickly gather the family. The Care Aide would be immediately won over by the realization of the easy, Ryen-less shifts that lay ahead. Hannah imagined Gina screaming in the background as the phone conversation came to a close.

Hannah would suggest upping her medication, as drug the bitch sounded a tad too harsh.

By the time the note was found she would have had a ten hour head start. Hannah took in a giant breath and let it out. This life was over; time to move on.

She slung the diaper bag over her shoulder, glided the suitcase off the bed and began to shuffle sideways through the door frame when she remembered the crumpled note from beyond the grave.

Almost. Almost.

She slid the heavy suitcase down her leg until it rested on the hardwood, repositioned the diaper bag, bent forward, and retrieved Travis's crumpled note from the floor.

It was then, that Gina finally acknowledged her.

CHAPTER XVIII

THE SOUND OF Gina's saliva as it rocketed from her mouth froze Hannah mid-step. She stood sad, silent, and still, awaiting the damp confirmation through the back of her t-shirt. Hannah slowly turned, placed one hand on each of the wheelchair's arm rests and leaned into her best friend's face; their noses literally inches apart. Gina remained silent, but her eyes, now furious and vibrating, finally met Hannah's dead on. As she stared back into the hollow darkness of Gina's eyes, Hannah suppressed the threatening shiver, veered back, then shot her face forward, violently returning the favor and spitting right into Gina's left eye.

Stepping back, she watched as Gina uncomfortably tried to blink away the acidic retaliation as it slowly streaked down her cheek and dripped onto her housecoat just above Ryen's light curls. Hannah looked on as Gina's brain failed to communicate with her broken body; the inability to just reach up and wipe away the shame was thick and humiliating. As Gina's soiled eye continued to roll in its socket, Hannah gently placed her hand on her friend's forehead and almost affectionately ran it through here roommate's jet black hair. Hannah carefully glided a few strands out from behind Gina's ear and smeared them in the sticky patch dripping under her eye.

Hannah backed off and watched as Ryen's tiny body rose and fell in slumber as she repositioned the diaper bag, lifted the giant suitcase, and made her way downstairs.

Without looking she slid her hand along the kitchen wall,

and blindly grabbed the car keys from the hook when she heard outside sounds inside.

Turning sharply, she stared at the back door.

The wide open back door.

Panicked confusion flip-flopped her thoughts as the luggage dropped from her arms. Hannah was in mid-turn when the first blow came screaming out of her left peripheral, caught her square in the jaw and sent her slamming against the wall.

The room swirled.

The follow up shot turned her stomach inside out and doubled her over as the air exploded from her lungs. Adrenaline and pain tore through panic as Hannah managed to dodge the third blow, wincing as it screamed inches by her face. She lunged for the knife block. Sucking air, her fingertips knocked it over, spilling its contents as her head snapped back. Her scalp burned and an arm wrapped around her waist lifting her off floor. Hannah screamed, thrashed her body and felt her hair tie pull free as she twisted a hand to her attacker's face. Fingernails tearing at eyelids relaxed the grip as Hannah spun her body free and threw herself at the pile of knives a second time. Her attacker went to a sudden Plan B and pushed her from behind, doubling her momentum and sending her smashing stomach-first into the edge of the counter.

Hannah's ribs exploded against the white marble counter top and scattered the knives. She bounced backwards, back towards her mystery attacker, who swatted the back of her head and dropped her to the floor. Hannah turned on her side just in time to see a pair of dirty jeans step and swing a field-goal kick at her ribs. Instinctively, she brought her hands out for the block and inadvertently stuck the paring knife, she didn't even realize she had managed to grab, blade out. The metallic point pierced denim and skin, hit ankle bone, then tore left as the follow-through from the kick still collapsed her arm into her side and lifted her off the ground.

The intruder/attacker screamed and toppled over Hannah. He came crashing to the floor beside her, shouting and grabbing at his punctured leg. A gush of blood emptied onto his shoe. "B-BITCH!" the man sputtered as Hannah blindly poked and stabbed at his legs while he flailed and kicked in her direction.

Ryen's cries slit the kitchen.

Christ, no.

Hannah continued to act in Survival Mode. She forced down the pain of her burning lungs and pushed herself to her feet, charging the staircase.

Gina demanded explanations above Ryen's cries.

Hannah crumpled against the bottom four steps and stole a look back. Her attacker tried to stand, only to topple behind the island and fall back out of view. With one arm clutching her ribs, and the small paring knife locked in her other hand, Hannah shakily began to ascend the large staircase on her hand and knees. Every stair shook her damaged insides.

The breath still refused to come.

Hannah shut out Gina and listened only to Ryen. Saliva dripped from her mouth as she shakily lifted herself from one stair to another. Scuffling noises emitted from the shadows below. In the kitchen, one by one, a pair of gloved hands slapped onto the island's countertop then struggled to pull the rest of the body to a standing position. Hannah blinked away the tears before she turned and improvised a more defensive strategy—one hand nursed her midsection, leaving all her weight on the opposite elbow. Hannah gnashed her teeth and focused on the new rhythm:

Foot
Foot
Elbow
Next stair
Foot
Foot
Elbow

Next stair

Focus on Ryen's screams

Foot

Foot

Elbow

Next stair

The hunched silhouette finally emerged from the shadows. The sight of the dark figure as he crept into the light, armed with a large shimmering steak knife, was something straight out of the movies.

Then it clicked.

This was Kevin Conner.

Kevin Conner wants Gina French

And Kevin Conner.

Kevin Conner wants another child.

Kevin Conner wants Gina's child?

Hannah abandoned her defensive position and bit through the pain as she turned and staggered up the stairs as fast as the explosions in her side would allow. Three stairs later a sharp tug on her pant leg sent her sideways into the railing as she turned and kicked at the blur of hands. She didn't even see the blade strike before it sliced through her pant leg and tore the skin below her knee. The knife pulled clean and whistled through the air as she retracted her limb and the knife stuck into the stair's thin carpet.

The mother/daughter's dueling screams meshed together as Hannah ignored the dark red liquid streaming down her ankle. Conner took a solid kick in the wrist as he slammed the knife down, he missed her ankle but tore through the denim, catching the knife on the thick hem. Hannah shook her leg but the blade was caught and Conner's grip was strong.

Rolling to her stomach with one hand furiously working the button on her jeans, Conner yanked the knife's handle, painfully bumping Hannah down two steps. With the knife still lodged in her pant leg, Conner clamped his free hand onto her back pocket as he continued to pull himself on top of Hannah and her bloodcurdling screams.

Hannah's body jarred as Conner released the knife and latched onto the back of her shirt. She swung the paring knife backwards. He grabbed her thin wrist mid-swing, slammed her hand down onto the stair and held it there. Getting his balance, he sat on her back and curled his free hand into a fist. Hannah felt him deeply inhale and then Kevin Conner went to work.

He savagely punched the base of her neck and shoulders. After the third blow the pain no longer registered.

Hannah's thoughts turned to gravy.

She imagined this exact scenario playing out between Conner and Gina and ending with Gina's twisted, broken body.

First it's my turn.

The punches slowed as Hannah's body melted into the stairs.

Both combatants froze. They panted and waited for the other to make a move.

White pops and flashes danced in the corners of her eyes as Hannah waited for the carpet to stop expanding and contracting in front of her.

He's going to snap my neck, he's going to break my spine, then he's going to kill Gina and then Ryen.

Warm blood ran down her leg and reminded her she wasn't dead; not quite yet.

He will not kill my baby.

Hannah flexed her upper-body into a push-up and sent Conner sideways against the wall. Everything moved in slow motion as she raised her sneaker and shot it back down, stomping her heel into his punctured ankle. It was once again Conner's turn to scream. Hannah rolled to her side, but he refused to let go and they began to dangle precariously, almost spooning, on the stairs. Again she smashed her heel into his ankle. Conner howled in pain, his other hand continued to dig into her wrist while Hannah swallowed and struggled to overcome the overwhelming urge to drop the knife. Hannah screamed along with the blinding pain and ground her heel into the large gash in his ankle.

He is not going to fucking touch you, Ryen.

The second she felt his hand slip from her wrist she drove the paring knife backwards and sunk it into his side. Conner's scream shook the house and momentarily silenced Ryen. He rolled off her back, bumped down three steps and slapped at the handle protruding from the side his stomach. Hannah staggered up the final stairs, collapsed at the top, crawled through the bedroom doorway and left a trail of bloody handprints across the hallway's eggshell carpet. She swung her body around and kicked the door shut just as Conner emerged at the doorway. Conner's body shook the doorframe the second the door closed.

Hannah pulled herself to her knees as Conner kicked the door back open. Reacting before the pain could stop her, Hannah pushed off the floor with her hands and sent her entire body forward, meeting the door halfway, slamming it shut on his elbow. His fingers arched into a claw with the bone crunching impact. Breathing through the pain, Hannah braced her feet against the bottom of the heavy wooden bed and used her throbbing shoulder to hold the door shut on his elbow. He howled in pain. His forearm floated in the room, alone and exposed. Conner pounded his free fist against the other side of the door. Hannah held her ground as she tightly grabbed Conner's index finger and forced it back.

Conner's screams dropped an octave. Hannah's hands fought to isolate his middle finger. Forcing it back, it grinded bone on bone before snapping.

Through the thick door she could heard Conner's body moving and sliding. Hannah wiped the hair from her face and braced against the retaliating blows on the opposite side of the door. She faked for his ring finger but grabbed the pinky instead.

Conner threw himself against his side of the door as he seemed to choke on his own screams.

Conner's door-slaps suddenly sounded more pleading than aggressive.

Hannah wiped the side of her face with her shoulder and wrestled his thumb into position.

The gunshot echoed through the house as the hole in the door splintered just above Hannah's head. The world rang silent as she spun to face Gina and Ryen.

Please God, tell me the shot didn't—

The door pushed Hannah forward then smashed open, nailing her in the ribs and the temple simultaneously. As she floated off balance, Conner booted the door a devastating third time and bashed Hannah in the back of the skull. Her knees buckled and she dropped to the floor. Conner leaned against the door, pushed Hannah's body out of the way and staggered forward into the bedroom. Hannah openly cried as she rolled back and forth on the ground, cradling her head. Conner took another two steps forward, wincing on his tiptoes, while he waved his smoldering gun through the air trying to keep his balance.

Ryen.

"Please."

Ryen.

"Puh—please."

Hannah quietly begged for the child's life as she crawled towards Gina. The knife, still lodged in the hem of her pant leg, scraped and slashed along the hardwood, slowing her down.

"Puh—puh—don't hurt the baby."

Hannah banged her head on the footrest of Gina's wheelchair before she used its large wheel to pull herself to her knees. Conner's eyes silently followed Hannah's painful journey from the door to the wheelchair, then rose from Hannah to Ryen.

Then from Ryen to Gina.

Hannah watched his eyes flash red. He winced and raised his gun in their direction.

Hannah screamed and turned her back to Conner. She covered the shrieking child and ducked her own head into Gina's lap, waiting for the bullets to tear holes in the back of her skull.

PleaseGodpleaseGodpleaseGodpleaseGodpleaseGod.

Ugghhh . . .

Silence.

Gina chuckled.

Hannah twisted at the neck. Conner had stumbled backwards and now clung to the door for support. Blood emptied from the paring knife-sized slit in his stomach. The gun hung at his side. His chin sunk into his shoulders.

The crazy look on his face was for Gina French and Gina French alone.

Hannah breathed through the tension and the pain. Gina chuckled a second time, then exhaled short and choppy through her nose, like she was still amused, but not enough for full-on laughter.

Their eyes remained locked.

Hannah and Ryen were suddenly invisible.

It was time to move.

Hannah painfully raised herself into a hunched position, threw the holder's safety straps and pulled the child from Gina's limp arms. Holding Ryen close, she turned and her own legs gave out. She protected Ryen's tiny head and neck and selflessly let her own battered skull and shoulders strike the floor. Dark stars fluttered around her. The baby's cries sounded underwater. Feeling her contentiousness flicker and spark, she rolled to her side on the red-smeared floor, cradled the infant and gently sobbed baby words of encouragement with her back to the killer.

Hannah listened as Conner and Gina ignored the pair of them.

The silence continued.

Their loud inhales and exhales remained in unison.

Hannah slid herself along the floor towards the bed's headboard. She locked her eyes on Conner's gun and slowly pulled the white blanket to the floor.

Conner steadied himself against the doorframe and somehow remained oblivious to her actions and Ryen's cries. She wrapped Ryen's trembling body in the comforter and began to quietly coax the terrified little girl.

She could hear Gina's choppy nose-snickers but didn't dare take her eyes away from Conner's gun and Conner, whose face was a sordid mixture of anger, skepticism and surprise accomplishment.

Conner turned his head to the room's empty corner and nodded.

Gina's nose-breathing became louder and took back his attention.

Gina's head hung forward, her eyes were murky and snakelike as she peered across the room through her spit-sticky black bangs.

Gina French spoke:

"Be honest, Conner."

A smirk slowly spread across her face.

"How much of that damage is from me, and how much is from my roommate? Gimme a girl-to-girl ratio if you can."

Hannah's jaw dropped.

She wanted to run over and backhand silence into Gina's mouth, but Conner beat her to it.

Gina was in the middle of using basic mathematics to mock the irregular angle of his nose when Conner pushed himself off of the door and stumbled towards her as it slammed shut behind him.

Gina looked amused as he feebly teetered forward. Three strides deep, his leg gave out, but Conner lunged forward and smashed the butt of the gun into Gina's jaw as he crumpled beside her on the floor. Hannah flinched, the wheelchair rocked, and Gina's head snapped back and rolled forward again.

Gina's eyes watered and her jaw trembled until her jaw snapped open, popping free her top two teeth from her bottom lip. Long dark strands of thin blood dripped from her now pouty lip as Gina probed her tongue into the pair of small, but deep tooth-sized holes.

Hannah hugged Ryen deep and covered her little face from the carnage.

Gina's bottom lip disappeared inside her mouth, letting it fill with blood before she released it all at once. Hannah watched in disgust as some of it trickled down the front of her robe and the rest splattered onto the floor in front of her feet.

Gina started laughing.

Hannah snapped her head back to get Conner's reaction. He shook with pain as he crawled back over to the foot of the bed.

"Get up!" Gina spat, "Get up! What the fuck can you possibly do to me?"

Conner silently nodded to the room's empty corner a second time before he pulled himself into a sitting position and leaned against the side of the bed. Gina's laughter returned and rocked the small room as she spat blood on the floor in Conner's direction. He kept nodding at nothing as he popped open the gun's chamber, rotated it, and clicked it shut.

Hannah and Ryen remained on the floor at the head of the bed, while Conner sat sideways directly in front of them, leaning against the bed's bottom corner. Conner had positioned himself directly between Hannah and the only exit. If she tried to escape she would have to crawl right between Gina and Conner, or try to sneak behind him—over the bed. Either way, she had an armful of baby and Conner had already tried to shoot her in the head. Hannah's only option was to wait. She clutched her side.

Gina's laughter died down as she continued using her tongue to flick tiny droplets of blood onto the hardwood floor. "Bitch!" she yelled at Conner, who still busied himself with the gun.

"Bitch, look at me!"

Her tight lipped smirk stretched into a mouthy grin. Every tooth was framed red with blood. The ends of her hair that hung in her face dipped and stuck against her gums. Her dead eyes hauntingly peered through the black strands.

"It took you how many months to get back to me, and THAT'S your opener?" Gina spat the bloody hair away from her mouth and continued, "A pistol whip? Are you serious? I sit here month after month daydreaming about the moment the great baby-napping Kevin Conner would burst through that very door branding a-a flamethrower? Or . . . or . . . a rocket launcher?"

Conner stared at Gina. Hannah stared at Conner. Two cooperative and three limp fingers applied pressure to the hole in his stomach. His other hand dangled the gun. His lips remained shut.

"At the very least, I pictured you exploding into this room and chewing up the walls with a rifle or an Uzi."

Silence.

Gina suddenly screamed the sound of gunfire.

"BANGBANGBANGBANGBANG."

Both Conner and Hannah jumped.

Gina inhaled and loudly exhaled another mouthful of blood and rocked with arrogant laughter.

"Instead, instead, you come crawling in here, on your hands and knees, unable to stand . . . and you pistol-whip me? You bloody my teeth and you call it a day? A job well done?"

His eyes slipped from the empty corner and back to Gina before his bloody hand fumbled a baby blanket from the foot of the bed. The tiny cloth slipped through his non-responsive fingers which triggered another dose of Gina's wet laughter. Suddenly the gun was moving. Hannah's body tensed as she prepared to dive across the bed to safety but Conner was merely fumbling and fighting with the cloth as he wrapped it around his slashed leg. The gun pointed to the floor as he tried to tighten it. Hannah watched his finger slide off the trigger as he struggled the blanket into a knot.

Jumpforit-grabit . . .

Gina's dark laughter abruptly turned to silence as her eyes bulged. She was choking.

Gina's gag reflex shook her throat and she violently coughed large clumps of blood down the front of her already soiled housecoat. She loudly cleared her throat before the grin returned. Her faint, childlike giggling soiled the room once again. Conner, through gritted teeth, stretched the blanket tight around the chewed-up section of his leg. Hannah exhaled after what seemed like a decade. She could feel pieces of her shattered ribs floating freely inside her, cutting and piercing everything internal. She held Ryen close and continued to mentally plead with the crippled laugh track.

Gina, please, PLEASE shut UP. Someone HAD to have heard the gunshot. Help is on the way. Just. Shut. Up.

Gina's giggles faded. The verbal castration resumed.

"Look at you Conner. Look. At. Your. Self." A tiny spray of blood spotted her robe as she hung on the F in "self".

"Geez, you gotta stop going toe-to-toe with all these women. I mean, what would your boyfriends in prison say if they could see this?"

Conner swallowed hard.

Hannah pulled Ryen closer to her chest and concentrated.

SHUT THE FUCK UP GINA.

Conner's finger slipped back onto the trigger as Gina's momentum built.

"Make no mistake about it, there's nothing humiliating about taking a beating from me, but her—her?" Gina rolled her bloodshot eyes in Hannah's direction.

Hannah slowly shook her head and desperately mouthed

NO at her friend. Gina remained emotionless through Hannah's tears.

Silence.

Hannah's skin began to crawl. She could feel Conner's gaze. She twisted her head back and reaffirmed that Conner who, for the first time since he locked eyes with Gina, had indeed, once again become aware of Hannah and Ryen's presence in the room.

Hannah shook the hair from her face and stared back at Gina with pleading eyes.

YOUR BABY, YOU STUPID BITCH, HE'S GOING TO KILL YOUR BABY!

Gina stared right through Hannah. "When my roommate uglied you up, now THAT—that was humiliating."

"Look at her. She's a waitress, Conner. A cute-as-a-button, coffee-pouring, pencil in the hair-bun, ripping your bill off a giant pad of paper and slapping it down on the table, welcome to 1952, Goddamn waitress."

Hannah tried to scream, tried to beg, but her throat had collapsed into itself, Her streaming eyes continued to plead with her roommate.

WHATTHEHELLAREYOUDOING? THIS IS YOUR CHILD!

Gina's bottom lip disappeared inside her mouth and she stared blankly back at Hannah.

Hannah wiped her eyes on the baby-hiding comforter then rolled them up to the ceiling, hoping whatever spiritual third party was watching this unfold would take pity on the baby, if no one else. Hannah slowly dropped her gaze back to Gina whose unwavering stare continued. Hannah lifted the little bundle underneath her chin and mouthed, "Ryen."

Gina's empty stare didn't break, but she pursed her lips into a kiss and blew it in Hannah's direction, arching another stream of blood onto her own legs. Her bottom lip once again disappeared under her row of top teeth.

Is she chewing her lip?

Conner began to move.

Hannah and Gina both turned their attention to the forgotten guy holding the gun. Conner had resumed nodding towards the bedroom's empty corner.

Gina dropped her voice, "They will fry you this time, Kevin Conner."

Silence.

Gina rolled her eyes to the empty wall, then back to Conner.

"Am I boring you, Big Kev?"

No reply came, instead every hair on Hannah's arms raised as Kevin Conner slowly watched nothing cross the room.

His jaw trembled and his wide eyes found a new location to fix upon—the empty space right above Gina French's black bangs. The girls watched as Conner came to terms with this strange new location before his eyes crept down and met Gina's.

It was Gina who finally released a giant, bloody huff.

It was Gina, who now seemed bored.

Once again she seemed to choose her words extremely carefully before she finally committed. Her dead eyes glanced to the side, then back at Conner.

"The whole time I worked at that prison, the years I spent wiping snotty noses and babysitting society's . . . " Gina seemed lost for the appropriate term, her eyes bounced back and forth before she curled the side of her mouth and settled on, "degenerate scum." Seemingly satisfied she continued with a dark intensity, "I never once thought of you things on the other side of the bars as people, as human beings." Now smiling, she squinted at Conner. "You have no idea what it feels like peering into those dirty cells, counting all of your sad little faces, all these super star macho men who thought they were something—such bravado reduced to a number, a barcode, each one more pathetic than the last."

Hannah closed her eyes, cleared away the tears, and questioned her friend's obvious suicide mission.

He's going to shoot you, but then what? What about the two of us? What about your daughter?

Waiting was no longer an option.

Hannah locked her eyes on Conner and painfully got one hand on the wall and her feet flat to the floor. Hopefully she could launch herself with enough momentum to carry the two of them over the bed and to the door.

Over the bed, through the door, down the stairs, outside, scream, scream, and scream, don't look back. If I can make it to the fence, I'll drop Ryen into the neighbor's shrubs.

Gina's tongue pushed her bottom lip away from her teeth as blood trickled from the giant moat. Conner squinted into the nothingness above her.

"No reaction, huh?"

Gina huffed and rolled her eyes again.

"Goddammit. Seriously, cards on the table. You made it this long, all this time. you ran from the police, you tracked me down, you let my burger-flipping roommate kick you upside down a few times so—so what? So you could sit there and listen as I read my diary aloud? If you came here to do something, I'm guessing that right about now would be the time to do it. Or are you going to just sit there and bleed to death with a stupid look on your face and for CHRISTSAKE—I'M DOWN HERE! What in the blue Hell are you staring at?"

"SHUT UP!" Conner screamed

Hannah jumped. Her ribs exploded. She swallowed hard.

"SHUTUPSHUTUP." He waved his gun in her face.

The yelling shook Ryen awake. Big brown eyes met Hannah's.

Gina emptied her mouth and beamed with approval.

Conner struggled to stand, his gun waived as he screamed at her, thick saliva popped with the hard consonants.

"You came after me, you stupid little girl, I never did shit to you but you came after me then lied about the child and now there's no other way to end this cause I ain't going back to prison a pedophile. Jesus Christ woman, just knowing you is a fucking prison in itself, you horrible, awful little bitch!"

Gina released her bottom lip and smiled a sticky smile of success.

Above Ryen's returning cries the words, "lied about the child," bleached Hannah's brain.

Oh. My. God. Gina.

Conner sneered into the air above Gina's head as he randomly waived his gun around the room. "Look at me? Oh no, kid—LOOK AT YOU! Look at this place, look at where you live! Aw, the poor little white girl gets hurt so let's make life as easy as possible for her—here's a mansion; I hope it's big enough for your servants to wheel your busted ass around in—"

Conner's gun suddenly angled towards Hannah.

GOD.

Her legs gave out from under her and she crashed to the floor, protecting Ryen from another gunshot that never came. Conner's weapon was nothing more than a prop as he pointed it at the large bristle board that hung above Hannah on the wall beside the bed. Dozens of push pins held up dozens of photos.

The Showcase.

Gina's darkly amused grin stayed constant. Playing along, her eyes floated above her terrified roommate and her own shrieking offspring as Conner began to point his gun at every individual polaroid.

A young Gina beside her uniformed brothers.

A goofy grinned Gina in front of the academy.

Hannah in a wicker chair, covered in cats.

A sweaty and puffy Gina in a hospital bed. A newborn angel in her arms.

Gina and Hannah at high school graduation.

Gina standing on a park bench proudly holding two open bottles of beer in outstretched arms, chest sticking out, face in the sky, "I'm Flying Jack," scribbled across the top in thick blue marker.

Ryen in a tiny pink dress.

Hannah lifting Gina's shirt from behind, revealing the words "Sexy Bitch" carefully sketched across Gina's stomach in lipstick block letters as patrons of the crowded bar unknowingly swirl around them.

The pictures went on and on.

Incredulously, Conner wiped his mouth and jammed the gun back at memory lane.

"You had every opportunity in the world, everything handed to you, and you fucked it away—"

"You don't—" Gina snapped before stopping herself. The shot had been fired and the nerve had clearly been hit. Hannah watched Conner succeed where she had failed. He had rattled Gina French, knocked her from her game plan. Gina tried to gloss over her overreaction by quickly composing herself and slyly countered, "You poor folk think you've cornered the market on all things unfair, doncha? Like you're all expected to screw up, like society owes the poor people, who don't murder and rob each other a service award for—for just not using their poverty as a crutch."

Gina's tone faltered to a horribly offensive over-the-top Ebonic slur, "I's sorry I stoe da car. I's sorry I dealt da drugs. I gots no choice. I ain't gots no daddy and my mamma and I's poe." Gina seethed, her voice shifted back to normal. "I've had to listen to that same story day after day my entire career, and guess what? Uh-uh."

Hannah lay on the floor unable to move. Her tears fell sideways; her insides flared and churned. She wanted to get back into her crouching position but her body flat-out refused. Ryen breathlessly sobbed, still shaken from the fall.

Gina flicked her bottom lip and sneered in disgust.

"When I was nine years-old, I lay in my bed and listened as my father came home from work. I wanted to see him, see my dad, but I assumed he would be angry at me for still being awake, so I tiptoed down the hall and stood outside my parents' bedroom door. I heard him place his gun and badge on the dresser. But then I heard something else."

Another thick strand of blood oozed down her chin.

"My father was crying. He was weeping and my mother was comforting him. I stood in the dark hallway and listened as my father whimpered and sobbed. The stories he told my mother that night ended my childhood right then and there. I stood there and listened to story after story after story about child abuse and domestic violence and people bound and beaten and robbed and raped and shattered skulls and missing eyes and mutilated genitals, and my dad—as strong and as big as he was—couldn't overcome it. It was too much for him. I was nine. I was nine and I learned the world was starting to collapse."

A single red dot dripped from her chin.

"So I watched it fall."

Her mouth curled at the sides.

"I let every horrible documented injustice sink in. The rest of the world? It went numb."

A dense strand separated mid-drip and another red spot appeared on her housecoat.

"But not me. I processed it all."

Gina cleared her throat and spat onto the floor. She paused to rub her tongue against her top teeth, smearing them with a fresh coat of sticky red.

"I was nine when my dad realized that nothing could stop the downward spiral. As long as the planet spun, children would cry in pain and babies would starve and husbands would beat their wives and people would be tortured for amusement, and strangers would fuck other strangers, and people would kill for food and for fun, and year after year, crime after crime, it would slowly become . . . common. Expected. Accepted."

Gina's tongue sank into the wound, its tip completely disappearing as her anger dripped back into a disturbing, stringy smile.

"But that's not the worst of it."

The smile vanished.

"That night I was too young to understand. My father had seen things no human being should be forced to see, yet he knew that was the price tag attached to his job. My father was a superhero, he was larger than life, but the terror that laced his words that night eventually embarrassed me. Made me pity his shortcomings. That night my father was petrified of something bigger than the crimes themselves and it wasn't until I held my own daughter that I finally understood."

Gina squinted.

"His fear was for me."

Her lips puckered.

"They know that people like you are waiting in the shadows, and because of people like you—no cop wants a daughter."

Hannah's eyes shot to Conner as his hand flashed silver. The revolver began a slow journey from The Showcase back to Gina who met it with a smile.

"That's right Kev, silence me with violence. Stick with Plan A, lash out at the first sign of conflict then act surprised when you're reprimanded."

Tears surged down his face.

"Really, you're gonna cry now? You're gonna cry now because you know I'm right?"

Conner's mouth became a thin line, the tears continued.

"You chopped your parents into splinters—what did you honestly expect was going to happen to you? I don't care what they did to you, I don't care if you got the green bike Christmas morning when you wanted the red one. I don't care if your oatmeal had lumps, don't care if they made you wear a dress and sing show tunes for the neighbors —here is how the world works: no one cares why you did something horrendous, they only care that you did something horrendous."

Hannah burned with each scathing syllable. She watched as Conner inexplicably nodded along with Gina's self-congratulating story, but her stomach dropped with the realization that Conner wasn't actually agreeing with Gina, he was agreeing with the empty space above her head.

"Life gave it to me hard and I took it and took it and took it and my shoulders never sagged, not even after—"

The two women locked eyes before Gina finished.

"Not even after they cut me open and pulled the cancer out of my back."

A calmness fell over the room as Conner and Ryen vanished and the moment belonged only to Gina and Hannah. Hannah swallowed and flashed a sad smile as Gina talked about it for the first time in fifteen months.

"Six months pregnant and terrified, still getting routine Hep checks and I can feel the kickin', but something isn't right with my back. Then came the numbness and the constant peeing, and when they showed me the x-rays and told me that the tumor had already spread, that the tumor had wrapped itself around my spine—around my fucking spine—I didn't feel sorry for myself. I didn't go public with it. I didn't rally support, or pin little ribbons on my clothes, because—"

Hannah silently mouthed Gina's cancer creed in unison.

"I would rather be fucking dead than pitied."

Hannah's eyes emptied down her cheeks.

Gina glanced down at her blood soaked housecoat covered body then back up to Hannah.

"Oh, they tried to scare me with their little charts and facts and statistics and threw around terms like limited mobility . . . "

Those two words produced the smallest flash of a smile.

" . . . and the little doctors sugarcoated the possibility of a quote: 'negative outcome'." Gina's somber eyes slowly bubbled.

"They slice me open and they tear it out, and they sew me up, and they show me a picture of it, and I've never hated anything so much in my life. Five days later I'm back at home and while I didn't have a stroke and I didn't go blind, walking was a bitch—but I rehabbed like a motherfucker, didn't I, roomie?"

Hannah blinked her eyes and faintly nodded. She had only heard Gina use this tone of voice once before, right before they sedated her for surgery and it scared the hell out of her. This was how someone reacted to the beginning of the end.

"They warned me to wait a few months, to be careful bending, no twisting or lifting. But I'm Gina French—I can't take it slow. So I rehabbed right away, every damn day. I rehabbed until I walked, until I jogged. I jogged until I gave birth. Then it was on to the next problem, then the one after that, then the one after that, and the one after that, because that's what I do. And I cut a pace that no one can match and when everything is clicking, even when everyone has counted me out, I spread my wings and Gina French fucking soars."

The tone abruptly changed cocky. The attitude reappeared full force. The moment had ended and Gina's fierce eyes were back on Conner.

"Cancer, paralysis, it's all the same, so Kevin Conner, baby stealer, parent killer, if you came here to do what I assume you are going to do, do it now."

Conner's eyes shimmered as they snapped from above Gina to Gina. Up and then down.

"See Conner, you broke me, but as we sit here, I promise you this. I'm going to get better."

Up and down.

"Yesterday morning I woke up and my toes were numb. I couldn't move them but I was aware of them. That was the beginning."

Up and down

"You can throw all the medical statistics in the world at me, but I'm going to heal, Conner. If it takes me two, five, twenty years. I'm going to walk out of this chair and out that door. And if you are still alive, I will find you."

Up and down.

287

"And let me remove any doubt you may have. I will kill you."

Up and down.

"Just to prove that I can."

Up and down.

"This is the one chance you are going to get. I'm right here and I'm unable to fight back this time, but deep down, we both know . . ."

Gina cut a wide toothy smile. A strand of bloody saliva dangled from the middle of her bottom lip.

"You won't do it. You'll drop the ball."

Up an down.

"See, you're not special in any way. You're a carbon copy. Everyone is so embarrassingly easy to set off. If you prod someone long enough, wind someone up tight enough, they will lose all gray area and their little world will become black and white."

Up and down.

"And then they react, and it's so fucking spectacular."

Up and down.

"The world spins because it's full of two types of people: those who use other people, and those who allow themselves to be used. When the weak finally realize they're being manipulated, it's THAT MOMENT they always retaliate, only they have no idea how to go about it."

Up and down.

"And that's when the bad things happen."

Up and down.

"That's why there's newborn babies in dumpsters. That's why schools get shot up."

The bloody saliva strand broke and fell to her thigh.

"Because people can't deal."

Up and down.

"And then there's me"

Up and down

"You can break my jaw, you can break my spine, you can give me cancer, you can beat me like a dog."

Gina's eyes fell to the floor.

"Hell, you can crush my bones into tomato soup."

Conner's endless nodding froze.

"But I will always come back and win"

Conner leaned closer, suddenly extremely interested and enraged.

Gina paused, took a deep breath as her mouth emptied and dribbled off her chin before her eyes slowly ascended and peeked at him through matted black bangs.

"I will never cave . . . "

Gina's voice dropped to a whisper.

" . . . under pressure."

Conner detonated forward catching Gina by the throat. He tipped her chair backwards, sending her back-first to the floor. Hannah screamed in pain as she pushed herself off the ground and stumbled forward clutching Ryen in her arms.

Gina made gurgling noises as Conner's accelerated inhales and exhales escaped between gritted teeth.

Hannah's ribs flared as she frantically readjusted the baby and the pain forced her to the ground.

As her knee hit the floor she saw it. The gun.

She looked up at Conner who was on all fours; the palm of his two-fingered hand supported his weight as his other remained clamped around Gina's throat.

Gina's gurgles were raspy and faint. Conner's screams continued endlessly.

Hannah snatched the gun and a hollow shriek escaped with all the air in her lungs as she snapped to her feet and swung one leg forward on her tiptoes. Without preparing herself for the inevitable burst of pain, she spun her body sideways and shifted Ryen under her left arm, the furthest place possible from the gun, as she cocked it and stuck it behind Conner's ear.

Gina's eyes remained open and bore into Conner.

Hannah's mind raced, her ribs screamed. She wasn't sure how Conner would react to the gun, but she thought at least he would react to the gun.

Gina's gurgles became choppy. Her eyes bulged. Hannah jammed the gun harder into Conner's skull, but neither said a word. Ryen screamed and struggled in the darkness of the blanket. Gina's eyes slowly faded. Her lips remained tight and serious. Gina concentrated on dying. Her eyes began to float upwards. Hannah mumbled, "I'll-I'll . . . "

Not even a full threat.

Conner did nothing. Hannah did nothing. Gina continued to die. Ryen continued to wail. The veins in Conner's arm threatened to burst with every pulse and Hannah could see the large red marks where the skin of Gina's neck stretched above his glove. Hannah's finger quivered on the trigger. Kill the killer? Or let him kill the monster that used to be her best friend? Ryen's little arm escaped and slapped at Hannah's damaged side. The flinch caused by pain almost pulled the trigger by accident. Gina's eyes were slits now, showing no pupil, only white. Hannah was pulling the trigger in her mind, but her finger refused to respond. Conner grunted and leaned into Gina, applying more pressure and crushing her neck just a little more. The wheezing stopped. Gina's eyes closed. Her head relaxed.

Nothing.

Ryen landed another blow to Hannah's side and then went quiet.

Gina didn't move.

Her robe had pulled open during the fall.

Gina's stomach no longer rose and fell.

Conner held on a few more seconds before collapsing onto his elbow and raising his busted hand off the ground. His "stranglehand" slid limp and lay on Gina's shoulder. Hannah followed Conner's movement, keeping the gun pressed behind his ear. He slowly turned his head. The gun folded his ear, then slid against his temple and was heading for his forehead when Gina's eyes snapped open and her body desperately sucked air, her chest heaved as it tried to force oxygen through her crushed throat and feed her brain.

Conner slumped back on top of Gina and clamped his large hand around her neck a second time as Hannah readjusted the gun back behind his ear. Gina gurgled and her bloodshot eyes suddenly snapped from Conner to Hannah.

They started wide, then slowly relaxed back to their normal size.

Hannah searched Gina for answers, guidance, sorrow, but only found an unmistakable look of curiosity.

A curious tinge that framed her horrible smirk.

That fucking horrible smirk.

Hannah's finger slid off the trigger.

Gina's eyes rolled up into her skull and again, the heaving stopped.

Seconds turned to minutes, but Conner didn't release her throat. No one wanted a repeat performance. He made sure she was good and dead.

Hannah's mind repeated self-defense over and over as she prepared to shoot Conner at the first sudden movement towards her or the baby, but he remained on his knees, his head slumped forward with the gun aimed at the back of his skull—execution style. Hannah imagined spraying his brains out the front of his face, showering Gina with a final crimson goodbye.

Ryen, with one free arm jutting out into the open, cooed warmly under the blanket.

Self-defense. Self-defense. Self-defense.

As Hannah focused on a spot at the back of Conner's skull, she noticed the trembling.

Conner slowly rotated his head towards Hannah.

Sobbing through clenched eyes.

The pain in Hannah's ribs ripped through her body as her numb arm forced her to readjust Ryen for the hundredth time. Her finger momentarily slipped off the trigger as she swallowed hard. Conner's clenched eyes turned to face her.

Mucus dripped from his nose and drool from his chin. He violently sobbed, but his eyes remained locked tight.

Is he waiting for me to shoot him? He's afraid to open his eyes. He doesn't even know I'm here. He's ill. He's—

Still sobbing, Conner's puffy eyes crept open.

The barrel of Gina's gun stared back into his face.

Hannah braced herself for the verbal part of the inevitable exchange but Conner prolonged it as he stared vacantly through the immediate threat of death. His eyes crept over to Hannah; his face unreadable. He carefully closed his eyes and slowly reopened them. They trembled. He ploddingly rolled them to the left. Hannah watched as the sobs of relief shuddered his body. His eyes moved back, briefly met Hannah's, then searched right. All the air emptied from his lungs as he lightly chuckled through squinted eyed. His head swung back and forth, his vision swept the entire room. After Conner's sixth or seventh visual tour ended, his head fell back and he rocked with laughter.

Ryen cooed.

Hannah held steady; the gun remained at his puffy-red eye.

Conner's fits of laughter escalated as his eyes, now warm with affection, returned to Hannah.

Hannah struggled to keep her stance. The .38 shook.

Conner, long past worrying about his injuries, laughed away as the thick redness continued to drain from his open wounds and pooled around his limp fingers.

Yet Kevin Conner was suddenly on top of the world.

Under the blanket, Ryen joined in and began to giggle.

This is so fucked.

Ryen's laughter made Conner laugh even harder. Happy tears streamed down his face. He let his body relax and he slumped backwards, the back of his head crashed against the side of Gina's wheelchair.

He winced and shook his head, the laughter unbroken. Conner continued to ignore the gun. He slowly raised his arms and pointed his hands to the empty corners of the room. On one hand, his middle finger extended. A look of concern finally silenced the laughter as he turned his attention to his other hand. The three fingers slumped loose and incorrect, explaining why he was only flipping-off one corner of the room. He brought his busted hand towards his face for a closer inspection and the laughter began again.

Hannah took a step back; the gun still pointing towards the giggling killer on the floor.

Trembling, Conner wrapped his arms around himself. The back of his busted hand forced pressure against the stab wound in his side while his good hand slipped down his blood drenched pant leg. Although he was still very amused, he no longer seemed able to laugh away the pain. Looking up at Hannah, he began to rock himself back and forth. His creepy smile remained.

He was done.

He rested his head against the giant wheel of Gina's overturned wheelchair and tried to make himself as comfortable as possible. His eyes drooped. His whole body seemed to beg for slumber.

It was over.

Hannah regrouped and used both hands, including the one with the gun, to properly position the child's weight against her hip. Ryen, apparently in on the joke, continued to giggle softly.

A flashing pain in her ribs reminded Hannah of her need for medical attention. She slowly moved the revolver back in Conner's direction and took her second step backwards.

She waited for Conner's response.

None came.

He remained in his slumped position using the dead as a pillow.

He had laughed so hard and so long he was hiccupping.

Conner's wondering gaze drifted back to Hannah and he nodded. His self-hug still intact. His smile disturbingly elated.

What did you do to this guy, Gina?

This killer?

Hannah took another step back.

She focused out the pain.

One more step found her back flush against the door. She blindly fumbled behind her waist, working the smooth doorknob with her gun hand. The metal of the revolver repeatedly clinked against the brass knob.

Just as the door unlatched, Conner made a sudden movement and Hannah winced as Ryen shifted and her body shook with pain. Hannah exhaled loudly and jammed the .38 back in the killer's direction.

Conner pulled a soggy red pack of cigarettes from his jacket pocket. He snorted as he squeezed it with his fist, sending blood—his blood—dripping from the package onto his pants.

Squeezed it like it was Gina French's neck.

Hannah turned and pressed her body and Ryen against the door. She rotated the handle with her baby-hand as she kept the gun pointed at Conner. She forced down another surge of agony as the locking mechanism released. The door creaked to life as Hannah walked forward, still facing Conner—who grinned as the door glided wider and wider behind her.

Then the screaming began.

The decibel level of the absolutely inhuman guttural sounds that came from Kevin Conner erased the pain from her ribs as he leaped to his feet—his wide eyes locked on the empty doorway behind her. His look of absolute unfiltered terror paralyzed her. His injuries were suddenly gone and he charged forward. His eyes staring past her and into the hallway.

Hannah steadied herself as Conner screamed towards her, the sharp smell of urine seared her nostrils.

SHOOT

His eyes threatened to pop from his skull as the inhuman noises tore through her sanity and he closed the gap between them.

SHOOT

SHOOT

He was five feet away and still coming. His incoherent cries firing past her, not at her.

SHOOTSHOOTSHOOT

She squinted and fired.

Ryen screamed.

Hannah snapped her eyes open just as Conner closed his mouth around the smoking barrel of Gina French's .38 and slapped both his hands at the base of the revolver, forcing the trigger a second time.

EPILOGUE

"**I'M GONNA PEE** my pants," Hannah whispered to the open road as she mentally kicked herself for not using the restroom half an hour ago when she had stopped for gas. With the next town at least forty-five minutes away and at this time of the night, bathroom availability was a little unpredictable.

She then made a brash decision her recently deceased best friend would have called, "very Un-Hannahish."

She managed to push pause on the stereo right after the, "Your mystery was all in your touch, you knew my history and we both got crushed" line of the best song on her playlist.

The car slowed to a stop on the shoulder while she cursed the empty size large styrofoam coffee cup. Hannah giggled to herself as she caressed the side of the cup before flicking on the hazard lights. As she reached for the door handle she slowly stuck her head in the backseat and listened to the sounds of Ryen sighing in her sleep. The little angel was snuggled comfortably inside her baby seat, the smoothest blanket Hannah could find tucked warmly around her. The Cadillac of blankets, she called it.

She smiled, popped the handle and slid into the cool summer night. She began to walk behind the car while the song looped in her head. She was happy to live in a world where technology gave you options past the car's radio. Hannah had quickly grown tired of the constant news interruptions. Despite the actions of her deceased roommate it was still hard to digest the news that Baby Amber's parents finally confessed and led the officials to the shallow grave in their own backyard. A tiny life snuffed out by monsters. Her thoughts returned to the backseat of her car and its slumbering contents. A slight breeze kicked up some dust and she ran a hand up her shirt checking the tightly wrapped tape. She remembered how Ryen had laughed through a never-ending game of peek-a-boo with the doctor whose diagnosis revealed two important things about herself:

Number One: her floating ribs were not in fact floating freely insider of her, shredding her guts as they drifted freely. In actuality, one rib was barely cracked.

And Number Two: when it came to pain, she was a complete pussy.

The uncomfortable need to urinate carefully guided her into the steep ditch. Raising the car keys above her head she triggered the automatic lock and popped the button on her jeans. She never ever thought she'd live the cliché, "just happy to be alive," but she was definitely living it now. She strained to hear oncoming traffic, but the highway was empty. Hannah held her breath, pulled her jeans around her ankles and crouched. After relieving herself from what seemed like a dozen large cups of coffee, she jumped up and down and threaded the button. A giggle escaped her lips. She knew full well she'd pay for the bouncing jubilation later, once the pain-killers wore off, but at that moment, Hannah didn't care. This was her moment and it was truly worthy of some sort of secret victorious gesture. She had turned a monumental page in her young life; one that was long overdue.

Finally, she was living in the present.

Falling silent she listened for Ryen's cries or approaching traffic. Nothing broke the beautiful silence. She began Part Two. Hannah dug into her jacket pocket and removed the large folded mess of dog-eared papers and smoothed open the memoirs of the dead. She had found Conner's pages on the stairs but didn't get a chance to skim through them until arriving at the hospital's emergency waiting room. As for Travis, she already had his final thoughts committed to memory.

Hannah crept out of the ditch, back to the car, popped the passenger side door and pushed the cigarette lighter. She chewed her hangnail and hummed the chorus until the lighter eventually popped.

Holding the silver cylinder like a cigarette itself, she quickly let the red dot guide her back into the ditch. She carefully pulled Gina's gun from her other pocket and sloppily wrapped it in the journals before dipping the lighter against every available corner. The crudely wrapped offering created a giant flame for all of four seconds before the paper charred, fell away, and smoldered onto the ground. Using the end of her sleeve as a makeshift glove, Hannah used her covered thumb and index finger as tweezers as she lifted the gun and hurled it deep into the bushes.

Would that really have burned off the finger prints?

Screw it. Should have watched more forensic crime dramas.

She stomped the puffy black char into the dirt.

Life was about to get interesting. She would continue to drive and drive, but eventually, inevitably, someone would find her and questions would be asked. She smiled as she scraped the bottom of her shoes along the rough highway. She'd answer their questions, but she had from now until then to get her stories straight and she didn't need a little thing like the truth to contradict her version of the events. Whatever she eventually decided they would be.

Gently clicking the car door shut, she glanced back at Ryen who didn't even flinch as the automatic lock announced their safety. The precious little gift more than justified Hannah's newfound selfishness.

Her version of the truth would be the one that benefited her and her daughter.

Hannah turned the engine, threw on the signal light, and veered back onto the empty highway.

Whenever she got to wherever she was headed the first call she would make would be to Aunt Kat. Or a publicist.

Hannah carefully removed her coffee from the holder with three fingers and her thumb, hitting PLAY with her middle finger as the cup passed the stereo. The music surged back to life.

"So while you're sitting here waiting for your colorful day, I'll watch mine pale in comparison with 12 shades of grey."

ACKNOWLEDGEMENTS

FEBRUARY, 2007, I blew the dust off of a very skeletal four-year-old writing project. I sat down with my laptop at Broadway Roastery and started pushing keys. "Hey world, I'm a writer" I was living the dream. I wrote the last page of (what would become) Draft One that November. If I knew what lay ahead of me—if I knew how truly broken and defeated the journey to publication would make me feel until the day I signed my contract with Kraken Press, I might have saved my tears and my liver and just scrapped the entire project. So right out of the gate I have to thank George C Cotronis, Max Booth III, and the rest of the amazing staff and support staff within Kraken Press for picking up Gina French and running with it. For supporting it. For believing in it. When I found Kraken Press and saw Cotronis's artwork my mind was simultaneously blown and made up. Kraken Press HAD to be the home for Gina French and I am so grateful I got my wish. Thank. You. Kraken. Press. All of my love to my wife and my best friend, Kazia. Your support was essential. Writing at this level requires a certain amount of selfishness and you did nothing but champion me during my years of private coffee drenched writing, rewriting and editing marathons. You know how people supposedly have a "devil" on one shoulder and an "angel" on the other? Danielle Korol was, is, and continues to be both. This book would have never seen the light of the day without her unfiltered advice. Special thanks to B. Shewkenek, Jonathan McNeil, Russell Isinger and Diane Nelson for, at four very different times in my life, saw something in me I didn't see in myself, and to Brock Andrews, Wes Funk, Kurt Dahl, Ian Goodwillie and Scott Kowalchuk for the advice and kind words along the way. For

Neil Fink and Jessica Babyck. You two know what you are to me and Jessica gave me the line "I can't stand people who are above getting even." I thought about that statement often. Although they will inevitably claim they did nothing, Jay Neufeld and the dedicated crew from "Stripped Down: The Music Show" literally chased away my crazies on a weekly basis. When things were their bleakest I would count down the days until it was Wednesday, knowing I would be surrounded by these amazing people who would instantly make me laugh and keep me going as I kept this book a secret from everyone. Their youthful enthusiasm played a bigger part in my life than they will ever know, so to Jay, Sal Accardo, Davis Baker, Caitlyn Barton, Patrick Brannen, Jordan "The Biz" Bzdel, Ian Cameron, Laura Churchman, Bennet Dobni, Douglas Evans, Dylan Evans, Jenna Giacomelli, Jesse Gordon, Spencer Gordon, Amanda Haughey, Tessa Hinz, Jennifer Juba, Brynn Krysa, Adan Lemus, Kathryn Morlock, Alex Stooshinoff, Mae Trohak, Zach Unger, Colton Wall and Alexa Woroniuk—again, I say, "thank you", as I walk with Big Legs. And finally, I have to thank Natasha Alexandra; a talented musician who goes by the stage-name NLX. If this book had a soundtrack—it would be her entire library of songs. It's no surprise that as I wrote something as dark as Gina French is NOT a Waste of Roofies, I was constantly inspired by a collection of raw tracks that would later be mastered and released under the album title Bitch Get Fit. The lyrics that end the book belong to NLX. Check her out—nlxmusic.com

AUTHOR BIO

Curtis Anderson is like the third bowl of porridge—he's just right.

Made in United States
Troutdale, OR
06/28/2023

10849900R00170